His face rela

been so concerne

stood by me, the

What was it about Benedict Swan that set my steady countenance adrift? Perhaps all my suspicions of the man. Suddenly I knew the urge to get away from him and everyone else, I rose from my desk.

"If that is all, Benedict, I must go down to the kitchen for luncheon." I went to pass him, but as I drew level, he grasped my arm gently but firmly, halting my progress.

"Kathryn, 'tis not my business but I am compelled to speak regardless."

I frowned and turned to face him. "What is it?"

"I worry for you," he said in an ominous tone. "Be careful with Gabriel. He plays a dangerous game." The sting of embarrassment spread across my cheeks as I realized he must have witnessed our embrace. Speechless, I pulled my arm from his hold and left him standing there alone.

Praise for *THE SECRET OF MOWBRAY MANOR*

"*THE SECRET OF MOWBRAY MANOR* is an elegant historic suspense that does a beautiful job reminding us that when you scratch the surface of dignified family, you don't have to scratch hard to find blood. Jude's bold and crisply defined characters felt tangible. I loved getting swept up in the stunning settings, and the mystery and angst locked me in. I couldn't put it down. The juxtaposition of dark vs. light and good vs. evil gets cleverly flipped on its head. I went from trying to solve the mystery to just hoping that the noble heroine Kathryn isn't killed before she can uncover the secret and find out what really happened to her friend."

~Amy Brewer, Literary Agent

The Secret of Mowbray Manor

by

Jude Bayton

This is a work of fiction. Names, characters, places, and incidents are either the product of the author's imagination or are used fictitiously, and any resemblance to actual persons living or dead, business establishments, events, or locales, is entirely coincidental.

The Secret of Mowbray Manor

Contact Information: info@thewildrosepress.com

Cover Art by *Diana Carlile*

The Wild Rose Press, Inc.
PO Box 708
Adams Basin, NY 14410-0708
Visit us at www.thewildrosepress.com

Publishing History
First Tea Rose Edition, 2020
Print ISBN 978-1-5092-3073-0
Digital ISBN 978-1-5092-3074-7

Published in the United States of America

Dedication

For John—
I would never have got here without you

Chapter One

Sunday, November 9, 1890
Dorset, Southern England

Completely alone, I glanced about the deserted platform, grateful for a dim light from one solitary gas lamp. My grip tightened on my small valise and suitcase. Swanage Railway station appeared as devoid of life as a ghost ship on the English Channel. I hastened to find an exit while my eyes chased shadows from the flickering, weak lamp. My mind battled the impulse to bolt, but I steadied my nerves, though it took every ounce of my composure not to run.

Outside the station and engulfed in darkness, I saw no other buildings, which fed my growing sense of unease. My eyes scoured the area, hungry for the welcome sight of Mowbray Manor's carriage. I had been assured someone would meet me. Discouraged, I set my bags down upon the sodden ground, pulled up the hood of my cloak to block the bite of November wind, and considered my predicament.

Wispy ribbons of fog floated like waifs through the dark canvas of night, while the moon sulked behind drab clouds like a child hiding in its mother's skirts. I shivered and pulled my worn cloak tighter. What if no one came?

An owl hooted, its companionable call a welcome

reprieve from my silent isolation. And on I waited, it seemed for an age. My back stiffened as I stood so erect and scared, and the blood in my veins turned frigid. I grew weary. Then a low rumble upon the ground broke the quiet, and a faint light materialized. As it swayed through the gloom, I felt immense relief. I was rescued.

The carriage creaked to a halt a few yards away, and the driver climbed down from his stoop and approached. An older man, stocky of build, his face coarse and bearded, inclined his head, yet avoided looking at me directly.

"Good evening, sir," I stammered. "Are you come from Mowbray Manor?"

The man grunted a low, unintelligible response and reached down to take my belongings. They did not weigh much, for my possessions were few, and he tossed them into the cab with ease.

"Get you in then," he mumbled gruffly and gestured for me to follow the course of my bags. I needed no further encouragement.

I quickly relaxed into the worn leather of the cab as the hackney traversed the road to Mowbray Manor. My body warmed slowly as my eyes grew heavy from a long day of travel, my healthy constitution no match for the torrent of uncertainty which plagued my mind.

After a time, our gait slowed, and we turned into a driveway. Although the dark windows of the carriage were closed tightly, a scent of saltwater permeated the atmosphere, and I inhaled deeply. Now wide-awake, I pressed my nose against the cold damp glass, and my eyes strained through the blanket of night to see my destination. Fortuitously, the clouds parted to allow a sliver of moonlight to shine down, and my breath caught in my throat. Mowbray Manor stood regal and imposing. Though wrapped in folds of gossamer fog, its austere mass pushed through the obscurity, as though even the elements could not veil its majesty.

With the same unfriendly manner he had displayed earlier, the coachman delivered me and my belongings unceremoniously before the front steps. I stood rooted to the spot. My gaze traveled upward, followed the grey rock of the building that rose before me like a monolithic stone giant. With trepidation, I picked up my bags, ascended the steps, and stopped at Mowbray's gargantuan oak doors. My hand shook as I reached for the bell-pull, and its trill ring pierced the quiet of evening. Footsteps approached from within and my emotions became conflicted. I yearned to be inside a warm safe-haven, yet felt anxious that I had arrived at my destination where I knew not one soul.

The heavy door swung open to reveal an elderly man, white-haired and somberly dressed. His clothing was dapper enough to be a gentleman's, but his diminutive bearing at once declared his status as servant. He did not ask me to come in, but I basked in the light which flowed invitingly behind him.

"Good evening, miss." His voice, eloquent yet disdainful, conveyed a tone which intimated that I should be stood at the servants' entrance. This impression was likely based upon my lack of finery. I looked as I was—poor.

I steeled myself. "Good evening. My name is Kathryn Westcott, and I am come to see Lady Clayton." His eyes flickered momentarily. He was no doubt surprised by my accent. He had obviously expected my speech to be that of a common girl.

The old man nodded. "You are late," he said without ceremony and gestured for me to enter. He closed the door behind me, and my relief was instantaneous now that I was out of the damp night air. I set my bags down and stared at the butler.

"Wait here," he commanded and walked away through the foyer down a well-lit hallway. As soon as he departed, I quickly examined my surroundings.

Several gas lamps were affixed to the walls, their sconces radiating soft yellow light which illuminated the scene before me. The space was immense, the floors made of polished marble. Two large pieces of statuary stood sentry either side of a staircase wide enough for a small carriage to pass between its carved bannisters. A majestic crystal chandelier hung like a stalactite, suspended from the painted fresco ceiling which depicted the heavens and what surely were gods, though which beings I could not say. Its magnificence exceeded my expectations.

A low murmur of voices escaped as a door opened and closed in the distance. The returning footsteps of the butler drew near. He stopped and extended a gnarled hand.

"This way if you please, Miss Westcott."

I glanced down at my valise and suitcase. The old man noticed my consternation and nodded to leave them where they stood. I took a deep breath and followed him down the hall.

As we entered the drawing room, its sudden warmth engulfed my cold bones, though my nerves still chattered. Inside the room, thick Aubusson carpets cushioned my step, and lavish fabrics and ornate furniture surrounded me. Yet I absorbed none of it in my present state of mind. The butler announced my name and, at once, a figure rose from a winged-back chair placed close to the blazing fire. As she approached, my eyes slaked across the woman's face, the elegant arrangement of her white hair and the length of her silken-clad figure. My feeling of uncertainty now I finally saw her in the flesh completely consumed me. Until this precise moment, the woman had been surreal, a fictional character in a popular novelette. Yet here she stood, the woman I had come to loathe through the words of her daughter, my dearest friend, Aramintha.

In a flash, I absorbed her features. The harsh jaw, thin lips, aquiline nose. Her skin like pale chiffon, soft with delicate creases, which changed the topography of her face. A striking woman, even in her sixties, she must surely have been a beauty in her youth.

"Ah, there you are, Miss Westcott." Lady Blanche Clayton inclined her head. "Good evening. I trust you had a pleasant journey?" She stood a few steps from me, and our gaze met evenly. She did not offer me a seat. I smiled and nodded, observing the cordial expression on her face, yet her eyes were cold and grey as stone.

"Thank you, my lady. I did indeed." I willed my voice not to betray the depth of my discomfort. "I apologize for the lateness of the hour. The early train was canceled."

She waved a gloved hand. "Tis of no consequence. Our housekeeper, Tricklebank, has your room prepared and will bring you a light repast." Lady Clayton turned away and went to a small ivory table. She grasped a small bell and rang it sharply. I watched her every move. The profile of her aristocratic face, the silver threads of her elegantly coiffed hair. Immediately the drawing room doors opened, and the elderly butler entered.

"Your Ladyship?"

"Baxter, show Miss Westcott to her room." She inclined her head toward me and gave a thin smile. "We will speak again in the morning at ten o'clock. We can go over your duties then."

Dismissed, I turned away and followed the butler from the room, elated that the first part of my plan had succeeded. Lady Blanche Clayton had absolutely no idea who I really was.

****

I awoke with the strange sensation I might still be dreaming. I lay cocooned within a large canopied bed, my body swaddled in linen sheets and warm wool blankets, my head cradled like a baby on soft feather pillows. I smiled with guilty pleasure, and then sat bolt upright as my mind cleared. Was I really at Mowbray Manor? Drowsy layers of slumber fell away as my thoughts arranged themselves in proper order. I glanced about the chamber. The morning light shone through chinks in the curtains, which offered clarity previously denied by lamplight last night.

The room was indeed pleasant. Sumptuous pink cabbage roses papered the walls, a busy backdrop to the multitude of small, framed paintings which depicted all manner of pretty birds. The mantel over a white fireplace was festooned with swarms of tiny china ornaments. At one side of the hearth stood a large wardrobe, painted white with gold trim embossing its doors, and on the other side, a writing desk situated beneath a generous window.

Curious to see what lay outside, I rose to pull back heavy damask curtains. Light swept into my room and painted the walls with bright honey. The winter sun was substantial, and I squinted until my eyes adjusted, only to be rewarded with a most spectacular view.

The grounds were impressive. A carpet of velvet, green grass was bordered by flower beds filled with a riot of heavy-laden rose bushes, the last blooms of the year. The center of the lawn appeared to be dissected by a narrow oblong pond, its somber steel-grey water littered with listless lily pads which floated aimlessly across its glassy surface. Beyond the gardens, my eyes were drawn to a remarkable landscape. For there in the distance lay the dark indigo of the English Channel, shimmering beneath the sunlight like molten sapphires. I could not help but be taken aback by the majesty before me, saturated with the delight of it, and then I thought of my darling, dearest Aramintha.

At Brampton Ladies College destiny had presented me with an education at the mere cost of my pride. All but a servant in status, I was given room and board in exchange for my abilities as a tutor. To the girls of the college I seemed inconspicuous, to its staff, insignificant. Yet to Aramintha Clayton I was a person, an individual whom she endowed with the generous gift of her friendship.

Aramintha had been my salvation. She alone had rescued me from drowning in a sea of loneliness when she plucked me from seclusion and called me all but sister. Indifferent to my social status and unconcerned with my lack of fortune and prospects, in Aramintha, I discovered purpose. My ambition had been solely to pursue knowledge and a good education, but Aramintha showed me the many possibilities within my reach should I acquire both.

"Miss Westcott?" Fingers lightly rapped on my door and roused me from thought.

"Come in."

Miss Tricklebank, whom I had met briefly the night before, entered my chamber holding a small tray in her hands laden with a pot of tea, boiled egg, and slices of hot buttered toast. She placed it down upon the desk and seemed surprised to see me still in my night attire.

"I trust you were comfortable?" she asked politely, her dour expression reminiscent of the headmistress at Brampton, stern and rather chilly. Her frown rippled with disapproval as she observed my disheveled state, my unbraided hair.

"Most comfortable, thank you, Miss Tricklebank." I glanced at the tray. "I would have come down to the kitchen—"

"It is customary to take breakfast the first day in your room. You may join the rest of the staff at luncheon and meet everyone then. It will be a full day, Miss Westcott, I can assure you." She smoothed down her stiff black skirts and absentmindedly patted the back of the brown bun in her hair. "Her ladyship will see you at ten o'clock."

As soon as the door closed, I set about my meal as though starved. I had never before been so spoiled with my breakfast served thus. I ate, my mouth savoring every bite, while my eyes feasted upon the scene from my window.

It was as I sipped my last drop of tea that I saw him. He strode towards the pond and then stopped as though taken by something which lurked in the water—a tall man, with the breadth of a laborer yet garbed as a gentleman. I could easily make out his form, his black, tousled hair, yet no other detail as he was too far from my vantage point. My mind conjured up the list of characters I had come to know from Aramintha's colorful stories and entertaining letters. I ran through the names in my head and landed upon his, for who other could it be than Benedict?

Aramintha had often referred to her half-brother as the devil in a sea of angels. For he alone had been the only child of Sir Nigel not gifted with the Clayton golden hair, blue eyes *or* the family name. She had said the late Lord Clayton's bastard son was half Romany gypsy, which would account for his swarthy complexion and raven hair. In truth, though I could not see much of the man, he did cut an imposing and formidable figure.

Suddenly his face turned, and he looked directly up at my window. I gasped and leaned back in surprise. Had he seen me watching? I composed myself and chased away my embarrassment for being so foolish. On this my first day at Mowbray Manor, I must settle down and keep my wits about me. I should dress and go downstairs, for I was to meet Lady Clayton within the hour.

****

I entered the drawing room escorted by the formidable Baxter to find Lady Clayton seated at her writing desk. But upon our arrival she placed her fountain pen down, then turned to look at me waiting self-consciously in my worn workaday dress. The butler departed, and she rose majestically from her seat and moved to a velvet settle.

"Miss Westcott, please do come and sit." She gestured to an intricately carved armchair, one of a matched pair which faced the sofa. I did as she bade, and rested my hands in my lap, my back ramrod straight as though I sat before a queen. Again, I was struck at the ethereal beauty of the older woman, the paleness of her complexion, the silver hair. Her ice-blue eyes assessed me, the cheapness of my dress, the cut of my collars.

"I trust your room was adequate?" The tone of her voice implied she expected an answer to the positive.

"Indeed, Lady Clayton, thank you, it was most comfortable."

"Splendid. Now I should like to discuss your position here. I was most satisfied with your credentials, though it is unusual for a young woman of your—" she paused to select her words, "…station, to have attained such a high level of education."

Attending a ladies' school without wealth or a position within society was highly uncommon. Therefore, her query seemed understandable. In my quest to be engaged as teacher to the youngest member of the Clayton family, I had intentionally withheld my relationship with Araminatha. My education at Brampton alone gave me the entrée required to join her staff. Lady Blanche would have been mortified to know her privileged daughter had been the best of friends with a personage as low in the social order as myself. But she would never make that connection. In our correspondence Araminatha had always called me Miss Victoria, after our Queen. She loved subterfuge, and it had been the easiest path to conceal a friendship her mother would have forbidden. Now I was glad of it, for I was determined to discover what had happened to my dearest friend.

"I count myself fortunate indeed to have an education, Lady Clayton. My father placed great value upon it. He considered knowledge the best security for my future. He did not wish me to be vulnerable nor dependent on any other but myself."

"I see," she muttered. Her tone suggested she did not. "I am sure you will prove worthy enough to instruct my son. Gideon is a bright boy, yet somewhat high-spirited, though no more than most thirteen-year-olds. My decision to educate him at home may change as I fear he has proven himself to be cleverer than his prior tutors. Not in scholastic endeavors, but rather with his stubbornness and cunning."

Aramintha had regaled me with many stories of her little brother. I was forewarned, and therefore forearmed. "Gideon and I will make the best of it, Lady Clayton."

"One hopes so." She raised her eyebrows. "You understand his past tutors have been men. This will be a trial period for the first month to see how you progress. Do I have your agreement?"

"Indeed."

"Good. Benedict will make the appropriate financial transactions based upon our contract." She rose with a rustle of fabric. "Follow me, and I will take you to the schoolroom and introduce Gideon."

****

The classroom was situated at the top of the house, along with what I presumed to be Gideon's bedroom, a nursery and a playroom. Lady Clayton led me down a short corridor into a spacious chamber, decorated with charts, maps, and diagrams of an educational nature. The front wall was covered in a black chalkboard, with three large desks facing towards where the teacher might conduct lessons. A young blond boy occupied the centre desk, and upon our entrance, he glanced up from his writing. I barely managed to conceal my sudden intake of breath as the boy stared at me with Arámintha's face. But for his gender, he could be her replica, the same pale blue eyes, butter-yellow hair, full mouth and upturned nose.

"Gideon, here is your new tutor, Miss Westcott," Lady Clayton spoke sharply. The boy rose to his feet, his fingers still rested on the desk as his gaze fastened on my face. I moved forward and held out a hand in greeting.

"Good morning, Master Gideon, it is a pleasure to make your acquaintance." He blinked at me but ignored my proffered hand, which I quickly dropped. I smiled, but his expression remained impassive, his demeanor far less attractive than his looks.

"Come, Gideon, where are your manners?" Lady Clayton's face crumpled with displeasure. "Introduce yourself to Miss Westcott at once."

"Good day to you, ma'am," he said begrudgingly and then sat back down.

Lady Clayton sighed. "Gideon can be rather sullen at times." She observed with a glance at me, her light eyes harsh. "I trust you will be able to manage him?"

"Indeed, Lady Clayton." My voice conveyed more confidence than I felt.

"Then I shall leave you to it," she stated flatly, and without further ceremony, Lady Clayton left the room.

I went to the chalkboard and retrieved a long piece of chalk, wrote my name, the date and then turned to my unhappy student.

"Well, Master Gideon, I look forward to us working together. To begin, we should discuss the lessons you have had in the past and determine where we shall start."

He was completely unresponsive. His pale eyes shimmered with obvious disdain; his chin tilted in defiance. Gideon Clayton was an angry boy. But why?

I tried again. "Master Gideon, I am in no doubt you are displeased with my coming. It is usual to feel this way when a new tutor arrives. Perhaps—"

"We have just met," he interrupted. "Therefore, how can you profess to know anything whatsoever about me?" His voice balanced on the cusp of breaking, teetered between boyhood and maturity, but the tone was clear. Gideon Clayton was irritated.

"True enough," I agreed. "But in my experience, it is natural to feel animosity towards an individual who implements a change in routine. I am here to teach. My intention is not to upset you nor cause any discomfort. However, I shall engage you in lessons to earn the salary your mother pays me, monies which ensure my survival. Lady Clayton insists you are to be educated, and if not by me, she will bring in another to teach you, or perhaps even send you away. If your objective is to make my task difficult, you only prolong the punishment by making new acquaintances each time a replacement tutor arrives." I looked straight at the boy who sat listening to my every word.

"Master Gideon, I am here to teach, and that is all. This can be a relatively decent experience, or you can render it more painful. The decision is yours. Please make it."

He seemed astonished. The expression upon his face spoke volumes. The boy had apparently never been challenged and seemed surprised by my frank words. I cared not. The most important relationship between pupil and teacher had to be respect. We would make little progress if the sulky boy did not accept me.

I recognized the precise moment Gideon allowed the tension to leave his shoulders. He leaned back in his chair, still unsmiling, but less combative.

"Now," I said. "Let us discuss how far you are come with your various studies."

****

The lunch gong sounded. Time had passed quickly. Gideon and I had examined his previous tutor's work and registered where my instruction should begin. Still reluctant to converse, he answered my questions with the barest of responses. At least his diminished pout was enough to encourage me our relationship might improve a little by our next meeting. I dismissed Gideon until after luncheon and went down to the kitchen.

I walked into a hive of activity downstairs, due to the preparation of dinner for a certain Mr. Reginald Plumb the parish Vicar, and his wife. I had met several of the kitchen staff after breakfast when returning my tray, but now felt somewhat at a loss. Fearful of causing any strife, I avoided Mrs. Oldershaw the cook, and instead asked a young kitchen maid where to partake of a bite to eat. She directed me to the servants' dining room off the kitchen, and there I enjoyed a slice of crusty fresh bread and a hunk of cheese.

Contemplating my plans for the afternoon, I opted to take Gideon outside for a nature ramble. Doing so might provide a better opportunity to get to know the boy away from the stern confines of the schoolroom. Gideon was dour to be sure. Cherubic in appearance, yet as sullen as a fish. I searched my catalogue of memories to conjure past conversations with Aramintha when she spoke of her family, but found little of him there other than his escapades. I had not learned much about the boy, but it would not take long to form my own opinion, and quickly.

The remaining brother I had yet to see was Gabriel, the current Lord Clayton. This sibling was a frequent subject of Aramintha's. Her elder by ten years, when she spoke of him, her eyes would grow misty with affection, her words revering as she described his admirable qualities, his handsome stature and pleasant ways. Perhaps I would meet him before the day was out? I considered the half-brother I had seen from my window that morning, Benedict. Of him, Aramintha had said little, yet the impression given suggested he remained somewhat aloof from the rest of the family, though why, she had not commented upon. For a bastard son to keep polite distance from the legitimate children of nobility was not considered unusual. Aramintha had told me Benedict was astute, adept at managing the Clayton estate for the legitimate heir, Gabriel. I had always surmised from her tone she cared well enough for Benedict yet adored Gabriel. I contemplated her opinion. Would mine be the same?

****

Gideon and I spent the better part of a chilly afternoon traversing a well-trodden footpath. We walked along the green clifftops of the Purbeck hills while the frigid sea pounded sandy beaches far below. The air felt damp yet invigorating, and we were both wrapped in our respective thick outer garments. The salty wind stung my cheeks like kissing bees, and my lungs hungrily sucked in the fresh, clean air, so vastly different from London.

As we travelled, I attempted to coerce Gideon from his unwillingness to make conversation, and after a time he begrudgingly began to relent. Initially, we discussed items we studied along our trek, flora and fauna, then identified the variety of seabirds wheeling in the skies and the colorful, comical puffins who inhabited the terrain. But more than anything, I desperately wanted to learn about the Clayton family.

I finally plucked up enough courage to steer the conversation away from our lesson. “Tell me, Gideon, do you spend much time with your siblings? I understand you have a sister and two brothers?”

He did not falter in his step. “Not really. I only have one brother, Gabriel. Benedict is half-brother to me, and he works for the estate.” He continued to walk. I kept abreast of him, my heart picked up speed.

“And what of your sister?” I endeavored to keep the tremble from my voice. “Is she at home often?”

Gideon stopped abruptly, catching me off guard. His solemn face turned to mine. His skin was ashen.

“My sister is dead.”

Chapter Two

Gideon walked on while I stood frozen to the spot with leaden feet. Araminitha dead? No! My addled brain struggled furiously to clear the confusion his words presented. That was impossible. How could she be? My eyes filled with tears, and my throat constricted as though a vice squeezed my neck. This could not be true. It could not!

Blindly, I followed him, as my thoughts crashed wild against my mind like the waves down on the shore below. Araminitha dead? No, I would not believe it. Certainly, I had accepted something was amiss with my darling friend. For why else had I come to Mowbray? But my goal was to identify her plight, offer assistance if needed. I had never considered for one moment she might be gone from this world - not once.

I swallowed hard and willed myself to calm down. Becoming emotional would benefit nothing and no one. My friendship with Araminitha *must* remain a secret. Hastily, I gathered my self-control, blinked away my unshed tears and caught up with Gideon. He strode on, his youthful legs collected yards as his lean young body barely noticed the exertion.

"Will you wait for me please, Master Gideon?" I requested, and he halted until I drew level.

"Might I ask another question?" I enquired, observing his bland expression. He did not answer, and

I took his silence as permission.

"How long ago did your sister die?" Asking the question sounded ridiculous to my ears, for how could Aramintha be gone? Her radiant face loomed in my mind, full of life and vitality.

"Five months hence, in June," Gideon replied, his tone nonplussed.

"What happened to her?" We commenced our walk. To an observer, we might easily be discussing the weather, yet a tumult of anguish ricocheted through me.

"They found her there." Gideon stopped and pointed down to an area where the gold sand gave way to the rocky shore below. "My brother discovered her body early one morning. He said she had fallen from up here." As his eyes swung to meet my own, I finally saw through Gideon's mask. There, beneath the boyish swagger and righteous indifference, lay the flicker of pain he fought to keep buried. As he spoke of Aramintha, I could see a young boy devastated at the loss of a beloved sister. If nothing else, Gideon Clayton was a master of disguising his feelings.

"My brother called for Doctor Beedles to attend her, but it was too late. Aramintha had been long dead."

"I am so very sorry," I said quietly and unconsciously reached out to touch his arm. Gideon flinched as though I held a flame to his skin. I withdrew my hand swiftly. I had not intended to upset the boy. With some effort I regained my composure. There was much to contemplate in light of what I had learned. Could Aramintha really be dead? I still could not conceive it. I had long determined the cessation of her letters due to something far less final.

"May we return to the house now, Miss Westcott?"

Gideon interrupted my thoughts. "This wind has turned chill, and I feel rather cold."

"Of course," I stammered, my mind still being pulled into uncomfortable shapes. "Let us stop here Gideon. We have learned enough for one day." I, for one, certainly had.

****

I carried a hot cup of tea up with me to my room, though my nerves could have used something stronger. The revelation from Gideon about Aramintha seemed surreal. How could I not have known? Had there been mention of her passing in the newspapers? Surely, I would have seen something, heard something? But in truth I knew better. I did not belong to the same social set nor mix with upper-class families like the Claytons. And if Lady Clayton had chosen to keep the knowledge of her daughter's death from the general public, then it was her right. Yet why did no one wear the shrouds of mourning? The house bore no black crepe upon the door declaring the death of a family member either. It made no sense, none whatsoever.

In the privacy of my room I went to my dressing table and opened the top drawer. At the back, wrapped tightly in a silk scarf, were the letters Aramintha had written over the past year. She had left Brampton to return to Mowbray Manor with a solemn oath to stay in touch. At first, she had been good to her word. We exchanged correspondence weekly, my letters not particularly interesting, hers full of color and excitement as she regaled me with vibrant tales of balls, hunting parties and the machinations of her family. I too had left Brampton to be employed as governess for a pleasant banker and his wife. I wrote about mundane activities and the occasional visit to a London museum or landmark.

I sat down at the desk and untied the ribbon binding the letters together. Tears streamed down my cheeks at the realization I would never see my friend again. Gently I lifted her last missive to me. The note had been sent back in the summer, during an unusually warm June. This one had worried me more than all the others. Though Aramintha's tone had been rather subdued the few weeks prior, nothing in her words had alarmed me. She frequently wrote of the family, especially her mother and their strained relationship. Lady Blanche had always behaved indifferently to her only daughter, and Aramintha had struggled and felt unloved. But in this particular letter she seemed terribly out of sorts and under the weather. A hot summer, many were affected with lethargy and the headache. But when this note arrived, it had brought an indescribable current of foreboding.

Aramintha wrote that she tired of Dorset and life at Mowbray Manor. She found the days long, her mother tiresome and they quarreled often. She also mentioned a matter of importance she needed to tell me but could not write it down on paper.

I had replied immediately, expressing concern, and asked if we could meet in person soon? Might she be able to travel to London in the near future? But alas, no reply was forthcoming. Aramintha never wrote again.

Almost four months passed, when by chance I discovered a post advertised for a tutor to the Clayton family. I had scoured my employer's newspaper after breakfast every morning for many weeks to find if there might be news of my silent friend. I imagined her engaged, married, off on a honeymoon, too busy and swept off her feet to remember me. Aramintha lived a life so different from my own. She owed me no loyalty, indeed it was quite the other way around.

I sipped my tea as memories soaked into my thoughts. At Brampton, I had been a quiet, melancholy person, well-used to solitude. I seldom spoke to others except in the role of tutor. I was grateful for the position which afforded not only the continuation of my education after the death of my father, but room and board, scarce as they were.

The staff at Brampton were predominantly female; however, there were three men engaged as teachers, and various gardeners and other laborers who tended the grounds of the school. One, in particular, a bull of a man by the name of Billy Scruggs was most unpleasant and therefore to be avoided at all costs. I'd seen his type before, belligerent, prone to drink judging by the mottled color of his complexion, and with the presence of mind to believe all women happy to receive his unwanted advances.

Scruggs had accosted me on several occasions, stepped in my path to stop my passing. He would grab my arm and pull me close to his face with an invitation to join him for a walk in the woods after dinner. I always vehemently declined, not only because he revolted me, but because of his forceful and overbearing nature. Though my work seldom brought me outside in the gardens, my love of horses did. Whenever I stepped out into the quadrangle on my way to the stables, invariably Billy Scruggs would not be far away.

Late one autumn afternoon returning from the

village post office, I walked up the driveway to the main building of my school and had the uncomfortable sensation I was being watched. With daylight fast disappearing I quickened my step. As I passed by the stables, a pair of thick arms suddenly shot out of nowhere, grabbed me from behind and pulled me inside. Before I could open my mouth to cry out, a dirty hand covered my lips, and I gagged at the smell and taste of skin.

Billy Scruggs pushed me into an empty stall and down onto the hay, the weight of his heavy body against mine tipping me over until my knees buckled. I struggled frantically, my legs flailed, my fists pummeled against any part of his body within reach. But Scruggs was a strong man, physically fit from the hard labor his work demanded. He kept a hand across my mouth and rammed one knee between my thighs as he unfastened his belt. I writhed in terror, my eyes cavernously wide with fear as I recognized his intent. I would not yield. I continued to fight him, wriggling my body to try and escape his vice-like grip. He moved suddenly and sat astride me, took a hold of my disheveled cloak and pushed it out of the way. Scruggs grabbed the bodice of my dress and with one strong jerk, split the fabric to expose my breasts. I bit down on his dirty fingers with every ounce of strength I could muster. He let out a roaring bellow of pain and tore his hand from my mouth. In that brief moment I filled my lungs with air and gave an almighty scream, which he stilled with a hearty slap across my face.

"You bitch," he growled. Spittle sprayed my face as he covered my mouth with his own and forced his thick, slimy tongue down my throat making me gag.

There came a loud thwack as something metal connected with an inanimate object, and suddenly Scruggs' putrid body went completely limp. He slumped against me, and I sobbed violently, pushing at his dead weight until I could get out from under his foul, unwashed body. And there she was.

Aramintha Clayton stood behind the inert body of Scruggs, the handle of a shovel in her shaking hands. Our eyes met, mine terrified and full of tears, hers bright with adrenaline. We stared at each other for a full moment until she broke the silence.

"Run and get help before he comes around!" she shouted, and without a thought I gathered my cloak around my naked breasts and did exactly as she bade.

By the end of the evening, the constable had come and collected Scruggs, the village doctor had been to examine me, and under Aramintha's strict orders I was confined to the sick room to be kept safe and warm overnight. And that had been the start of our friendship. Aramintha Clayton had saved me from Billy Scruggs and certain harm, a debt which could never be repaid. From those sordid events, our relationship had formed and grown steadily. She had protected me while placing herself in certain danger. Now it was my turn to do the same.

I finished my tea, returned the letters to their hiding place, and then glanced in the mirror to wipe away my tears. I did not understand why my friend had died. I was uncertain why no one had spoken of her since my arrival, other than Gideon. Something was not right, and though I could not identify my unsettled feeling, it still gnawed on me. I thought of my darling friend, the letters she had faithfully written, and her words came back to my mind. Why had Aramintha become so unhappy at Mowbray Manor? What was it she had wanted to tell me, information too important to write in her letter? I was too late to save her now, but deep down inside, I knew I would not rest until I learned what had become of Aramintha Clayton.

Chapter Three

I had long dried my tears as the sun descended upon the horizon. Soon it would be time to dine. I tidied myself as a knock sounded on my door. I opened it to reveal a pretty redhead dressed in grey surge standing on the threshold. She gave me an appraising look and a friendly smile.

"Good evening, Miss Westcott. I am Campbell, Lady Clayton's maid." Her voice was soft, with a trace of a highland accent.

"Pleased to meet you, Miss Campbell."

"Och, it's just Campbell if you will, miss. Lady Clayton requests you join the family at dinner tonight. Seven sharp, if you please, and I would highly recommend you are not late." She raised perfectly shaped eyebrows to emphasize her point and rolled her eyes. "Her ladyship is most particular about punctuality."

"Thank you for the advice."

My expression must have conveyed dread because her smile grew warmer. "Her bark is worse than her bite, don't be too nervous." With a nod, she turned and walked away. I closed the door. I was not completely surprised by the command. This was my first full evening at Mowbray after all. No doubt Lady Blanche wanted to speak with me after my day with her son.

With a sigh, I opened the large wardrobe and stared

at the total sum of my possessions—three gowns, two skirts and two blouses which hung sadly in the voluminous space. Two of the dresses were muslin, one navy, one grey—I currently wore the black—and the other a peacock blue silk evening gown, made from fabric my father had purchased in Granada. Although there was scant use for the dress in my life as a servant, I would never part with the piece. It was all I had to show from another more prosperous time.

I had lived in the gothic quarter of Barcelona many years earlier. But images of our beautiful home stayed with me. The wonderful fragrance of pink almond trees in our courtyard, the smile of my ninera Ana, who cared for me in place of my mother, and upon whose love I had thrived. We had not been wealthy, but my father's occupation paid him handsomely, and our lifestyle was more than adequate. I had wanted for nothing.

I took my hair from its pins and enjoyed a moment's pleasure as the tresses tumbled down my back and gave my head a reprieve from the weight. My hair had always been my best feature. I was no beauty, not by English standards. My mother was Catalan, a native of Catalonia, and from her I had inherited my Spanish black hair, dark brows and complexion. But my eyes were all my father's, 'grey as the skies o'er Dartmoor,' he would say, his nostalgia for his home in Devon readily prominent in his thoughts. I smiled sadly. Seven long years he had been gone, yet I missed him more by their passing. For my mother I harbored no emotion whatsoever. She had run off before my sixth birthday.

I brushed my hair vigorously and then painstakingly pinned it back up into a chignon, though it took some effort. I dressed, and then sat at the writing desk to wait for the sound of the dinner gong.

****

In my usual attire, I seldom felt self-conscious of my appearance, content in the knowledge I blended with my surroundings. But when I joined Lady Clayton in the dining room, I immediately felt the perusal of several pairs of eyes fasten to my form. I stopped short, taken aback by the sensation and kept my gaze fixed upon my employer.

"Ah, Miss Westcott, there you are. Do come and join us." Her imperious voice found my ears. Baxter appeared at my side like a rabbit from a magician's hat and directed me to a place at the food-laden mahogany table. He pulled out a chair, and I humbly sat down.

Lady Clayton was to my immediate left at the table's head, but I became aware of an extremely handsome man sitting directly opposite her, beside a middle-aged woman.

"Gabriel," said Lady Clayton. "This is Gideon's new tutor I spoke of, Kathryn Westcott. She arrived late last evening." The man bestowed me with an admiring stare and smiled. So here was Gabriel, the beloved brother Aramintha had spoken of so frequently and the current Lord Clayton. I returned his smile and noticed the same blond hair and pale eyes as his sister, yet his nose and cheeks were more aquiline, his chin chiseled and firm. Had he been a woman, he might be considered exquisite. His face was that of an angel, all perfection and light, yet something in his eyes spoke of a less than virtuous personality.

"It is indeed a pleasure to meet you, Miss Westcott. And how do you find my rascal of a brother? I trust there have been no frogs hidden in your bedsheets, or dead mice in your shoes?" He grinned with a display of even white teeth.

"Fortunately, no, Lord Clayton, but thank you, I shall heed your warning."

"Really, Gabriel, you speak such nonsense," his mother admonished. "Miss Westcott allow me to introduce you to our Vicar, Mr. Reginald Plumb and his wife, Avril." The woman seated beside Gabriel smiled with a display of front teeth a horse might envy. The remainder of her features seemed undersized for the chubby dimpled face, but her raisin eyes twinkled pleasantly.

"Delighted to meet you." Her contralto voice hummed like velvet on the air, unexpectedly bewitching and in direct contrast to her appearance. Next to me, a man cleared his throat.

"Ahem, good evening to you, Miss Westcott. I trust we may look forward to seeing you at our service this week." I nodded politely at the rotund Reverend Plumb. His bald head shimmered with sweat, his shape that of a person who had long over-imbibed with too many sweetmeats and steamed puddings. His eyeballs looked as though they wished to jump from their sockets, his nose red and bulbous, his lips thick and slack. What an odd couple he and his dulcet-toned wife made.

"Thank you, Vicar. If my schedule allows."

Gabriel's eyes rested upon me, and I glanced back at him. A smile played about his lips as though he had read my unflattering thoughts.

"Baxter, dinner may be served," Lady Clayton commanded. The old man nodded and gestured for one of two young footmen in attendance to pick up a silver soup tureen from the sideboard and ladle a measure into our bowls.

The light consommé was delicious.

"My mother tells me you attended Brampton Ladies College?" Gabriel commented as we enjoyed our first course.

"Indeed, for many years."

"And did you perchance know my sister Aramintha?" he asked casually, and Lady Clayton's soup spoon clattered against the bowl. I stared at the older woman. Her complexion had paled.

"Excuse me, Mother, that was indelicate of me," Gabriel exclaimed, though I did not believe him to look particularly sorry.

"I was not acquainted with her Lord Clayton." My lie came easily. "The college has many pupils. I was employed there, and not encouraged to socialize with the young ladies."

"Of course. Forgive my assumption," he said. "How many years were you there?"

"Six."

"Ah," he said. "You were there from a young age?"

I could not decide if he paid me a compliment or was genuinely curious—I chose the latter. "I went to Brampton as a student when my father fell ill and could no longer tutor me. It was his wish I receive a proper education. Unfortunately, due to his ailments it became necessary for me to seek employment. Brampton gave me much-needed work, and I was able to continue my studies as part of my compensation. I remained there after the death of my father."

Lady Blanche cut in, her voice stern. "Gabriel, must you really interrogate Miss Westcott? Pray, allow her to finish her soup while it is still tepid." Duly chastised, the heir to Mowbray did as he was told.

Mrs. Oldershaw had cooked a wonderful dinner, each course a savory delight. I could not remember how long it had been since I had enjoyed food so elaborate as this fare. Small talk ensued during the remainder of dinner, primarily led by Lady Blanche and the Reverend. They discussed the upcoming Christmas services and the conditions of various poor families within the parish—this I found ironic as we imbibed in such rich and opulent food.

After a large quantity of delectable lemon sorbet was consumed, we ladies left the gentlemen to their cigars and brandy and went into the drawing room where a large fire crackled a warm and inviting welcome. I was somewhat out of place, unused to being included at a family dinner. Tonight was hopefully the exception, and tomorrow I would resume taking my meals in the servants' dining room.

Avril Plumb and I sat down upon the pretty settle, while Lady Clayton, stunning in her silver gown, laid claim to one of the armchairs. Baxter brought around a small tray with tiny glasses of sherry, and we three politely sipped the amber liquid.

"Miss Westcott?" Avril asked. "Are you originally from London? I take it you are not a native of Dorset?"

"Indeed, no ma'am, my father's family was from Devon, and I spent many years of my childhood on the continent."

"I see." The raisin-eyed lady gave a little nod and left it at that.

"Pray, what were your parents doing abroad? Were they missionaries? Artists?" Lady Clayton demanded.

Her eyes narrowed as though she expected me to tell her my parents were highwaymen.

"My father was employed by the Spanish Railroad, and he spent many years in Barcelona until the Revolution. We returned to England when he took a position at Durham University as a Professor of Language."

"Very interesting," Lady Blanche remarked unenthusiastically and hastily averted her eyes so I would not elaborate further.

Mrs. Plumb began a discourse on the appalling shortage of knitting wool in the village haberdashery shop when the doors were opened by a footman, and Gabriel, along with the Reverend Plumb, joined us. The large, portly man squeezed himself into what now resembled a Lilliputian armchair while Lord Clayton stood in front of the roaring fire. I took in his measure.

Gabriel was tall, built with the figure of an athlete, not bulky and strong, but lean and sinewy. He wore his blond hair short and neat, and his dinner suit was crisp and exquisitely tailored. Lord Clayton was a very handsome and eligible man. My cheeks burned as he caught me staring. I quickly looked away.

"Marvelous dinner, Lady Clayton." The Reverend gushed; his sentiments cheerily echoed by his wife. "It is always such a treat to join you here at Mowbray. I do believe you've the finest cook in the county."

Lady Clayton gave him a polite smile but did not seem particularly interested in the compliment.

"Our cook can burn a pot of tea," Avril Plumb added. "Just the other day—"

"Lady Clayton does not care to hear about our household problems dearest," her husband admonished, his eyes barely perceptible above his fat cheeks.

Gabriel strolled over to join us, rendering the awkward moment broken as he leaned against his mother's chair. "Miss Westcott, have you had a chance to see the grounds here at Mowbray?"

The Reverend blustered, "Indeed Miss Westcott, you'll find no better in Dorset I'd wager."

"I have not seen much as yet, Lord Clayton. Though I did walk with Master Gideon along the cliff path this afternoon for our nature lesson." An instant change enveloped the room as the atmosphere unexpectedly grew tense. Had I said something wrong?

Lady Blanche placed her sherry glass down loudly and threw a disapproving stare in my direction. "Miss Westcott, under no circumstances are you permitted to take my son along the coastal walk. I shall overlook it this time as you were not given prior instruction, but please ensure it does not happen again." Her jaw clenched and she raised a hand to her breast as though to catch her breath.

"Really, Mother, calm yourself, there is no harm done. I am certain Miss Westcott provided Gid with proper supervision and a spot of fresh air."

I gave Gabriel a grateful smile. "I do apologize, Lady Clayton. Rest assured it will not happen again." I received an imperious nod of acceptance, and then she rose abruptly, the evening now apparently at an end.

Reverend Plumb attempted to get respectfully to his feet but displayed great difficulty ungluing his generous torso from the confines of his chair. With a deep grunt he managed to extricate himself, and quickly thanked his hostess for a delightful evening. He glowered at his wife, who finally grasped the hint, and she too rose to bid farewell for the night.

I stood and said my goodbyes to the ample pair and remarked it had been pleasant to make their acquaintance. As they departed, Lady Blanche bade me a good evening, gestured for her son's arm, and followed her guests from the room, leaving me alone. But as I made towards the door, Gabriel returned having seen his mother to the stairs. I hesitated as he stood between me and my escape.

"Oh no, you do not run off, Miss Westcott?"

"Lord Clayton, I thought to retire as well."

"Come, come, madam." His smile was honeyed. "Do not go, I beg of you. It is most enjoyable to have another's company for a change, especially someone not yet forty or wearing a clergyman's frock." He gestured for me to return to the settle and took his mother's empty seat. I sat across from him, at a loss what to do or say. I had scant experience with men, especially the gentry.

"Good Lord, Miss Westcott, please stop looking so fearful, I shan't bite." He pulled out a slim leather case from his inside pocket. "Though I might smoke a cheroot if it will not offend you?"

"Please do."

He struck a match, and a swirl of smoke drifted into the air. The scent was unusual and exotic, with a strong hint of anise, which I found not unpleasant at all.

"I apologize for my mother's curtness this evening. I am certain you do not know much of our family history, but my sister recently fell tragically to her death from the very path you walked today with my brother."

Summoning every ounce of composure I possessed, I forced what I hoped was a look of surprise upon my face. I must disguise my despair and plead ignorance of Aramintha's plight at all costs. I managed to keep the tremor from my voice.

"I am so sorry to hear of it. No wonder Lady Clayton was distressed. How devastating. Was this recent?"

"Yes, early June." He pulled on the cheroot, and I reflected on the months past when I had worried about my dear friend.

"It was a great shock to my mother and to the rest of the family also. Mother should have informed you, especially as Gideon still suffers from her absence." He looked straight at my face and again I felt a sense of wonderment at the perfection of his features. His eyes were such a brilliant hue, for even in the subdued lighting of the room, they pierced the space between us.

"Aramintha was a dear sister to us both and a dutiful daughter. My mother is at a loss without her here. She refuses to wear mourning and has forbidden the servants to speak of what happened."

"How unusual." I could not help but speak my thoughts.

"Indeed, it is. But we do not live in London, Miss Westcott. Here in the West Country, we are not observed by society nor judged quite the same as those in the capital. I am certain the local gentry find her actions somewhat eccentric, but in truth, my mother's name is lofty enough none would dare pass comment. Tis my belief she cannot accept Aramintha's passing, and this way she can pretend it never occurred." He rose and walked to the fireplace to toss in the remainder of his tobacco. "Easier for us all to believe she has gone away for a spell."

"I am most truly sorry, Lord Clayton."

He returned to the chair. "Please, when we are informal, do address me by my given name of Gabriel."

"I am not sure if—"

"I insist. Do you go by Kathryn?"

I nodded.

"Then I shall address you as such when we converse like this." He smiled. "It has been quite a time since I have had the pleasure of conversing with a young woman at home. Since my sister's tragic death, Mowbray Manor has been a very lonely place."

My hesitance to be on first name terms vanished as the sadness of his tone echoed the very sentiment of my own when thinking about my dear friend. But the voice in my head warned me not to be too familiar with a man I barely knew, and I shrugged it aside. Perhaps I would learn more of Aramintha's life at Mowbray Manor if I spent time with one brother in the schoolroom, and become a friend to the other?

"Very well, Gabriel." The name slipped from my lips with ease.

His eyes glowed with what I took to be acknowledgement, though something else I could not identify shone there also. The clock on the mantel chimed nine o'clock and jolted my mind into a semblance of reality. The hour was late, and I should go up to bed. Spending too long in the company of a single man unchaperoned might be considered improper. I quickly rose to my feet.

"I believe it is time to retire for the night, Lord Clay—I mean Gabriel. Thank you for welcoming me. I am very happy to be at Mowbray. I hope I can fulfill your mother's expectations, and of course yours as well."

Gabriel stood up and gave me a little bow. Then he regarded me with his lovely smile. "Why, Kathryn, I believe you already have."

Chapter Four

Sleep proved difficult, for each time my eyes closed, an image of Gabriel Clayton presented itself. His beautiful blue eyes, his rakish smile, and then suddenly his face would melt away to be replaced by that of Aramintha's, her expression haunted. I fidgeted under the covers and willed my thoughts to settle and quiet. But what a day it had been. My first at Mowbray Manor, and in the space of a few hours I had discovered my dear friend had not only died a tragic death, but one shrouded in mystery.

How had these months passed with my ignorance that Aramintha lay in a cold grave? I shuddered and pulled the covers closer. The Claytons would have a family crypt where I might at least visit her tombstone and pay my respects. I would pursue the inquiry at breakfast. One of the kitchen staff would know. This notion settled my rambling thoughts. I would teach in the morning and then go in search of Aramintha's resting place on my midday break.

****

I awoke rested and went down to the kitchen, only to realize most of the servants had already been up hours before me to prepare the house ready for the day. I helped myself to bread, jam and a hot cup of tea. As I passed one of the kitchen maids whom I had met the previous day, I called her name.

“Yes, miss,” she replied with a bright smile.

“I plan to study the Clayton family tree with Master Gideon today. Where might I find the family graveyard where we could read some of the inscriptions?” I hoped it did not sound like a ridiculous request but, judging by the girl’s face, she did not find it an odd question.

“Why, there’s a small chapel where the family all lay, miss. Tis in the other direction from the cliffs, on the way to the village, not ten minutes’ walk away.”

I thanked her for the information, and as she walked off, I caught sight of the kitchen clock. I still had another hour until today’s lessons began.

Since my arrival at Mowbray Manor, I had been pressed for time and had yet to see the stable. Horses were in my blood. My mother had been a skilled equestrian. Her family in Catalonia had once been wealthy, her father’s stable legendary. My grandfather, Francisco Santiago, had amassed one of the finest collections of Andalusian horses in Europe. Though my grandparents had died in a tragic accident when I was five years of age, my scant memories of them always included their black and grey Andalusian horses, the finest Iberian breed.

My father said I had practically been born on the back of a horse. He had regaled the story to me all through my childhood. It seems my mother, Valentina Sofia Santiago, had continued to ride her beloved beasts even while heavily pregnant, and one such ride had induced labor. Horses had been in my life for as long as I could remember, but after my father’s return to England, we were no longer able to afford our own livestock, and it had been several years since I had ridden.

I made my way across the back courtyard to the Clayton stables. Bert Hogg, the head groom, had a desk in the tack room just inside the building. I thought it best to stop and speak to the man.

"Good morning, Mr. Hogg. Would it be all right if I went to see the horses?"

Bert looked up from the newspaper he read with a quizzical look on his face. He knew who I was for he had brought me from the railway station. Since then our paths had crossed in the kitchen, but we did not know one another at all. Bert seemed surprised at my sudden interest in his part of the estate. He was a short, squat man whose physique would fare well in a boxing ring. Bert scratched his bald head, and then his full beard and shrugged broad shoulders. "All right by me, miss, though watch yerself as they don't know you and might be skittish."

"I will," I said solemnly, and left the man to his paper.

My nostrils drank in the sweet, familiar scent of horses and hay which flavored the air, and I was at once transported back to happier times in my childhood. The place had a quiet, calm feel, which spoke highly of Bert Hoggs management of the horses. The stable itself was impressive, housing four stalls either side of the building. Natural light filtered through many windows which illuminated the dust motes in the air like tiny fairies.

I walked between the stalls and marveled that each held an occupant, or at least the name of one. Two of the largest stalls were reserved for the Clydesdales, magnificent creatures who pulled the heaviest loads for the farmers, with their massive quarters and their strong legs. At every stop I gave each horse a small treat I had collected from the kitchen, pieces of fresh carrot which were like sugar to their palate. The English thoroughbreds were beautiful, I counted two chestnuts, two greys and a black mare. I spoke softly to each animal as it nuzzled the treat from my open palm, then pressed my face against theirs and felt the connection I had thought forgotten.

"They like you, miss." A young man's voice broke the comfortable silence, and I turned to find Johnny Dainty the stable lad one stall down, a horse brush in his hand.

"It is mutual." I smiled and stepped back from a black mare. "You and Mr. Hogg keep a fine stable, Johnny. The horses are well cared for and very content." The young man beamed, his smile advertising the gap in his front teeth. He sported a thatch of ginger hair, and his face was a riot of fine freckles. With a body the size of a petite woman, Johnny appeared far younger than his actual years.

He nodded towards the black horse. "That a'one be Jezzabel, she's my favorite, miss. Want to help me give her a brush down?"

Now it was my turn to beam with pleasure. "I would love to."

****

My time in the stable was wonderfully cathartic. At least the horses were happy to be with me, which was more than could be said for the youngest Clayton.

Back in the schoolroom writing on the chalkboard, I awaited my pupil, who upon his arrival uttered not a single word, but took his place at one of the desks with eyes downcast.

"Good morning, Master Gideon." I greeted him and tried to inject a positive and happy note to my words.

"Morning," he replied without looking my way.

I sighed. His morose disposition did not encourage my desire to teach. I took a deep breath and approached him, taking a seat at an adjacent desk.

"Master Gideon, we should establish a few ground rules before we go any further in this arrangement."

He glanced up at me, and again I was so taken by his strong resemblance to Aramintha. "What are you talking about?" He frowned.

"We are fated to spend inordinate amounts of time together. I should prefer it if we could make this an amicable situation rather than one full of disinterest and boredom." I had his attention. He appeared somewhat confused, but at least he was listening.

"As I mentioned yesterday, if not me, your mother will ensure someone is here to tutor you. That, or you will be sent off to boarding school. I have no notion of your past experiences with other teachers, but here you have an opportunity to work with me and start the way you mean to go on." I shrugged. "To become educated is not simply a case of cramming books and reciting Latin. The pursuit of knowledge should also be an adventure. Consider this. We can get the basics lessons covered early each morning and then spend the rest of our time together outside. Or we might conduct scientific experiments, travel to nearby places of interest and learn about the area, perhaps even venture to London to see some notable landmarks. Truly Master Gideon, learning can be a wonderful voyage of discovery."

The boy seemed to be riveted to my words, and his eyes shone bright with curiosity.

"Or," I continued, "it can be a monotonous drudge. You could spend hours inventing ways to be disrespectful and childish, while I conjure up punishments and detentions, wishing I was somewhere else and not teaching you." I reached out and touched Gideon's shoulder, he flinched but did not pull away.

"Tis your decision Master Gideon. This can work or not. There are many other pupils I can teach." I dropped my hand and rose. I had said enough. Now it was for him to determine the road we would take. I walked to the board and wrote out the morning lesson.

"Do you mean that?" His voice broke the quiet. I turned. His light brow was drawn.

"Will we really be able to go out and do other things, experiments, take trips?"

I nodded. "Yes. Obviously, we would need Lady Clayton's permission to venture away from Mowbray, but I do not see why she would take issue." We stared at one another for a long moment, and then much to my complete and utter amazement, Gideon Clayton smiled.

****

The remainder of the morning flew as we studied arithmetic, literature and French. I left Gideon to spend the last thirty minutes translating a paragraph of Latin, with luncheon to follow immediately afterwards. I went to my chamber and procured my cloak, collected my hat and gloves and set out from the manor to find the family chapel. I walked the long driveway under a weak mid-day sun and harbored a sense of wonder that it had only been two days since the coachman had driven me along this very road. I reached the end of the driveway where it met the country lane and happened upon one of the gardeners, who kindly pointed me in the direction of the chapel.

Before long, a small spire came into view, with its iron cross pointing up to the sky. I rounded the corner of the lane and there it stood. A lovely little chapel constructed from crude stone, capped with a thatched roof, so prevalent in this part of the country. The small graveyard bordered with healthy hedgerow was still a vibrant green despite the time of year. Several headstones of various ages poked out from the grass like scattered giant's teeth, and I found comfort that Aramintha did not lie here alone.

The wrought iron gate swung open with a gentle nudge, and I walked along a small footpath towards the chapel. As I passed some of the stones, I paused to read their inscriptions. As expected, many Claytons were buried here, but they were interspersed with other names, probably those who had married into the family. Some gravestones were dated as far back as the sixteen-hundreds, their dedications barely legible. The newer stones appeared to be placed closer to the bordering hedges, and I stepped onto the damp grass to investigate further.

This group were certainly far more recent. Lord Nigel Clayton's parents, Lord Nigel himself, and two smaller stones which appeared to be infant children of the current Lady Clayton. I searched among the headstones yet could not locate Aramintha's marker. I walked back the way I had come, along the same row of stones. No, I was not mistaken; she was not here. Puzzled, I went around the perimeter of the graveyard and stopped at each grave, then made my way around the remainder of the area. Aramintha's tomb was nowhere to be seen.

"Are you in search of buried treasure?" The deep voice jolted me from my task, and I spun around, my heart pounding. My breath came fast, I had thought myself alone and now felt somewhat vulnerable by the arrival of another. As I quickly regained composure, I recognized my interloper. Aramintha's half-brother stood with his hand rested lightly on an old tombstone, with the appearance of a dark specter himself. He made an arresting portrait. Tall and well-built, his indigo coat added to the imposing figure he presented. I observed his strong jaw, the angles of his cheekbones, the Roman nose. My eyes then settled upon his, deep blue and brooding under thick black brows.

"No, sir," I replied to his question. "Everything buried here should stay under the ground where it belongs."

A smile played around his lips, and in an instant, the harshness of his expression melted away. He moved closer. "Miss Westcott, is it not? Allow me to introduce myself. Benedict Swan."

I nodded. "Kathryn Westcott. It is a pleasure to meet you, sir."

"Benedict, please," he said firmly. His eyes narrowed. "I carry no title at Mowbray Manor, I am an employee, not unlike yourself."

I smiled. "Indeed."

"What brings you to the chapel?" he enquired as he casually removed black leather gloves from his hands.

"I took a walk for some air," I lied. "One of the maids mentioned the chapel and I was curious to look about. After all, it is not often one can view a church with a thatched roof." Had I imagined it, or did Benedict Swan relax a little at my explanation?

"Have you ventured inside yet?" he enquired.

"No." I glanced over at the large wooden door. "May I?"

"Of course," he replied kindly. "I'll give you a guided tour if you like?" He moved towards the building and beckoned me to follow.

The chapel was dark inside. Sunlight glittered through leaded stained-glass windows, casting soft hues of blues and reds across four rows of rustic pews. Though barely larger than my bed chamber, it did not give a sense of being closed in. At the stone altar lit by two candelabra, there were baskets of pink chrysanthemums and rose hips placed upon the ground. Above the altar, against the wall of the chapel hung a large crucifix, with a depiction of Jesus with his eyes raised to the Heavens.

"What a lovely place," I muttered without thinking, and then realized I had spoken my thoughts aloud. "I have never seen anything quite like it." I was being honest. The churches and cathedrals I had visited in London and Barcelona were vastly different.

"It is rudimentary in decoration," Benedict commented and came to stand right behind me.

"Yes," I agreed. "Yet somehow its simplicity only adds to the elegance. Humble, yet regal. Simply charming Mr. Swan."

"Benedict." He stepped beside me and turned his head to glance around. "I used to come here often as a boy. Gabriel and I would hide here when he was called in for his nightly bath."

I chuckled. "Boys are like cats with their mutual abhorrence for water." I stepped away and went to one of the low windows to look at the design.

"The chapel dates back to the seventeenth century." Benedict moved to an adjacent window. "The glass also, somewhat gothic in design, wouldn't you agree?"

"Yes," I concurred. "It is fascinating." The images on the stained mosaics were basic and primitive. My window had a depiction of the disciple Paul. This I knew not from my scant religious instruction, but because his name was written underneath.

"Does the family use the chapel at all?" I stepped away and walked about the place. Benedict stood still, the hue of the glass shifting over his form.

"Seldom. It is far too small to conduct services, but as you saw, the family are buried here keeping with tradition."

I glanced at the fresh flowers and candles. "Who takes care of everything? It certainly looks as though someone does."

Benedict left the window and walked towards the door. I followed behind.

"Juniper Blessing, a local woman. She's unable to work due to a disability which makes walking difficult and is paid a small stipend in exchange to tend the chapel and the graves. No doubt she saw us coming and went off, Juniper doesn't like to be around people."

"Oh." How odd? *A sanctuary kept in good order for the dead*?

Benedict opened the chapel door and we stepped back out into the chill of the early afternoon. What remained of the sun peeked shyly between the clouds and the wind collected bluster. We walked up the pathway to the gate and I had to ask the question burning upon my lips.

"Benedict. I was told of the recent death in the family?" He came to an abrupt stop and turned to look at me, his eyes hard as flint.

"What of it?' he said, his tone at once menacing.

I swallowed and willed myself to be confident and not flinch under his imposing glare. "I saw no new headstone, and I wondered—"

"I would suggest you keep your thoughts to yourself Miss Westcott. You are new to these parts and this family. It would be somewhat reckless for you to busy yourself with the private affairs of the Claytons." He drew on his gloves.

I blinked in astonishment at his words, not expecting such a curt response. I had been reprimanded and warned off. But why?

"I would walk you back to the manor Miss Westcott," he continued. "But I have business in the village. Good day to you." Benedict gave me a curt nod and then strode away while I remained where I stood at the gate, speechless. I let out a deep breath and regained my composure, annoyed for becoming quite so rattled. What was amiss here? I could not for the life of me begin to guess.

I set off back down the lane towards Mowbray, my step a little quicker than it had been on my way to the chapel. It unnerved me, this constant aversion to any mention of dear Aramintha. Why was her death kept quiet? It made no sense. How could something as tragic and terrible as her loss never be spoken of? This broke my heart, for everyone behaved as though she had never existed at all.

The wind persisted. I pulled my cloak tighter about my neck when out of the corner of my eye, I saw a splash of color against the backdrop of trees at the edge of the lane. I came to a halt and spun around just as a small figure moved in the woods. A woman, too far to see her face, just the outline of her crooked body and the deep blue of her shawl. She stopped and stared at me for just a moment, and then began to move away in the direction I had just come. It appeared to be an effort for her limbs to move her slight form. For as she walked, her legs dipped severely at the knees as though she might fall at any moment, then rose up awkwardly again. Each step was choreographed the same way as the previous, and I felt guilty for taking my own agility for granted. This must be the woman Benedict had spoken of, Juniper Blessing. Small wonder she was unable to work, the poor thing was practically a cripple.

****

Upon my return to the manor, I sought out Baxter in order to request a meeting with Lady Clayton. He assured me he would let me know as soon as was convenient. I went into the kitchen and looked in the staff dining room to see if there was anything for luncheon.

"You look all windblown I must say," Mrs. Oldershaw greeted me. The cook sat at the table spooning broth into her mouth, a huge chunk of crusty bread on a platter beside her. "Get you some broth from the hearth Missy and come and sup wi' me if you will." I went back into the kitchen and procured a bowl of soup and returned to take a seat across the table from the robust woman.

Fanny Oldershaw had the build and countenance of a northerner. Pasty-faced, rosycheeked with arms the size of hams. Her frizzy blonde hair wriggled out from under the mooring of her cap, and her bright eyes shone like pieces of sea-glass. "Sorry I've not 'ad much of a chance to speak wi' you, miss. It's been a might busy since you came the other night."

"Please," I remonstrated, "do not apologize, you have your hands full running a large kitchen like this." I sipped the broth finding it delicious.

"Here," she gestured to the platter of bread. "Have you some. It'll put a lining in your stomach." I took a hunk of bread and dipped it into my soup.

"I stay right busy and no mistake. Her ladyship likes to feed her boys, so she does. The masters eat more than the laborers out in yonder fields." She took a spoonful of broth.

"Have you been with the family a long time Mrs. Oldershaw?"

"Aye, you could say that." She dabbed her mouth with her serviette. "Nigh on twenty-nine year give or take. It were just after Master Gabriel were born when I started here, though back then I was only under-cook."

"My goodness, that is a while. Where are you from, up north somewhere?"

"Aye, Lake District, near Graythwaite, do you know the place?"

"Why, yes." I was pleased to find a common footing other than our employer. "I spent several weeks in the area as a child. We roomed in Hawkshead. I believe that to be quite close to your village?"

The cook beamed. "Aye, it is. Just a few miles down the lake from there. 'Tis a lovely place, and if it weren't so pretty here by the sea, I would have long since returned home." She was wistful, as though she had travelled back there in her mind. Her eyes clouded.

"Do you have family still there?"

"No," she said sadly. "The last one was me brother, Thom. Now he's gone there's nowt there to go back fer. No, the Claytons are the closest I have to family nowadays." She took more of her broth and a reflective silence settled between us. I wanted to ask Mrs. Oldershaw so many questions but was mindful not to arouse any suspicion of my interest. I trod lightly.

"Mrs. Oldershaw, I wonder if you can help me with a matter?"

She glanced up at me. "Well, I'm sure I'll try, miss."

I took a breath. "I would like to get to know Master Gideon better, it is important we get along well. But he seems terribly unhappy, and for the life of me I cannot guess what could trouble a lad his age? At first, I thought my arrival had upset him, but it seems to be something more." I paused to look at her, and there it was again—the subtle stiffening of the face, a shift in the atmosphere, a change of disposition.

"Well I shouldn't worry if I were you, it's just the Master being difficult, boys are like that when they're ready to leave childhood behind. His brothers were the same." Cook gathered up her dish and spoon and prepared to leave the table. I took a chance.

"I am convinced it is more than that. When Master Gideon spoke of his late sister, he seemed very distressed about her loss. I do not want to cause anguish by asking him questions, though if I understood what had happened, it would be easier to help."

The cook rose to her feet and glared at me, all traces of amenability gone. "Then you should take your questions and ask her ladyship. I'll not talk ill of the dead." With that, Fanny Oldershaw turned on her heels and left me alone in the dining room.

I was annoyed. I had taken on the role of tutor and now felt as though I acted in a play without being given any lines to speak. Everyone here knew something of Araminta's fate, though none were willing to share their knowledge and I alone remained ignorant. Other than her death, I knew nothing about what had happened to my dearest friend. I was appalled.

Baxter's outline loomed in the doorway.

"Lady Clayton will see you now in the drawing room."

I thanked the old man as he shuffled away. Going from the kitchen to the main part of the house, my heart raced under my irritation. I had more than a few things to say to Lady Blanche Clayton.

Chapter Five

I knocked, and at her response, strode into the room. The heat rose in my cheeks. I took a deep breath to control my feelings. As before, Lady Blanche sat at her bureau, placing a document down on the desk. She did not move but slid her attention over to me.

"Miss Westcott, how may I help you?" Her tone was polite, but her expression conveyed annoyance at the interruption.

"Lady Clayton, a few words if I may?" My voice was firm, gone was the nervous girl of just two days hence.

One elegant eyebrow arched, and then reluctantly she gestured for me to approach. This time there was no offer of a seat, I was to stand before my employer and deliver my speech. Undaunted, I drew closer.

"I would like your permission to speak frankly, Lady Clayton." She nodded assent.

"I am come to talk to you about Gideon."

She sighed, her obvious assumption likely that I was there to report bad behavior on Gideon's part, or some such action. "Go on," she instructed, her tone already laced with frustration.

"I am worried about your son. He has a very sad disposition, and I believe he suffers from a depression of the mind."

Lady Clayton's face registered a look as though I

had said my father was the Prince of Wales. I ignored it and continued.

"In conversation, Gideon spoke of his sister and what happened to her." Lady Blanche made a slight sound, but I looked at her directly without pause and continued.

"The tragedy has made a marked negative impression on Master Gideon. I have endeavored to discover the circumstances of what happened in order to understand what he struggles with, so I might assist. Yet I am met with disdain, bordering on dislike when I have asked even the politest of questions."

Lady Clayton got to her feet and took a step towards me. I held my ground, even though I could see the mixture of anger and hurt which gleamed from her bright eyes.

"Miss Westcott, I do not know who you believe yourself to be, so let me remind you. You are an employee of this house, neither friend nor family to the Claytons, yet you determine to have the right to snoop and busy yourself with my private affairs?"

"Indeed, you are wrong, Lady Clayton. I have no desire to intrude or cause any slight to you and your family. But I am employed to tutor your son, and as an outsider, it is apparent that Gideon is troubled. I have a duty towards his wellbeing. Therefore I thought it only right to speak to you."

Blanche Clayton sighed. I stood not two feet from her, and with our similar height we were eye to eye. I sensed the conflict raging within her. Was I friend or foe? For a woman of her station she could dismiss me with a flick of her hand, bid me to leave Mowbray Manor and be done with me and my enquiries.

"Sit." The word left her lips as a command. I obediently walked to the sofa and took a seat while she chose a chair. Once again, we sat opposite one another.

"I am well aware of my son's mental state these past few months." Her voice wavered with discomfort. "Gideon and my daughter were close. They spent time together when Aramintha—" she paused, "was home with us. It is understandable he feels her loss deeply; we all do."

"It is to be expected," I interrupted. "But why will no one speak of her?" The question burst from my lips. "Everyone at Mowbray acts as though she was never here, surely that cannot help Gideon?"

"Enough," she hissed. "You know nothing of the situation, and after one day with my child, you certainly cannot claim to understand him!" Her face was taut and ghostly pale. "My daughter died because she threw herself off a cliff, for reasons I choose not to share with you. Suffice it to say she killed herself, and I will not have my family bear the shame nor responsibility of her selfish actions." She rose to her feet, still ashen, her silver eyes blazed. "These are the circumstances, Miss Westcott. And I strongly suggest you either abide by the rules of my house and respect my wishes, or pack your bags and return to London. I will not tolerate your interference on this matter. You were engaged to teach my son in his lessons, and therefore I advise you to stick to your duties." She glared at me for another moment and then strode to her desk and sat down. "You are dismissed."

Her tone conveyed my insignificance. I rose from the settle unsure what to remark, and decided it better to hold my tongue. I walked to the door and left the room, my mind a whirl with her words. Suicide? The word sat uncomfortably in my head and I pushed it away with distaste. Aramintha would never have given up her chance to live, a person with more vitality and spirit I had never met. Yet it would account for the aversion to speak of her. When a family member took their own life, it devastated the survivors and often cast a poor reflection upon the family and friends of the dead person. I could easily see how someone of Lady Blanche's noble standing would evade what had supposedly occurred. She mixed in a society which would potentially snub her because of such a stain. These reasons for the bizarre behavior exhibited at the mention of Aramintha's name made complete sense to me—except I would not believe for one single, solitary moment that my friend Aramintha Clayton had killed herself.

With a heavy heart, I ascended the staircase to the schoolroom to find Gideon waiting patiently for my arrival. He appeared less downcast than earlier that morning, though he radiated no warm welcome either. At least we had made a little progress.

"Good afternoon, Master Gideon." I gave him a half-hearted smile. "To start, I would have you read two chapters of your book please, and then we shall work on Geography."

He picked up his book as I took a seat at my desk.

"Have you spoken to Mother about my taking a lesson away from Mowbray?" The anticipation in his voice was evident. I had unintentionally discovered a pastime the boy was excited to begin.

"Not yet, but I shall as soon as possible. I would like our first expedition to be Corfe Castle. Are you familiar with the place?"

His lips pursed as he thought. "Yes, I went there many years ago, but I must have been quite young, because I can't really remember it."

"We will need to take the train, but it is only one stop down the line. I will ask permission from Lady Clayton, and then we can make plans."

"Plans for what?" a male voice asked, and Gabriel Clayton sauntered into the room. "Where are you off to with young Gid?" His handsome face stared at me while the smile reached his sparkling blue eyes. I blinked and wondered if the man had an uncanny knack to unsettle all females, or just me. I fought to keep the stain of embarrassment from my cheeks after our encounter last evening.

He walked over to his brother and tussled his curly hair. "What adventure does our Miss Westcott plan to take you on, Gid?"

Gideon's face glowed with pleasure at this attention. He was obviously in awe of the older Clayton. "To Corfe Castle, Gabriel, well if Mother says we may. I do hope she does. It's been an age since I got to go anywhere."

"Indeed? Perhaps because you've been so ill-mannered? Can't go on daytrips with your teachers when they do not last more than a few days, eh boy?" He smacked him on his back lightly, and then came over to stand at my desk.

"When do you go on this outing?" he enquired.

"With Lady Clayton's permission, we would go on Thursday. We can take the train from Swanage to Corfe in the morning, spend a few hours, and return before dark." I glanced up at him. "Do you think your mother will approve?"

He shrugged his shoulder. "I doubt it." He saw my crestfallen face and let out a laugh.

"Come now, Miss Westcott, do not be so disappointed. She will not want her precious Giddy out in the wilds of Dorset with naught but a young slip of a girl like you to protect him."

"I beg your pardon?" I got to my feet, my pride wounded. "Lord Clayton, I do believe myself more than capable of taking care of your brother." Gabriel held out a hand to stop me from going further.

"Of course you are. I did not intend to imply you weren't. It is Mother you have to convince, and that will not happen."

"It's not fair," Gideon moaned.

"For goodness sake, Gid, stop whining, boy." He regarded me. "Have no fears, Miss Westcott. I will see to it Mother gives her assent. Please make your plans for Thursday and do not worry over it any longer." With that, he spun on his heel and walked out of the schoolroom leaving myself and Gideon, staring at one another with bemused expressions.

We resumed our previous actions, Gideon read his book while I pretended to look through a textbook, all the while attempting to harness my meandering thoughts. Gabriel Clayton had blown in here like a busy wind and set the dust to scattering. Now at his departure the room seemed a little duller. My mind conjured up his lovely face, the rascal smile and the hint of wickedness in his blue eyes. My pulse quickened, and I bit my bottom lip hard. I was being foolish. Had I not come to Mowbray for one purpose and one only? I must clear my mind, take stock and straighten my wits. In a scant two days I had discovered the loss of someone very dear. Was I to be distracted now by a handsome face and a smatter of attention? Indeed, I would be a terrible friend if that was all it took to steer me from my sworn course. I silently admonished myself, a man of Lord Clayton's social rank would never be interested in an ordinary woman like me. The quicker I stopped thinking such nonsense, the better. After all, I was here to discover the truth. What had happened to Aramintha?

Chapter Six

I was not invited to join the family for dinner that night, thank goodness. Was the lack of invitation down to my position as staff, or if it had been encouraged by Lady Clayton's displeasure with me? Either way, I was happy enough to eat with the other servants downstairs.

We ate before dinner was served upstairs, I sat next to Campbell, but she was not talkative. Instead, she gulped her meal down and exclaimed she had to be back to dress her ladyship before dinner. Though the servants' food tasted far less exotic than the dishes served to the family, I found it nonetheless a hearty fare. Thick stew and fluffy dumplings, followed with apple pie, the fruit so tart it almost made my eyes water, and pastry as light as a snowflake. By the time I ascended the stairs to my room, my stomach felt full and content. I spent a little time with my book and fell into a deep and dreamless sleep.

Wednesday morning arrived quickly, and the day passed easily as Gideon and I read about the history of Corfe Castle, and its strategic importance during the English civil war. Our studies were heightened, when a note arrived from Lady Clayton, with permission for us to venture there on the morrow. Gideon beamed like a lantern, his eyes bright with happiness at the prospect of a journey away from the house. I reminded him it was because of his brother's intervention. I felt certain

Gabriel had persuaded Lady Clayton and won her approval. I would thank him when next we met.

We took a short walk that afternoon into the village, where I purchased ink for my fountain pen while Gideon spent his coin on a currant bun from the bakers. Mowbray Village was a small hamlet, the larger town of Swanage being only another two miles farther on. It consisted of a cobbled lane with houses and small shops on either side.

I counted a baker's, butcher's, greengrocer's and the obligatory fishmonger's shop. Situated a scant half-mile from the sea, fresh fish must be a daily staple. On the opposite side of the street stood the apothecary's shop, an ironmonger and the post office, which doubled as a grocer. The last building was a public house on the corner named *The Bull and Boat*. Its massive wooden sign depicted a menacing horned bull goring the side of a sinking vessel.

Gideon and I strolled through the village and many of the locals smiled and nodded at us both, then whispered to one another as we passed by. We stopped at most of the shops to look in the windows. As we reached the pub, I saw a solitary stone house and then the grounds of the church and rectory, where I assumed the Plumbs made their home. Gideon had been regaling me with stories about the various inhabitants of Mowbray Village, and now he pointed at the house.

"And that's where the surgeon, Doctor Beedles lives. You'll probably see him at Mowbray, I imagine. He often comes to attend Mother and gives her powders. Though I don't know what's wrong with her, she looks healthy enough to me." Gideon continued to chat as we passed the large village graveyard and the tall spire of the church.

"Good day to you, Miss Westcott and Master Gideon!" The dulcet tones of Mrs. Plumb reached us as she rushed down the path from the church to catch us before we passed by.

"Good day," we replied in unison as the heavyset woman reached the gate, her ample bosom inflated and deflated like bellows as her lungs fought to catch air.

"Oh my." She flustered and held a hand to her chest, "I am quite out of breath."

"Then please rest a moment," I encouraged. "Master Gideon and I are off back to the manor. We took a walk to escape the schoolroom and stretch our legs."

"Tis a chilly day," Avril Plumb declared with a shiver. "Perhaps too cold for even two as hale and hearty to be out for a stroll."

"On the contrary," Gideon replied. "It is good to get exercise and keep your muscles strong, at least that's what Benedict says."

The Vicar's wife smiled indulgently. "Indeed. But be careful you don't take a chill, this time of year is always so damp, gets right into my lungs." She then began to regale us with a litany of every ailment she had endured since her relocation to the coast. I could feel Gideon's desire to bolt and run, so at the first possible opportunity, I extricated us from both the conversation and her company. We bade Mrs. Plumb a friendly farewell and set back on the road home.

After an affable walk, we arrived back at the manor and parted ways for the remainder of the day. I went to the kitchen and made myself a cup of tea to take up to my room.

"That you, Miss Westcott?" Cook enquired as I poured hot water into the teapot. The older woman was in the pantry, but she came out to join me. "I thought I recognized your step. Will you be needin' a picnic made for your outing tomorrow?"

"No, thank you, Mrs. Oldershaw, we will not want to carry anything, there is a tearoom in Corfe Village, I thought we'd have luncheon there."

"Well, it's as good a place as any to get a meal." She smiled good-naturedly. "It'll do the young master a world of good having a day out of the manor."

"It most certainly will." I went to the pot, stirred the brew and poured a cup for myself. I offered the cook a cup and she accepted with a smile, a much different expression than when last we spoke.

"Come and sit with me in the dining room for a spell if you would Miss Westcott, I've a mind to have a word." I followed her in, and she closed the door behind us. We sat down at the table.

"Is something amiss?" Unease laced my words. Had I inadvertently offended someone or overstepped my line?

"No, nothin' of the sort." She spoke kindly. "I wanted to talk to you without nosy ears listening. "Look, miss, it's mighty sorry I am for being so testy when we spoke yesterday. I was a bit rushed off my feet, but it were no cause to snap at you when all you wanted was to help my young master."

Her words brought relief and a small twinge of guilt. I had used Gideon to try and pry information regarding Aramintha, but my intentions had been honorable. "Mrs. Oldershaw, you have no need to apologize, I did not mean—"

"Hush now, Miss Westcott, tis a mess you're found yourself here I'll be bound. Ever since the young lady of the house passed away, things have not been right at Mowbray Manor. In all the years I've worked here there's never been a hair's breadth of scandal, not even with the old Lord's bastard mingling with the family."

My thoughts flew to dark, brooding Benedict.

"When poor Miss Aramintha fell from the cliff, there's many said she jumped. An' though I don't know the real story, I think she might have done just that, an' brought shame to her family. Why else would Lady Clayton have no mourning gowns worn or mention of her bein' gone. Miss Tricklebank told the staff we were to behave like Lady Aramintha had never lived in this house." She shook her head solemnly. "There'd be no talk, or we'd be sent away without references."

I felt no surprise by her words, for had not Lady Clayton issued the very same warning to me?

"Now see, I don't hold with her sentiments on this, for Lady Aramintha was a dear girl. An' no matter how she died, tis not right to behave as though she never walked the earth, let alone grew up in this very house." She leaned forward, and her eyes shone with tears. "But hear you this, Miss Westcott. What's done is done, an' no harm can befall a dead girl, nor can her sensitivities be hurt. But the living? Well 'tis another matter entirely, and poor young master Gideon, he struggles with it all and his mother don't seem to worry none about it. So, long as you care for that boy and what befalls him, then you'll have my support. I've told you what I know, and I'll encourage others to do likewise in the interests of the young master. But mind my words well, I'll not help if 'tis for any other reason." She paused and gave me a harsh glare. "Do you follow?"

Numbly I agreed while my mind raced like a horse out of the starter's gate. "Thank you so much Mrs. Oldershaw. I am most grateful."

****

The morning of our outing, I woke with great anticipation and eager to begin the day. Hopefully, the changeable weather would stay dry for Gideon and me to explore.

At breakfast, Campbell came to sit by me. Again, I was struck by her prettiness as were several of the male staff who turned their heads with approving stares as she passed by.

"Morning, Miss Westcott," she said cheerily and sat down. The maid helped herself to toast from the large platter on the table, and then spread a liberal amount of marmalade across it. "Have you settled into Mowbray now you've been here a wee while?"

"Yes, thank you." I noticed her skin was like alabaster, which made me even more conscious of each freckle and mole upon my face.

"How do you find Master Gideon?"

"Very well, slowly coming out of his shell I believe."

"Good. I hear you are off on an expedition today to Corfe Castle? Now there's a wonderful place for a field trip."

"Indeed, I thought so too. It will be good for Gideon to spend a day away from home and get some fresh air."

Campbell agreed with me, yet something in her eyes belied her words. What was really going on in her thoughts?

After breakfast, Gideon came in search of me in the schoolroom, his face beaming with the anticipation of adventure. Though I had accomplished little else as tutor, at least the boy was happier than when I had first arrived at Mowbray. As we arrived downstairs, Lady Clayton entered the foyer once she heard our voices. I tensed, slightly awkward at our first meeting since the discussion a few days earlier. She kept her manner distant and polite, her usual demeanor, and from that I gathered all must be well. She instructed Gideon to keep his warm coat on and not to venture away anywhere on his own.

"Please stay with your brother at all times." I heard her comment. I opened my mouth to speak just as Gabriel approached.

"Ah, there you are Gabriel." Lady Blanche greeted her son and then glanced over at me, her face stern. "Lord Clayton will join you, Miss Westcott. I prefer you and Gideon do not travel unaccompanied as one can never be too careful."

I looked away so she would not see annoyance ripple across my face. This was supposed to be an outing for Gideon and myself, I had been anticipating the chance to bond with the boy, get to know him better and perhaps gain an ally in this strange house. As Gabriel donned his heavy coat, I did not pass a remark, but followed the Clayton brothers out of the house where the carriage awaited.

Gabriel sat opposite me, and as we set off, he glanced over and smiled kindly. "I hope you don't mind my tagging along Miss Westcott. Mother would not consent to your day trip, and it was only after some convincing that she finally concurred, but with the proviso I accompany you both.

"Indeed," I said stiffly, and then seeing the wide grin on his face, relented. He seemed as happy as his younger brother at the prospect of a day out.

"Then thank you for offering your time. It would have been a blow for Gideon if we had not been allowed to go."

"Yes," Gideon agreed strongly. "I might have gone off on my own anyway just to spite everyone. It's quite boring being home all the time."

Gabriel ruffled his brother's hair and told him not to even think about going anywhere by himself. "Besides," he laughed, "you have no sense of direction." His eyes smiled over at me. "When Gid was five, he got lost walking in our own gardens and went missing for several hours. We finally found him tucking into Cornish pasties at one of the gardeners' cottages. He thought he'd gone as far as London!" We all laughed.

We reached Swanage Railway Station. The place appeared far less formidable than the night I'd first arrived in Dorset. Gabriel purchased our tickets at the counter, and we waited for our train. Within ten minutes our party was Corfe bound.

Corfe Village lay but a few miles away from Swanage, and the duration of the trip lasted barely thirty minutes. As the ruins of Corfe Castle came into view, all the reasons for my being at Mowbray disappeared momentarily, and I took time to absorb my interesting surroundings.

From the train I could see the castle. The ruin was situated high on the rise of a hill which overlooked Corfe Village. Gideon and I had studied the history of the place, which made it far more stimulating to see. The castle, built by William the Conqueror in the eleventh century, had seen many battles over time. Oliver Cromwell and his Roundheads had succeeded in breaching the fortification during the English Civil War, and left the castle in ruins, rendered unfit for use by the Royalist Army ever again.

Though fragmented, with only the large walls of the structure left intact, Corfe Castle was nevertheless beautiful. It had stood for more than seven hundred years and yet still emanated a sense of dominance, a watchful eye over the beautiful Dorset countryside.

We left the train at Corfe station. Though the chill in the air nipped at our faces, we were sensibly dressed for the occasion and the November sun offered some comfort. We walked into the village, famous for the cutting of clay, and as a supplier to the great Josiah Wedgewood. The village was not considerable in size, but most pleasant to behold. The houses appeared well kept, constructed from local limestone quarried close by.

The castle, unlike most completed under William the Conqueror's reign, had been built of stone and not timber and consequently ranked as higher in status and mentioned in several historical documents. Corfe Castle was intended to guard the principal route through the Purbeck Hills, and therefore had been assembled on a steep rise in a gap between many other hills in the area. Its name *'Corfe'* derived from an old English word *ceorfan*, the definition of the word was 'a cutting,' in reference to the gap.

We passed a variety of shops, a post office, a pub, and finally the tearoom where we would take refreshment after our walk. At the approach to the castle there were a number of people come out to take advantage of the dry day. Some apparently working, but others like us, purely enjoying part of our shared history.

As we walked through the gatehouse Gideon bolted towards the castle, running up the path through what had once been the outer bailey but was now a large expanse of grass. I began to call him back, but was stilled by Gabriel, who lightly touched my arm.

"Let him go, Kathryn. He'll come to no harm here. The place is safe enough."

"But your mother—"

"I am responsible for my brother today, not you, so please stop worrying and just enjoy yourself."

I smiled at him, and he returned the gesture. I was again struck by his handsome face, the arresting eyes. I also enjoyed the way he spoke my name. He made it sound almost pretty.

"Miss Westcott, Gabriel, do come and look!" Gideon called out as his face poked out from a window of the keep.

"Come along, Kathryn," Gabriel commanded. "We are in for a time of it I think."

****

By two o'clock that afternoon when I finally took a seat in the tearoom, my feet ached as though I had traversed miles. Gideon had talked non-stop since we arrived. I purported for a thirteen-year-old boy, the castle had conjured up many adventures in his imagination. He was especially fascinated to learn of the vicious battles waged so close to his own home.

"And imagine. It took a woman to defeat Oliver

Cromwell the first time. Lady Bankes had been left in charge of the castle as her husband was away fighting for the Royalist army. Cromwell had to return a second time to best her. He razed the castle in order to take it by placing gunpowder in the foundations of the castle to make it unsafe. Awfully clever that, but at least he allowed Lady Bankes to leave before he lit the gunpowder." Gideon managed to convey the entire story while simultaneously devouring a thick chocolate éclair, his mouth full of pastry and fresh cream.

Gabriel chuckled at his young brother. "For goodness sake Gid, do stop talking, you're getting food everywhere." Gideon grinned with a display of cake covered teeth, and his older brother shook his head. His gaze settled upon me. "What did you think of Corfe, Miss Westcott?"

I finished my last bite of a delicious iced bun and sipped my tea. I dabbed my mouth with the serviette.

"A fascinating place," I crooned. "I am stunned to think it so very old. How such buildings were constructed in times when their tools were limited, well it is beyond my comprehension."

"Indeed, especially when you allow for the fact that although razed by Cromwell's gunpowder, it still did not demolish the castle so well was it constructed," he agreed.

"Limestone must be very impermeable," I declared.

"And they cut the walls thick too, don't forget," Gideon interrupted with his mouth still full. Gabriel and I exchanged glances and laughed.

We passed the rest of our refreshment in pleasant conversation about the sights we had seen, and then took our leave to catch the train. Gideon, still full of youthful energy, walked ahead of us, his attention caught by this and that, which left Gabriel and me to saunter along together. I felt much at ease with the Clayton heir. His manner was gentle, his attention generous, and we soon settled into an amicable companionship. So much so, I grew a little bolder with my topics of conversation and eventually steered them towards Aramintha. Though hesitant to raise a subject which caused him sorrow, my pledge to discover my dear friend's fate won out.

"You must miss you sister," I stated.

Gabriel sighed, and his face became drawn. "Yes, I do. Each day I still expect to see her come down for dinner, or out strolling the grounds. There is a huge void at Mowbray none can fill."

"Your mother seems to bear the loss stoically, which is fortunate. I imagine that must bring you relief. To see her mourning has to be difficult."

He glanced at my expression as though to read my true meaning, and for a moment I thought he might be successful. I strengthened my guard. I would not fail my friend.

"My mother is a strong woman with a great sense of duty. She will never display her emotions publicly. But don't be fooled, Kathryn. Just because Mother has the curtains pulled open each day and is not dressed in black, do not think for one moment she does not mourn. The loss of a child to a mother is unnatural, a tragedy which can never be assuaged." He fell quiet.

"The loss of a daughter especially," I commented. "For one would think they must have been close, in a house full of men such as Mowbray." I fished for anything I could catch. "Was Lady Clayton close to Aramintha? I would imagine they were. I grew up without my mother, but I like to think had she been there we would have had a good relationship. As I do not know Lady Clayton personally, it is difficult to tell how she feels. What little I have heard of Aramintha has been very favorable."

"Aramintha was a joy," he stated flatly. "We were all drawn to her. She was a beautiful young woman with a very kind heart." I noticed the soft edges to his voice and heard the sincere affection he had for his sister. It warmed me to him. We had both loved her, though socially and economically far apart, this was the one thing Gabriel Clayton and I did have in common though he did not know.

"Come now." Gabriel turned to me. "Let us not speak any more of it today. Let us enjoy the remainder of our outing." He pointed to the distance at a large plume of steam. "See, here comes our train. We must hurry or we shall miss it. Gideon?" He called and gestured to his brother who was about to turn down the wrong street. "Gideon, this way, the train comes!"

I picked up my pace and hurried on.

****

By the time we arrived at Mowbray and alighted from the Clayton carriage, we were laughing and chatting about our day at Corfe. How quickly such a lightness of spirit had grown between us, a kinship developed from sharing an activity so enjoyable. As I stepped from the carriage, I lost my balance and would have fallen had not Gabriel placed his hands deftly upon my waist to arrest my descent. His fingers lingered longer than necessary, and I was given the full assault of his warm gaze.

"I must speak with you, Gabriel." I had not noticed Benedict standing close by. His stern voice pierced the moment, and in those words the revelry so pleasantly come was sent running at the tone of his command. Gabriel quickly released his hold on me and turned to his half-brother. They moved away, out of earshot, yet I could not help but observe the two. The angel and the demon, one head golden and touched by the sun, the other black and kissed by midnight. I walked from the carriage towards the door and cut a wide berth so not to disturb them. They paid no heed, for whatever their subject, it was not a happy one. Benedict's face wore a mask of anger and Gabriel's countenance appeared flushed. I passed by and went inside the manor.

****

Fully engulfed in my book, I started at the knock upon my door. Miss Tricklebank had a message—I was summoned to the drawing room by Lady Clayton. I felt some trepidation at the order. Was I in trouble? Thoughts tumbled through my mind as I descended the servants' stairs. Baxter met me at the drawing room door and ushered me in, his face drawn with age and worry.

"Miss Westcott, do come in." Lady Clayton was dressed in a pale blue silk gown, which heightened the paleness of her complexion. She could have been an ice maiden.

I approached as she remained seated in her usual chair, regal as the queen herself and surely as intimidating. She did not give me leave to sit, so I stood quietly before her.

"I gather your outing today was a great success,"

she stated. "Indeed, Gideon can speak of little else. It was good for the boy."

I remained silent, but I could not deny I was pleased she admitted my idea had been sound.

"Thank you for your consideration of my son's situation. It has been a time since I have seen him so happy."

I nodded in acceptance of her compliment. She rose from her seat and walked past me to the hearth. I followed her with my gaze. She turned and fastened her silver eyes on me, her face carved from marble.

"Miss Westcott, you have only been with us at Mowbray a few days and so are naturally unaware of some—" she hesitated as though having trouble selecting the correct words. "…some of our arrangements." I frowned, what was she speaking of?

"The Claytons are an old family and owe a great responsibility to the people of our community. Those responsibilities include the management of the estate, our farms and industry, and partnering with other distinguished families to keep the bloodline going."

I still did not understand what any of this had to do with me and my outing with Gideon, so I held my tongue.

"Miss Westcott, do you have any designs on my son, Gabriel?" The question was shot like an arrow and penetrated my skull with as much force.

"I beg your pardon?"

"I wish to know if you carry a personal interest in Lord Clayton, that of—" she stammered, "…a *romantic* nature?"

I opened my mouth to speak and found no words, because I was still processing her insinuation. I was insulted and a little embarrassed. Of course, I had no serious interest in Gabriel. Yes, there certainly was an attraction, though I would barely admit it to myself, never mind to his mother.

"You see," she continued. "Gabriel is an attractive man and often the target of young women's imagined desires. But I feel it my duty to inform you my son is engaged to be married to Lucy Ditton-Jones, a delightful girl. Our families have been friends for many years."

Something in my stomach flipped, the surge of disappointment almost a surprise to me. How ridiculous! Between Gabriel and me, there was no understanding, no alliance. Yet perhaps the notion there might be a spark of interest awakening there, had appeal. My memory played back images of our day out at Corfe together. It saddened me to recognize that in Gabriel's flirtatious behavior there had been deceit now I knew him engaged to marry another.

"Do you understand my meaning, Miss Westcott?" Her commanding voice splintered my thoughts.

"Absolutely," I replied. "I can assure you, Lady Clayton, my interest in both of your sons is purely in the role of tutor. I congratulate Lord Clayton on his engagement."

"Excellent." She smiled. "That is all." She turned her attention to the fire, and I left the room.

I lay down on my bed, exhausted. Physically, from our busy day in Corfe, and emotionally from the weight of the Clayton matriarch's words. So, Gabriel was engaged? He did not act like a man betrothed. Could he be in love with this Lucy Ditton-Jones? I certainly had no idea and without experience of my own to speak of, how would I? Yet I still felt foolish. Had I smiled at him too many times? Stared into those eyes longer than necessary? I remembered the touch of his hands upon my waist, and how his fingers had pressed into my body with purpose.

I turned out my lamp and lay back among the pillows. I closed my eyes and waited for my thoughts to go where they had each night at Mowbray. But tonight, instead of Aramintha's lovely face haunting my last waking thoughts, it was her brother's.

Chapter Seven

Morning classes went exceptionally well. Gideon was in fine fettle, his face bright with a ready smile. What a difference a few days had made, and how marvelous a single expedition could encourage such a positive turnabout. Though I had made scant progress discovering more of Aramintha's fate, at least there was some sense of satisfaction in the knowledge I had helped cheer Gideon up.

At luncheon, Mrs. Oldershaw informed me the family were going out for the afternoon to visit a neighbor, Viscount Royston Munt. I had never heard of the man, but Cook told me he was the wealthiest landowner in the parish, the county's most eligible bachelor and in Cook's opinion 'a tad bit odd if you ask me.' The Munts and Claytons were allies of old and visited one another regularly. Therefore, my charge was let out of the schoolroom at luncheon. I changed into my walking clothes, once the carriage departed down the driveway with the family inside.

A sudden sense of liberation took hold of me. I had been at Mowbray Manor for five days, and other than time in my room, this was my first opportunity to be alone and not at another's call. I gathered my cloak as the day was chilly but at least not wet. I decided to walk to Mowbray Village and then return to read my book in front of the fire. I left my room and went down the hall to the servants' staircase which led to the kitchen. I hesitated and peered in the other direction, where the hallway beyond my own room led to the center of the manor and the main stairs. Though I had ventured up to the schoolroom and the nursery floors, I had not yet seen any other part of the house. I was curious. It certainly was strange to have been here so many days yet still be ignorant of my surroundings.

I made an impulsive decision. With the family gone and most of the servants on their afternoon off, I could have a quick look around before going on my walk. Surely there was no harm in that? After all, I lived here, I had even dined with the family. It was only natural to have an interest in the rest of the house. But I was fooling myself because I knew what really drew me here—the desire to find Aramintha's bedroom.

Mowbray was a large building of four tiers, five if one included the basement, which also housed the kitchen, servants' dining room, Cook and Baxter's rooms and the wine cellar. The ground floor consisted of the drawing room, dining room, billiards room, library and study. The Clayton family resided on the first floor, while guest rooms occupied the second—the smallest of these apportioned to myself and Tricklebank. The third floor was for the children of the house, taken up entirely by the schoolroom, nursery, children's dining room and Gideon's chamber. This left the top of the house for all the staff, and an attic used for storage.

I went along the hall to the staircase and made my way down to the first floor, my eyes and ears alert to any unusual sound. All was quiet. I stopped at each door, opened it a crack to peek in and guess the identity of its occupant. The first room appeared empty, the next, very masculine, and most likely Gabriel's. Then came another empty chamber and finally the last, a grand, feminine room that could only be Lady Blanche's. I retraced my steps back to the staircase and went down the other side of the hall. Again, there were two empty chambers, but my heart picked up rhythm as I approached the last door. Would this be Aramintha's room? I cracked open the door and the breath left my lungs. I spied beautiful feminine furnishings and knew at once I had discovered her bedroom.

I glanced over one shoulder and stepped inside, closing the door softly behind me. Pink curtains on the huge windows were open and pale sunlight illuminated the space. I saw a large four-poster bed dominating the centre of the room encased in fabrics of pink and gold. Rich salmon-colored Aubusson carpet hushed my footfall as I leisurely explored the ornate furnishings and possessions of my dearest friend. The walls were adorned in pale pink wallpaper, the furniture all white, trimmed with gold piping. Upon a large settle sat a group of dolls in a row, and I stopped to touch their soft, ribboned hair.

A painful weight tugged my heart as I stood where my friend had spent so much of her youth. She had slept in this bed, looked up to this chandelier, sat by this fireplace and played with these dolls. But no more. Tears pricked the backs of my eyes as I allowed her image to come into my mind, but the lovely face disappeared only to be replaced by a vision of her broken body lying on the sand. I shook my head to clear my thoughts and told myself to get a grip on my emotions and quickly. This was no time to mourn, but to investigate. I must look for something, anything to explain what might have induced Araminitha to take her own life—if indeed she really had.

I approached her desk and opened the drawers. They were filled with expensive notepaper, pens, ink and envelopes, yet they were untidy, as though someone had rifled through them. There were several notes written by others, but none from me. Had she not wanted to keep mine? Of course not, Araminitha would have destroyed my letters, knowing full well her family would never approve of her friendship with someone of my class.

I picked up one of the pens and held it in my hand, realizing as I did that her fingers had held it long ago. Again, I felt a stab of tears and the thick blade of sorrow sliced my throat. It would not do to cry now. I lifted my hand to wipe my eyes, and the pen slipped from my grasp to the floor. It bounced on the carpet and landed underneath her desk. I dropped to my knees only to find it just beyond my reach. I moved beneath the desk until I was head and shoulders below and stretched as far as I could.

But what I saw caused me to pause. At the very back of the desk was a tiny hidden shelf affixed to the underside, small and flat, barely discernible to the naked eye. But there it was, and something appeared to be lodged within. I stretched out my hand to touch it. The place was cleverly concealed, discoverable only if one was completely underneath. My brain began to fire. Carefully, I grasped the object and pulled it free, along with a light amount of dust.

No larger than my hand, it appeared to be a small blue book. Gingerly, I opened the cover and gasped with delight to see Aramintha's own handwriting! Whatever this might be, to me, I had discovered a treasure. I got back to my feet and put the book in my pocket. I left the room quietly and closed the door securely behind me.

I walked cautiously down the hall to the stairs. Was I still alone? A faint noise caught my ear, like the click of a door being closed. I froze but heard nothing else. Satisfied, I ascended the stairs until I reached the third floor. Going down the hall and into my own room I locked the door, panting as though I had been running. Had someone seen me? Surely not. One of the maids was probably going into a room to clean.

I retrieved the book from my pocket and set it down upon the desk. I pulled up a chair, took a deep breath and opened the cover. The front page announced it to be a diary, with an inscription dated from the previous year, 1889. My pulse leapt. What a find! If I had not dropped the pen, I would never have known it there. No wonder it had lain undisturbed in such a clever hiding place.

The first entry was dated July 26th, 1889, a date I knew well as it was Aramintha's birthday.

I cannot believe today I am nineteen! A lump formed in my throat at her words. I swallowed and willed my tears not to come. I continued.

Benedict gave me this darling book which I shall use to record my thoughts and feelings. I have had a wonderful day. Mother presented me with a pearl necklace she wore at the same age, and it is truly lovely. Gideon has bought me paper and pens, and Gabriel has given me my very own horse! Her name is Poppet, and she is a beautiful grey mare with the sweetest disposition. I am happier than a girl deserves to be.

I remembered her letter to me last year where she had recounted the gifts. Aramintha had been so delighted, her joy had practically radiated from her words. I sighed and turned the page to another entry.

I am so clever, I have found a secret hiding place for this book, no one shall ever be able to find it! Today was marvelous. I rode to the Munts with A, and we raced one another. Of course, he won, and told me the prize was a kiss from my lips. I obliged. So long have I yearned to kiss him. He is a darling, and he is all mine!

I blinked and re-read the entry. Who on earth was 'A'? Aramintha had never mentioned a man with that initial, and she certainly had not spoken of anyone she harbored feelings for. What was she about? Who was she kissing? I moved on to the next entry.

Today A took me to Lulworth Cove as the sun was radiant and the weather perfect for the sea. There were many others there, but none we recognized. We managed to slip away to a beautiful secluded spot near an abandoned fishing hut. Dear God, it was blissful. I never knew it could be like this, that a person could elicit such feelings from me. I know I tread a rocky path, but when he holds me, I care not and fear not!

I was astounded. This could be a stranger's hand, not the Aramintha I knew. My friend had been a level-headed girl with a wonderful imagination, this person wrote like a love-sick schoolgirl. I flicked through a few more pages, more entries of places visited by Aramintha and the mysterious 'A'. Her words were romantic, gushing with her apparent love. Frankly, I felt it almost obscene to read her personal thoughts. I closed the book and stood with a sudden desperate need for fresh air. I plucked my cloak from the bed and placed it around my shoulders. I glanced at the diary and paused. I did not like to leave it anywhere in my room. After all, it was not mine, and I should not want to be found out and labelled a thief. I grabbed the book and put it back into my pocket. It was safest kept close.

A brisk walk would be the tonic. I ventured out the back of the manor, past the pond and down stone steps to the tree line and a distant view of the sea. The skies had become overcast, the scene dulled by sullen clouds and very little sunlight. But it felt good to breathe and calm my furious mind. One week ago, I had been in London, employed by the Buckleys, a middle-class family who had hired me as a governess to their twin daughters, Imogen and Ingrid. Now I found myself living on the Dorset coast, residing in a beautiful manor house with a family I did not begin to know or understand. Was this a fool's errand? Had I been wise to make the decision to leave my comfortable employ and unearth the fate of my dear friend?

Arabintha's notes trickled through my thoughts, and I balked at them, the silliness of them, the flight of fancy which seemed so far removed from the sensible girl I had known. The anguished cry of a seagull pierced my attention, and I stared up at the sky and watched the large bird circle down closer to the water until it became a grey dot below.

I paced along the edge of the gardens, the ocean to my right, the manor to my left, I walked, still deep in thought until I spied a small iron bench situated at an ideal viewing spot. Here I might sit for a moment and read more of the diary. I found where I had stopped reading and began to scan the pages. There were more outings, declarations of love and stolen kisses with the mysterious 'A.' I was tiring of it once again until I reached the centre of the book. Here was written a list of names in two columns, on one side masculine names, the other female. Odd? I read through the list and there seemed no pattern to them, or any surnames. A tiny suspicion budded in my mind, and I chased it away. Going back to the previous few pages, I read each entry in its entirety.

...and I thought it something I had eaten which was making me so ill. Only once I looked at my calendar did I realize what was really wrong with me. It is true! Inside my body, grows a wonder, a proof of our love. I am so very happy. I cannot wait to share this news with A.

An audible gasp left my lips. I checked the journal entry date—April 15, 1890. My mind calculated the time, my brain almost numb with shock. Aramintha Clayton had been with child.

****

My head spun as I got to my feet, battling an impulse to run into the house and find someone to tell. I could not grasp what I had read. Aramintha having a baby? This was too much to comprehend! My mind spun into a tangled web. I struggled to accept what I had read with my own eyes. And then it struck me. If Aramintha had been pregnant, it would have rendered her even more unlikely to have taken her own life and that of her unborn babe. I began to pace back and forth in front of the bench, and my feet lost the battle to keep up with my thoughts. I must walk and dissect this shocking information.

I headed towards Mowbray Village at a steady pace. I could not believe in the course of one week, my knowledge of Araminitha's fate only seemed to grow more complex and difficult to understand. First to find she had died, then to be told it had been suicide. Now to discover she was in love with a mysterious person and with child? It was too much. Had I not known Araminitha at all?

My legs carried me on to the village and, before long, I found myself outside the doctor's surgery. I had not made a conscious choice to come here, yet something had propelled me to the spot. Why? Did I think to confide in the doctor? Had he known of Araminitha's pregnancy? Before I could decide upon my course of action, the door opened, and an elderly lady stepped out. I obstructed her passage as I stood poised on the top step. She cleared her throat, and I quickly stepped aside and glanced into the surgery. Hesitantly, I went in and closed the door behind me.

The waiting room was small and dull, the only occupant a man who sat quietly reading a newspaper. I did not meet his eyes, but instead approached a desk where a stiff-backed lady sat making notes on a pad of paper. She paused and glanced up at me with a watery smile.

"May I help you?" Her voice was autocratic, and she reminded me of Matron back at Brampton.

"Yes please, might I be able to see Doctor Beedles?"

"Do you have an appointment?"

"No, I do not."

Her grey eyebrows rose, and she inspected a large clock on the wall. "Doctor Beedles will be leaving on a house call when he finishes with his patient. If you care to wait, I can ask if he has time to fit you in?"

"Thank you, that would be most kind."

She nodded and passed me a small card and a pencil. "Please be so good as to fill out your name and other pertinent information for the doctor." Her smile looked as if it had been painted on with a thin brush.

"Oh, I do not think I—" she stopped me with the wave of her blue-veined hand.

"Young lady, if you wish to see the doctor, you will have to fill out the notecard."

I smiled. She was Matron all right, to a tee. I took the proffered card, sat down in one of the chairs and did as I was told. I put the barest of information on there, but it would suffice for my purpose. Once finished, I returned the card.

Not five minutes later, the door opened, and a middle-aged lady came out looking the worse for wear. Her husband folded up his paper and got to his feet, his expression full of concern. She crooked her hand into his bent arm, and together they left the surgery. The doctor's assistant disappeared into the examination room and I heard a low murmur of voices. She reappeared.

"Doctor Beedles will see you now." She gestured towards the doorway as though I had just been granted an audience with the Pope.

"Thank you." I stepped into the room and closed the door behind me.

"Miss Westcott?" I was unprepared for the doctor's voice when it came, small and reedy. But as I turned to meet him, I realized it matched the man perfectly. Doctor Beedles came towards me with an outstretched hand, and I was astonished at his resemblance to a large rodent. Sinewy, his face narrow, features sharp and a mouth that seemed too close to his nostrils. Above his lip sat a flimsy puff of wiry hair, which mirrored the scant handful on the top of his head. He grasped my hand in introduction, and it felt as though I shook a handful of bones.

"Take a seat, my dear." He pointed to the chair on one side of his desk and I obeyed.

"I recognize your name, Miss Westcott. Are you not the new tutor engaged at the manor?" His eyes were small and dark, through the round lenses of his spectacles.

"Yes, I arrived earlier in the week."

"Hmm, good. I hope you are settling in with the family?"

"Yes, the Claytons have been most welcoming."

"Excellent, excellent." He leaned on his desk and steepled his fingers. "Well, Miss Westcott, how may I assist you? Are you unwell?"

I had not formulated a plan and was ill-prepared. It had been an impulsive decision to come. "Actually, no, Doctor Beedles. I want to speak to you regarding Master Gideon."

"I see." He bent forward and surveyed me. His eyes appeared to shrink as small as a rat's.

"I was unaware before coming to Mowbray Manor, that there had been a loss in the family. In fact, Gideon himself was the one who told me, and the boy is beyond distressed." I noticed the unmistakable bristle of his posture. I continued regardless. "I am his tutor, and though I have some experience with boys his age, it is a strain on our relationship in the classroom. I would appreciate your advice how to help him through such a difficult time? After all, you are the family doctor, and you more than any other would understand their situation." I managed to speak without alluding to the nature of Aramintha's death and fervently hoped I was not wrong-footed coming here. If the doctor took offense, he could report me to Lady Clayton, and my tenure at Mowbray would be at an end.

Doctor Beedles took his time to answer. "Miss Westcott, I do admire your heartfelt concern for young Gideon." He sat back in his chair with an authoritative sigh. "The Claytons have suffered terribly these past months with the tragic, senseless loss of a beloved daughter and sister. However, Lady Clayton has seen fit not to draw attention to the event, hence the lack of mourning or for that matter, any public display of sorrow or emotion. I would suggest it is her way to manage grief." He frowned through his glasses. "Unfortunately, it may not be so for someone of Gideon's age. It is likely he is depressed and probably unable to process her loss due to his mother's mandate. It is commendable you recognize his need for understanding and that you make allowances for his behavior."

"Thank you, Doctor Beedles. Any advice you might have would be welcome." I was disappointed. The man was not going to tell me anything.

"Indeed. It seems to me you are already on the right course Miss Westcott. Being sensitive to the nature of the boy will aid you. Alas, there is nothing you can do to remove the sadness he feels at his sister's passing but being supportive is the way to continue forward. It is unfortunate his mother is determined to remain in denial about what happened, but there it is." With that, the gaunt man got to his feet. The interview was at an end.

I rose as he came around the desk and walked to the door. I followed him. As I drew level I paused.

"I would appreciate your directness under the circumstances, doctor. I understand Aramintha Clayton fell to her death from the cliffs near the manor?"

"That is correct."

"There seems to be some confusion as to the nature of her death, and her condition?" I threw the word out there to see if he would make a remark that would be telling. He did not.

"Miss Westcott, I do not believe the exact manner of her death has any real bearing on young Gideon's state of mind. It is the fact she is gone which upsets the boy. Now I must be getting along, my dear."

And there it was again, another person who refused to say anything about Aramintha. I recognized his dismissal.

"Thank you so much for taking the time to speak with me, doctor, I do hope you understand my intentions are only for the best."

He smiled, and again I felt the same disdain at his rodent-like features. "Absolutely, Miss Westcott. Please do not hesitate to come and see me if you have any other concerns. Good day."

I left the surgery with a frosty farewell from the doctor's assistant and made my way back out into the street. Passing the church, my mind was full of questions when I blindly knocked against another pedestrian.

"Miss Westcott, are you feeling all right?" My eyes

met the dark blue gaze of Benedict Swan, his black brows drawn. I blinked to clear my head.

"Oh, excuse me. I was not paying attention to where I was going."

"Indeed, you were miles away." He smiled, and I noticed how his chiseled face softened under the humor. "Do you walk back to the Manor?"

I nodded. "Yes, and you?"

"Indeed. May I accompany you?"

In truth, I yearned to be alone and think. But not knowing how to decline, I agreed, and we set off down the lane.

"I trust you enjoyed your outing to Corfe yesterday?' We walked in unison, me a little faster to keep up with his pace. He noticed my hurry and slowed down.

"Yes, it was pleasant and most interesting. There is so much history in these old castles is there not?"

"There is. I am sure Gideon found it most entertaining."

"I believe so, it did him good to be out in the fresh air instead of being confined to the classroom."

"And apparently Gabriel had need of a diversion also?" he said drily, and without realizing I came to a stop. I looked up at Benedict with an explanation on my lips but found his painted with a grin.

"Relax, Miss Westcott," he said with a nonchalant air. "I am teasing. I imagine Lady Blanche would not let Gideon out of sight without her champion at his side."

We continued along, and I decided the regard he held for his half-brother did not extend to his stepmother. What a fascinating dichotomy there was between this family.

"How do you find Mowbray Manor after your first week here. Do you like the place, is it what you imagined?" he asked.

"Which question shall I answer first?" I replied, although I smiled at him. He returned the gesture.

"All right," I said. "I will answer in order. I rather like Mowbray. The manor is a comfortable home and the staff friendly. The area is quite lovely, and yes, it has very much matched and perhaps exceeded my expectations."

"Splendid," he commented, and I thought how easy he was to converse with, especially when he was of a jovial countenance.

"I have lived here my entire life," he continued. "Well, other than a brief stint in the army. So, I am of course very partial to Mowbray. Though I never stay at the manor, I have always been welcome. I enjoy my work helping run the place."

"I envy you your childhood somewhere this idyllic." My eyes cast over the rolling green hills either side of the lane, with the promise of the sea off in the distance. "I had no idea Dorset was such a pretty county, no wonder you stay on."

"I can assure you my remaining here is for quite another reason than its beauty. I stay because of a promise given to my father, Lord Clayton, to prepare Gabriel for the responsibility of the estate."

That surprised me, for I had imagined the brothers close in age. "When does he inherit?" Perhaps there might be some sort of stipulation to the deceased Lord Clayton's will.

"Gabriel inherited immediately after our father

died." His eyes creased at the mention of the loss, and he let out a sigh. "Unfortunately, Gabriel does not share my interest in managing the estate. My goal is to persuade a change in his mind, but it is taking longer than I originally expected." He tried to disguise the trace of irritation threaded through his voice, but ever the listener, I caught it and somehow was not surprised.

"Of course, once Gabriel marries, he will have to change his tune, perhaps employ someone else to manage his affairs."

That surprised me. "You will not stay on?"

"Absolutely not. Gabriel will need to be the head of the family, and not just in name only." He shrugged his shoulder. "Besides, I have other avenues in life I would follow if given the opportunity."

"Indeed?" Our conversation was more thought-provoking than I had anticipated.

"Yes, I would like to see more of the world, perhaps even return to Africa."

"Africa? When were you there?"

"I fought in the Boer War in South Africa. I was an army man. But I've a mind to try the Eastern side of the continent, Kenya. The place intrigues me. There are many British people with the same ambition."

"My, that is a long way from sleepy Dorset, what would you do in Kenya?" I noticed the distant bark of a dog. We were nearing the outlying farm of Mowbray Manor.

He looked around, hearing the animal as well, then glanced back at me. "I am most interested in the coffee plantation business, or even sugar cane farming. I have learned much of agriculture from my life here." He indicated the ploughed fields as we passed by. "I think I might be able to make a success of it with enough capital."

"My goodness, it sounds quite the adventure, Mr. Swan."

"Please do not be so formal. As I said before, I would prefer you call me Benedict. After all, we are both on the same social footing, wouldn't you agree?"

He was correct. The formality was a little out of place given both our circumstances, though he was the son of a peer, albeit a bastard son.

I conceded. "You are right of course, but I insist you do the same and call me Kathryn." We smiled our easy truce, and he guided me into the drive of Mowbray Manor. It seemed we had just left the village, yet here we were arriving back so quickly. Perhaps it felt that way due to the pleasant conversation we had shared? I certainly had not expected to enjoy his company, especially after our last encounter at the chapel, where Benedict Swan had essentially warned me from asking questions about Aramintha.

We made small talk the remainder of our journey until we reached the back entrance to the house. There, Benedict took his leave politely and walked off towards the stables, where I understood he lived in a nearby cottage within the grounds.

The kitchen was in the throes of preparing tea and the servants' meal. I did not stop to speak to anyone feeling more than ready to shrug off my cloak and rest my feet before dinner. In my short stay at Mowbray, my room was already a safe sanctuary after a long day, a place for solitude and calm. The fact it was such an elaborate bedroom did help encourage my time spent there. I felt as though I were not a lowly servant but a lady myself, surrounded by such finery.

I hung my cloak in the wardrobe and left the diary where it lay on the bed. I had been so ensconced about my conversations with both Doctor Beedles and Benedict Swan, I had stopped thinking about the revelations written in the book. Now my mind snapped back to my enquiries. I felt an urgent need to re-read the letters my friend had written even though I knew there had never been any mention of Aramintha's condition, or her love affair. But perhaps if I studied them yet again with the knowledge I now held, I might discover an inkling, the merest of hints hidden between the lines. I opened the drawer and rummaged through my items of clothing for the small packet of letters.

They were gone.

Chapter Eight

Was I going mad? I emptied the contents of the drawer onto my bed. Nothing. I did the same with the remaining drawers, and still the letters were nowhere to be found. I began to panic. Frantically I went through the wardrobe, the bureau, my bags and even under the bed. Aramintha's letters were gone.

Sinking down onto the bed, my body began to tremble slightly as I realized the implication of this. Dear God, who had come into my room uninvited? Why had they gone through my things? Had they looked specifically for my letters? Had they discovered my identity? My thoughts scrambled in chaos. I had last read my letters not three days hence, which meant they could have been stolen at any time since then.

I felt physically sick. Violated by the knowledge that someone had rifled through my personal belongings and stolen treasured possessions which could never be replaced. Why? The question wove my thoughts into a web of uncertainty, which grew with every thread. I rose and went to the window where I stared out at the dimming sky, while my hands wrung in anguish. I must compose myself and not become frightened! I could do nothing to change this turn of events, but I could make an impact on its outcome.

Though Aramintha had spoken of her mother in an unfavorable light, my cherished letters betrayed naught but a young woman's idle chatter to a friend, with a few references to Brampton. One small condolence was the use of my pseudonym, Victoria. It might yet offer me anonymity and hide my real association with Aramintha if they thought the letters written to another. If confronted, however, I would need a plausible reason why the letters were in my possession yet not my name.

I was alarmed, the full realization of my precarious position startlingly clear. I calmed myself. I must not panic. After all, had I not realized this ruse I played carried an element of risk at its conception? As I willed my fear into submission, so my anger began to bud. I disliked feeling scared, no doubt a relic of abandonment by my mother at such a young age and left as vulnerable as a kitten. This was no time to become feeble and addle witted. I was at Mowbray under false pretenses, and there was a chance another might now be aware of my trickery. My guard must always be kept up.

The diary! I retrieved the book from my clothing and decided I could not risk the loss of this as well. But where could I hide it? I cast my eyes about the room in search of a secret spot, yet none was forthcoming. I would have to keep it with me always. Deep in my pocket, Aramintha's private words would remain safe.

I readied myself to join the servants for dinner. My mind began to settle and re-focus. I quelled my concerns about my friendship with Aramintha being exposed. Whoever took my letters knew something, but they would not know of *my* true relationship with Aramintha, just someone by the name of Victoria. I should be more careful. In time I would discover the thief and demand they return my letters. For they were all I had left of my darling friend and I would not stop until I found the person responsible.

****

I slept fitfully and dreamt a tapestry of stories full of ghosts. My parents, Aramintha, even a baby. I awoke tired. Fortunately, today was Saturday. I planned to take it easy and spend time in the schoolroom preparing lessons for the following week. I was determined to keep Gideon interested in his studies, regardless of my reason for being at Mowbray Manor.

During breakfast, Baxter asked me to come to the Butler's pantry. I followed him to a small office near the kitchen, where he went to his desk and picked up a piece of paper. He handed it to me.

"Came this morning," he muttered and walked away.

I frowned, not recognizing the seal. Much to my surprise, the missive contained an invitation to lunch from the Vicar's wife, Avril Plumb, for that very day. My first instinct was to refuse, for she elicited no interest from me one way or the other. Yet on second thought she might be a source of information, and I was certainly in dire need of help. I made my decision and went to Cook to ask if anyone might be going into the village who could pass on my acceptance to Mrs. Plumb.

The church bell tolled midday as I knocked upon the Vicarage door. A young slip of a girl answered, and with a smile asked me into the parlor where my hostess awaited. Avril gasped with delight as I entered and proffered a seat near the fireplace, which was warm and toasty. Small and cozy, the room was delightful, full of a myriad of knick-knacks strewn about the place. That the carpet was threadbare seemed testimony to the financial status of most village vicars, yet the parlor still exuded a pleasant welcome.

After a cup of tea and a sandwich, I found my initial impression of Avril Plumb reversed. In her own home the vicar's wife seemed relaxed. Her ample cheeks full and smiling under dark button eyes. Quick to laugh, her over-large teeth drew my attention each time she grinned. But Avril's velvet voice was a delight to listen to, a boon if there ever was one as she seldom took a breath.

"Tell me, Kathryn," she asked. "How long were you on the Continent with your family? I find it fascinating to speak with people who have lived elsewhere. Where were you again, dear?"

"I was born in Barcelona. My father was from Devon and my mother from Spain. We lived there until the political unrest became too much for my family's safety. My father accepted a position at the University of Durham, and then eventually we moved to London when he became ill."

"Spanish," Avril smiled, "now I understand where you get your dark beauty from."

I felt a warm blush touch my cheeks, unused to being studied.

Avril reached out a chubby hand and patted my own. "Oh, please don't be offended by my compliment, Kathryn, I wish no disrespect. I only commented as your heritage is very prevalent in your lovely black hair, your smooth skin and captivating bone structure. Your mother must have been quite lovely?"

If Avril hoped to learn any more of my past, she would be greatly disappointed. I did not discuss my mother under any circumstances. I asked for more tea, certain the pot was empty, and by the time Avril had called the maid to replenish our drinks, I had already changed the subject.

In a short time, I learned much of the village and its occupants. But now I hoped we could move on. What I wanted from the friendly woman was information regarding the Claytons. I decided to nudge her in that direction.

"How long have you and the Reverend been acquainted with the Claytons, Mrs. Plumb?"

"Now dear, no more of that—you'll call me Avril, and there's an end to it." She took another bite of pastry while considering my question. "Let me think, Plumb and me, well we came here right after we were married. We must have known them going on for seven years now." She beamed at the memory. "Ooh, I can't believe it has been so long." Avril took another sip of tea. I kept my silence. She would continue speaking if I did not interrupt.

"Of course, when we moved here, Lord Nigel Clayton was still alive."

"What was he like?" I knew from Aramintha he had been a fine individual.

Avril paused. "He was a good man, well respected by all. Even though he was of the nobility, he did not have the arrogance which often comes with those born higher up in life. He knew everyone by their given name and was always willing to work alongside his men."

"And what of his son, Benedict Swan. Do you know him well?" I grew bolder.

Avril set down her teacup. "Not that one. Nor do

many as far as I can tell. He's not amicable the way his father was. He keeps to himself, more like the mother I wouldn't doubt."

My interest piqued. "And who is his mother?" For some reason I had never considered her.

"Lavender Swan. Now she died before we moved here so I never met her, though there was plenty of gossip. Seems the woman was with the gypsies when they came through Mowbray one summer with the county fair. Lord Nigel took quite a shine to Lavender, and she to him. But when the girl became with child, her people left Lavender and her sister behind. His Lordship gave them a cottage to live in and kept her and the babe well-looked out for. Of course, the boy did not get the family name, but young Benedict Swan was schooled up at the manor with the other children. He was taught the running of the estate, to be of help to the Claytons."

The story was intriguing. Though Benedict was somewhat imposing, I did like him. He had shown kindness towards me, and the conversations we had shared were enjoyable. His father must have been a good man. Not many of such eminent standing would honor a by-blow.

"Of course," Avril continued. "He's always been a loner, and stand-offish too, not like his brother Gabriel." She gave me a knowing look and cackled. "Now there's a fellow with an eye for the ladies, and them with an eye for him." She chuckled merrily. "A handsomer gent you'd have trouble to find in the whole of Dorset I'll be bound. And charming?" She feigned a tiny swoon, "'tis no wonder he's the pride of his mother's eye." Avril finished her tea and offered me a cake. I declined.

"Were you friends with the daughter, Aramintha?"

The cheeriness dissipated and was replaced by sadness. "Now, that was a terrible business." She sat back in her chair, and her fingers worried the slip of a handkerchief. "We're not to talk of it in the village, but I can tell you there's many do when their doors are closed."

"Why is no one supposed to speak of it?"

"All I know is what dear Plumb told me the night that poor girl died." I leaned forward to ensure I did not miss a word.

"Lord Gabriel himself came to the village to fetch Doctor Beedles. Plumb, hearing all the commotion so early in the morn got out of bed to see what was amiss. He's a good man, my husband, he cares deeply for his parishioners." She was already sidetracking.

"Why was Gabriel there?" I steered her back on course.

"Well, 'twas his sister, Aramintha, seems she'd taken a terrible fall from the cliffs. Doctor Beedles was to see to her, though she was already gone from this world. Plumb wanted to go with them, give the girl a prayer and attend the family, but Lord Clayton would have none of it. He told Plumb he'd be sent for later in the day, and under no condition was he to come near the manor until asked for. Most unusual, so it was."

"Unusual?" My mind was furiously busy, snatching Avril's words while I aligned them with all I had learned to this point.

"Yes. The vicar is always sent for with a death. The good doctor is first, but if it is a serious ailment, he calls Plumb out on his way to minister them. Doctor

Beedles likes for my husband to care for the family while he tends the patient. But this particular night, Lord Clayton would have none of it, he was adamant the doctor come alone."

"Why was that do you think?"

Avril shrugged her thick shoulders and shook her head. "I don't rightly know. But odd it was indeed. Since then, when we go to the manor and dine, I find it sad that no one speaks of Aramintha. It is not very Christian-like, now is it?"

"No," I agreed. "Had you met her often?"

"Not really, for she was away at school you see, and back then we were not invited to dine at the manor as we are now. Oh, to be sure I would meet her on a Sunday at church." She grew wistful. "Aramintha was so much like Gabriel they might be mistook for twins. She was outgoing, friendly, a chatty young thing and a lovely girl with such pretty eyes—" Mrs. Plumb was back in the past.

"Avril," I hesitated. "Do you believe she fell from the cliff?" I had to ask.

Her chubby face registered surprise at my blunt question. She did not answer immediately but ruminated over her words before she spoke.

"Now there's the thing." Her small eyes fixed on my face. "I've heard some say she fell, and some say she was pushed. Then there's others—well they say she might have jumped. But I'll tell you what I think, Kathryn, and I'll not mention it again to another soul Lord help me." Avril lowered her voice to a whisper. "The last time I saw Aramintha Clayton, her face shone like the sun. She was smiling and chattered to everyone outside the church like a starling, not a hint of sadness

’pon her pretty face. Yet it wasn’t but days later she lay broken on the shore. No, I do not think for one moment she killed herself.” She raised her eyebrows to emphasize her point.

“Could she have fallen?”

“Perhaps, but she grew up on those cliffs, and the weather that day was very fine.”

I suddenly felt as though my reason for being here made sense. My desire to find out what happened to my friend was not the product of an over-active imagination.

“Avril, do you believe Aramintha might have been pushed?”

She frowned. “God help me, but I do. Though her family does not think so.”

She was right. The Claytons seemed convinced Aramintha had killed herself.

“And here’s something else I thought very odd mind you.” She added, a hint of conspiracy in her voice. “No one besides the good doctor and Lord Clayton ever saw that poor girl’s body.”

Chapter Nine

My visit with Avril Plumb had been most enlightening. Her speculation was a welcome addition to my own suspicions, and it gave me confidence in the pursuit of my enquiries. But her last comment had unsettled me. In normal circumstances, when a person died, their body would be kept until the cause of death was established. This usually took a few days if there had been no disease or illness to account for loss of life. In the case of an accident, there would be an inquest to determine the cause and rule out foul play. A person of Aramintha's social rank would demand that at the very least. There would have been strict observances paid because of her status. If the matter had been expedited and simultaneously kept quiet, it stood to reason there may have been just her brother and a village doctor in attendance.

I walked briskly from the vicarage back to Mowbray deep in thought. A local magistrate still would have been required to sign a death certificate with the doctor. Gabriel might be that person in authority, but as she was a member of his own family, would it not require an unbiased signature?

So many questions remained unanswered. My friend had died, by whose hand I was not certain. Her body had been whisked away quickly, and I could not find her grave. Even the vicar's wife had remarked upon the lack of a funeral. Aramintha had been taken to Dorchester, some miles away, not brought to Swanage as was local custom. Therefore, I could only ascertain something was amiss. What was being hidden, and why?

I walked down the drive and around to the back of the house. The kitchen was in complete upheaval. Cook was bellowing like an old bull at her many maids scurrying around the kitchen like frightened mice, weaving between footman who carried meats and other goods from the cold pantry.

I spied Sally and tapped her arm, causing her to almost drop a large jug of milk.

"What is amiss, Sally? Why is it so busy?"

She dabbed her forearm against her glistening brow. The poor girl was overly warm. "'Tis company we have, miss. It be the master's fiancée come to dinner." She bobbed a quick curtsy and carried on her way. I hurried to the servants' stairs and went up to my room. I had no desire to be among the Claytons this evening.

Since the disappearance of my letters, my bedchamber did not harbor the welcome it had before. The violation of my privacy was still quite raw, and the sense of loss. Aramintha's diary had remained safely on my person at all times, yet I constantly checked the room to see if anything looked out of place or disturbed in some way.

All appeared to be in order. I slipped off my cloak and washed my face and hands. I would wait a short while and then go down to the kitchen, make a tray to bring up to my room and retire early. At least I could lock my door once settled for the night. I glanced at the small clock on the bureau. I would stay put for another hour.

Miss Tricklebank rapped on my door and came inside, her face taut and lips pinched.

"Miss Westcott," she said sternly. "Lord Clayton requests you join the family for dinner this evening."

My heart sank, and for a moment I debated what to say. I had no desire to be among them. I needed time to myself. "Miss Tricklebank, please convey my apologies, I have the headache, and would prefer to remain in my room until it passes."

Her expression did not change. She simply nodded and closed the door behind her. I felt no shame in my lie. Dining with the family was certain to bring on an aching head as I would have to keep up my guard, given someone now had my letters. I was in no mood to play the demure tutor. My mind had other avenues to explore.

The dilemma presenting itself was my knowledge of Aramintha's condition. If Doctor Beedles had attended the body, surely, he would know of her pregnancy? Would he not be honor-bound to speak of it to the Claytons? At the very least to Gabriel as the head of the family? That might be an additional reason Aramintha's name was never mentioned. I dearly wished for someone to share my discoveries and concerns. But the choices were few. There were three people I might speak to, Gabriel, Benedict and Avril Plumb. Yet I knew so little of them, how could I feel secure enough to place my trust in their hands? What if one of the brothers had stolen my letters? Yet I had not seen Benedict inside the manor since my arrival, so did that mean the thief was his half-brother? Or might a servant have taken them on someone else's behalf?

I retrieved the diary from my pocket and thumbed through the pages until I reached the part where Aramintha believed herself to be with child. I had not read beyond this point as my mind had been intent on the loss of my letters. I flipped to the next page which had been dated April 1st.

"April Fool's day and I must be one for thinking I was important to A. When I told him of our baby, he was not at all pleased! He became angry, asking how I could have let it happen, as though it was I who had brought my condition to its situation. Oh, how I cried! Of course, then he was filled with remorse, and held me close whispering loving words and begging my forgiveness."

I turned the page to the next entry.

"Miss Westcott?" Baxter's voice came from outside my room. I was startled and snapped the book shut and hastily returned it to the safety of my pocket. I opened the door quickly.

"Mr. Baxter?"

"A word if you will, miss." He gestured for me to join him in the hallway, it would be unseemly for him to step inside my bedchamber.

"What is it?"

The old man cleared his throat. "I received a message from Miss Tricklebank. She informed me you would not attend dinner with the family due to a bad head?"

"That is correct," I said stiffly, feeling the lie spread in a blush across my cheeks.

"Miss Westcott." His watery eyes narrowed in disapproval. "I do not know how you have conducted yourself in other houses, but here at Mowbray, an invitation from the family should be interpreted as a command."

"I beg your pardon?"

Baxter let out an exaggerated sigh of disapproval. "If you have a fever, then you are not to put the family in danger of contracting an illness. However, that is the only exception. When the family deigns to invite you, they do so politely rather than make it an order. I highly suggest you ignore your malady and make yourself ready for dinner. It will not go well for you should you fail to appear."

Irritation prickled my skin. "But I—"

"I assure you," he cut in. "I tell you this simply for your benefit. It matters not to me if you find yourself a subject of her ladyship's displeasure. I merely offer you very sound advice." Before I could utter a response, the old butler turned on his heel and strode off.

****

As before, I was brought into the dining room after the guests had already been seated. This time Baxter escorted me to a chair farther away from the head of the table where Lady Clayton sat, and closer to the opposite end where Gabriel took his place. Across from me, sat a beautiful blonde woman, with youthful cheeks and bright hazel eyes, her cupid's bow lips painted a soft pink, a small black mole by her mouth. Beside her was Benedict Swan, dark and handsome in his evening suit. To my left was another gentleman, older than both Gabriel and Benedict, and rather debonair.

None of the men had risen to their feet when Baxter showed me to my place. But all three had given a welcoming smile. The young lady had stared at me curiously.

"Thank you for joining us, Miss Westcott," Gabriel said pleasantly.

I nodded and kept my eyes in his direction and not towards Lady Blanche, whose disapproving glower burned the side of my face.

"I would like to introduce you to my fiancée, Lady Lucy Ditton-Jones." We nodded at one another in greeting. "And next to you our dear family friend Viscount Royston Munt." The attractive stranger bowed his head. "Benedict, I believe you have already met."

"Good evening, Miss Westcott." Benedict smiled kindly. I could see by his expression he recognized my extreme discomfort being included in their dinner plans.

"Mr. Swan," I replied with a nod.

"Well now we are all friends," exclaimed Lady Lucy in a bright falsetto voice, which sounded as though it might have come from a child. "I've so wanted to meet you, Miss Westcott. Gideon could speak of little else when I arrived." Her narrowed eyes regarded me with more indifference than her words conveyed. But at least she attempted to be civil.

"Indeed," added Royston Munt. "The boy could hardly stop gushing about his new teacher. I actually thought we'd come to the wrong house—Gideon always dislikes his tutors." He grinned at me. His eyes were dark like sherry. "I believe you have made a conquest there, madam." He and Lady Lucy laughed. I glanced at Munt's face and estimated he was somewhere in his thirties. His light brown hair fell onto his forehead and almost covered one eye with a curtain.

"Master Gideon is a good pupil," I said quietly. "He attends his lessons well."

"As he should." Lady Clayton's voice rang from the other end of the table. "He had better if he desires to remain home and not be sent off to Eton." Her cold words killed the moment of levity, and we all attended to our soup.

The conversation soon steered towards the current political situation. Lord Salisbury was in his fifth year as Prime Minister, and the gentlemen found him 'tolerably better than Benjamin Disraeli, and a vast improvement on the Liberal, William Gladstone.' The topic then turned to the exciting news of the first deep level underground train station which would open soon. A debate began on the safety concerns of rail travel, and I learned Swanage railway station had been a recent addition to the area a scant five years earlier. I declined to participate in their chat, I listened instead, noting how little Lady Ditton-Jones appeared to know of current events, and how much she relied on her coquettish comments and flirtatious laugh.

During the remainder of dinner, I glanced up several times to find Benedict Swan's dark blue eyes resting upon my face, though I found it difficult to read his expression. *Amusement?*

My attention was frequently drawn to his half-brother, who sat at the table-end holding court like a golden prince. His handsome face glowed with good humor, his eyes bright with pleasure as he regaled his audience with anecdotes from his past, and amusing stories of local eccentric characters.

"Never mind the butcher, what of Juniper Blessing?" He chuckled. "Now there's a sight to scare a babe."

His fiancée's laughter tinkled like a bell. "Oh, isn't

she the hideous old crone who walks in such an odd manner that she appears to be bouncing?" Lucy giggled like a naughty schoolgirl.

Gabriel nodded. "Yes, the very one. I remember when she used to scare the devil out of me when I was a lad. I was convinced she was a witch!"

"Really, Gabriel?" Benedict's eyes were hard as he stared at his brother. "Yet I believed you were scared of her because she once slapped you across the face for calling her a cripple." His deep voice dropped the words and scattered the nasty comments away like he had blown dust from his hand. I knew a sudden surge of pride at his championing the poor woman, and disappointment in Gabriel for his cruel mockery.

"You would be on her side, Benedict." Lady Clayton said coldly from the opposite end of the table. "She is your aunt after all."

An awkward silence fell upon us, and then Lady Ditton-Jones laughed under her breath. I was not sure where to cast my eyes, and the atmosphere felt charged with an energy which was uncomfortable. Fortunately, Lady Clayton rose with an invitation for Lady Lucy to join her in the drawing room. She began to walk away, and then as an afterthought turned.

"Miss Westcott, your company is no longer required this evening, you are dismissed until the morning."

Humiliation stung my face, but I held my head high as I left the dining room for the staircase and sanctuary of my room.

As I recounted the conversation in my mind, I was surprised to have learned the relationship between Juniper Blessing and Benedict.

But I was more perplexed why he had not mentioned it to me before.

Chapter Ten

Monday morning arrived with a fierce rain shower. I gazed out of the schoolroom window at the tiny silver spears of water which darted through the air. I shivered. Storms seemed more violent when near the coastline, I felt fortunate indeed to have warmth and shelter, unlike many. Gideon was in a quiet mood. His golden head bent as he read a book I had brought with me from London entitled *Treasure Island.* The boy was completely absorbed in the wonderful adventure of young Jim Hawkins, while he sipped on my untouched hot chocolate, having already gulped down his own.

My mind jumped about like a fly at a picnic, unable to settle upon any thought for long. I ruminated over my conversation with Avril Plumb and the uncomfortable time spent at dinner last evening. I had been startled at the identity of Benedict's aunt, surprised he had not surrendered his kinship when we were at the chapel. It had been interesting to meet Lucy Ditton-Jones, the future Lady Clayton. She had not disappointed. The girl was a spoiled, overindulged young woman, like many I had encountered at Brampton.

Had I really been at Mowbray for more than a week? In that time, I had learned much about the family and Aramintha, yet still had so many questions. The theft of my letters worried me. I had considered mentioning the loss to Baxter but was hesitant because I knew the staff would be suspected immediately. My instinct told me it was not my coworkers, but a member of the family. But who? Certainly not Gideon. I glanced back at the boy as he drank in his story and my chocolate. Lady Blanche? Perhaps. The woman did not like me and was obsessed with keeping her daughter's supposed suicide a secret. Gabriel? The image of his handsome visage filled my mind, his laughing eyes, generous smile, surely not. Which left only Benedict Swan, whom I knew little about. He was friendly but undoubtedly secretive. I was trying to unscramble a complicated riddle. And then what about the mysterious 'A'? How would I ever learn his identity? The only other male I had encountered thus far was Royston Munt, but Aramintha had mentioned him by name in the diary.

"Miss Westcott?"

"Yes, Master Gideon."

"May I be excused? I have the gripe in my belly." I walked over to Gideon and saw he did look a little flushed. His hand rested on his stomach, and he gave a low moan.

"Go to your chamber, Master Gideon, and I will inform your mother." Gideon loped away, still clutching his book, and I quickly went to find Baxter. He would ensure the boy was cared for.

****

The afternoon offered respite as the rain clouds moved away. With my student indisposed, I took the unexpected opportunity and ventured outside for fresh air. With my umbrella in tow, I set off down the driveway in the direction of the chapel. Though unsure why I felt compelled to return there, I carried some sense of curiosity about the woman who tended the place, a woman now known to me as Benedict Swan's aunt.

The lane was soggy, which quieted my approach, the gate ajar, and I reached the chapel door with no announcement. I turned the heavy brass handle and pushed open the door and stepped inside. Immediately I heard a sudden intake of breath, and there sat Juniper Blessing in the first pew. She rose to her feet, a look of alarm stretched across her face.

"Please," I said calmly, reaching out my hand. "Do not be startled, and do not leave on my account. I have only come to sit a few moments." The older woman hesitated, and her eyes darted to the door as she tried to decide what to do.

"I mean you no harm, Miss Blessing, I wish only to have a few words." Her dark eyes were not scared, rather she seemed apprehensive, as though she did not relish the company of another.

"What would the likes o' you want to talk to me about then?" Her accent was broad West Country, her timbre deep for a woman. I took a step closer and finally saw her clearly.

Her posture was crooked, I surmised because of her lameness, but Juniper's features caught me by surprise. Her hair was thick as a horse's raven mane, her face arresting, despite the ravages of time and hardship. Eyes black as pitch, were both bright and intelligent, I could see at once her likeness to Benedict and the remnants of what had once been a very striking woman.

"I wish to speak of Aramintha."

She blinked, stared at me for a moment and then

relented with a sigh. She nodded. "Come sit you here then." She gestured to the pew. I took a seat, though not too close. "Why do you want to know about that poor thing? Why not leave the girl in peace?"

I considered my words carefully. "Because something feels wrong at the manor, and I want to know the truth to determine if I should stay or leave." I gave her an earnest look. "I worry for Gideon. He is a good boy, yet troubled. I want to help him, but how can I without knowing what happened? Everyone I ask will not answer my questions, in fact they encourage me not to pry. The servants are all too scared to talk about her. Can you help me?"

Juniper studied my face intently. "You're not tellin' me everything. I can see it in your eyes." She regarded me thoughtfully. "Secrets, they do be dangerous things to keep, miss, an' even worse to tell. I'll be bound you've more than Gideon's welfare in mind. No—" She angled her head. "I've a notion there's more to your bein' here than you're lettin' on."

I struggled to keep my expression blank. Goodness, was the woman a mind-reader? I decided not to respond for fear of giving myself away.

The black eyes stared towards the altar. "Aramintha Clayton, now there was a fine one for keepin' secrets. She had her family fooled as to her game she did."

"Game? What game was that?" I had a feeling I already knew.

"Not fer me to say, but I saw 'em enough times to know."

"You speak of her lover, do you not?" I stated and watched surprise ripple on Juniper's weathered face. I continued. “I know Aramintha was in love with someone, which is partly why I do not believe she would take her own life.”

“An’ how would you know what a girl like that might do? Not as if you knew her, Miss.” Her tone was questioning, but her eyes seemed all-knowing. There was something decidedly pagan about this woman. After all, she was Romany.

Her compelling gaze held mine. “I’ll tell you what, Miss Teacher. That girl is gone, God rest her. But did she fly from the cliff like a bird? I think not. I’d be lookin’ close to home if ’twere me. There’s a baddun there, an’ that’s a fact.”

“Juniper!” A male voice made us both jump, and I leapt to my feet only to find Benedict Swan stood in the threshold, his countenance fierce, the angles on his face hard. “Leave Miss Westcott at once and return to your duties.”

Juniper Blessing rose slowly and graced me with a sly smile as she passed by. Benedict came over to me. He was not pleased.

“What nonsense has my aunt been regaling you with?”

“Nothing, Benedict, she and I were simply chatting about Mowbray. She was nice to me. You should not be cross with her.”

“She’s a relentless gossip,” he growled. “And loose tongues cause naught but trouble and sorrow, so pay no heed to anything she told you.” I immediately thought of her admission of seeing Aramintha with a man, I believed every word she had said. But I alluded to none of that now.

“Have no fear, Benedict. We had idle conversation.

The woman was but friendly." I pulled on my gloves. "I must get back to the manor and check on Gideon. He was unwell when I left."

He frowned and his black brows drew with concern. "What ails the boy?"

"I know not. But I believe it might be something he ate."

Benedict elected to accompany me back to the manor so he might check on his half-brother. He too seemed to have a soft spot for the boy, as we all did. While walking back down the lane, he recounted several amusing stories of Gideon's antics as a small lad.

I was tempted to question Benedict about his aunt but decided it could wait. As he talked, I wondered what kind of man he really was. I could tell a propensity to sternness there, yet also good humor. He seemed distant and a loner, yet spoke warmly of his half-brother. Those swarthy, dark looks persuaded a person to be wary of the man, yet he also had a strong, kind streak. No two ways about it, Benedict Swan was an enigma.

It struck me as being odd Aramintha had said so little of him during our friendship. It had always been Gabriel she bragged about. And no wonder now I had met him, for Lord Clayton was like a sunny day, a warm wind, a brilliant sky. There seemed a light burning within him, luring us like moths to a flame, heedless of any danger, only hungry to be touched by his presence.

"You are far away, Kathryn."

"Oh, I am sorry. I am lost in thought."

"No matter," he said kindly. "Well, here we are."

We had reached the kitchen at the back of the manor. "I'll away up to see Gideon." He stopped and gave a curt nod. "Good day, Kathryn." We parted ways and I went in search of a hot cup of tea.

****

By nightfall Gideon fared no better, and a footman was dispatched for Doctor Beedles. I kept out of the way but saw the worried look upon Baxter's face as he came and went from the kitchen to the drawing room, where Lady Blanche consulted frantically with the family.

When the doctor arrived, there was a unanimous sigh of relief, and though I cared not for the man I was glad of his skills. He must set Master Gideon to rights. But Gideon worsened as the evening progressed. Campbell reported her ladyship would not leave the boy's bedside, that his fever was up, and he could keep naught in his stomach. A vigil was to be kept, and the doctor would stay through the night.

The entire house seemed paralyzed by the overwhelming cloud of fear and anxiety. Mowbray Manor was no stranger to death, yet the tangible feeling of fear in the air was palpable. The dark hand of doom hovered ominously over a young and previously healthy boy. Would it snatch another of the Clayton children and devastate the family once again?

My mind knitted worry. I tried to discern what could be wrong with Gideon. I had not heard of stomach flu raging through the area, and no one at the manor had taken sick. Might he have eaten something tainted? Indeed, if that was the culprit, surely more of us would be ill, for we all ate from the same pantry.

I doubt any of us slept that night, wracked with

concern for the young boy lying ill in his chamber. But as morning broke, thank God so did Gideon's fever. Baxter came to the dining room, his face devoid of the usual frown, it shone with relief. He happily announced the most welcome news, Gideon was weak, but he would live. Yet amid the cheers and hearty wishes for his speedy recovery, I could not help but notice there was no mention of what had ailed him.

I kept to my room that morning, thinking it better to remain out of the way while the servants attended the family and got back to a normal schedule. But by late afternoon I could stand it no longer and went upstairs to the schoolroom. As Gideon's tutor, I was in no position to visit my student, though I desperately longed to see him. Our relationship was still in its infancy, yet I was nevertheless attached to him already. At least here I was closer to where he lay a few doors down in his chamber.

The room was quiet. Creeping dark fingers of the gloomy afternoon crawled inside and cast shadows on the floor and furniture. I sat at my desk and picked up Gideon's last essay which he had written about Corfe Castle. I smiled at his clumsy use of descriptive words and buoyant enthusiasm when writing of the battles which had taken place there.

"What amuses you, Kathryn?" said Gabriel. I put the papers down.

"I was just reading your brother's last essay. He has such an odd way with words, and it pleased me to read them. How is he?"

Gabriel came to my desk and perched on one corner. He looked exhausted. "Beedles says he will be fine with plenty of rest and nourishment, but he was a very ill chap last night, and for a moment we thought we might lose him." His face contorted with raw emotion as he spoke. My heart went out to him.

"Does the doctor know what ails him?"

"No. Beedles thought the grippe, or perhaps bad food. Mother has ordered Cook to throw away all the meat and vegetables from the cold room, just to be on the safe side. After Araminţha, I don't believe she could take the loss of another child."

"Of course," I consoled. "And it would be very hard for you too, Gabriel, would it not?" He sighed and then lifted his gaze to meet mine. The light and laughter were gone, replaced by an expression I can only liken to weariness. He was done in.

"I could not stand it, Kathryn," he stated. And in that moment, I wanted to go to him and put my arms about his shoulders. I got to my feet and went to where he sat. I rested my hand upon his arm.

"Take heart, Lord Clayton. Gideon is well now, and all will be right again before you know it." He nodded, and gently placed his own hand on mine. The soft warmth of his touch passed through me as if he'd held my body against his. Our eyes met, and I was drawn into a heady moment with emotions entirely foreign to me. Before I could examine them, a noise came from the hallway. Gabriel quickly rose from my desk and my hand fell away.

Campbell had come to tell Gabriel his brother asked for him. She eyed us suspiciously and then accompanied him out of the room. As they walked away, my senses still full of Gabriel's image, his scent, his presence, a warning bell tolled in my head. Gabriel Clayton was not a person I should form any attachment to. He was to be married to Lucy Ditton-Jones come spring.

Chapter Eleven

The next days passed quietly. Gideon continued to recover, and after three days, I was granted permission to visit him and even give a short lesson as he grew bored with his bed. Doctor Beedles suggested a return to the schoolroom after a full week's rest, so I spent the remainder of my free time exploring Mowbray's grounds, the village and then planned to attend the Sunday sermon, a chore I had avoided since my arrival.

I held no religion; indeed, I had seen enough poverty and illness in the city of London to believe no god would allow such suffering to exist. Yet in me was an obligation to go if for no other reason than because of Avril Plumb's kindness. I had taken tea twice with her this very week and promised I would be at the service.

The Clayton family attended church most Sundays, but due to Gideon's illness they would remain at the manor. This pleased me. I preferred to be by myself. It provided a better opportunity to encounter those who might enlighten me with information. I needed as much help as possible to derive what had really happened to Aramintha.

Juniper Blessing's insinuation of someone close to the manor being 'a baddun' had stayed with me, though in truth I had been somewhat sidetracked by Gideon's illness. As I walked into Mowbray Village, I contemplated what she had said and tried to determine who in the manor would wish Aramintha harm, and why? Was it probable the same person stole my letters? And if so, did it that mean I too was in danger?

The vicar, Reginald Plumb, expounded on the wages of sin and the glory of God. I fought the will to lapse into unconsciousness in an attempt to escape the monotonous drone of his voice. As I sat next to his adoring wife, I found new respect for the woman. How she suffered through his weekly sermons and remained awake was a mystery to me. But suffer she did, with a loving smile on her face as pride radiated from her eyes.

After an eternity, the sermon finally concluded, and the flock gratefully abandoned their pews and spilled out into the chilled November morning. I wasted no time and quickly bade my farewell to Avril and set off back to the manor.

As I walked, someone called my name, and there was Campbell running behind in an effort to catch up with me. I stopped and waited for her. She was quite fetching in her lavender coat. It made the brown of her eyes shimmer like liquid. Her fine russet tresses were scooped into a neat chignon, and her skin glowed with the bite of cold air.

"Miss Westcott, may I walk with you?"

"Of course." I smiled, glad of the company. "Were you at the service? I did not see you."

"Aye, I was. Though I barely managed to stay awake." We both laughed out loud, and for the first time since my arrival in Dorset, I recognized I might have finally found someone from the manor to befriend.

"He is rather awful," I admitted. "I commend Mrs.

Plumb for attending each week."

"Och, I know." Campbell's accent seemed stronger now she was away from the house. "An' it's no' as if he makes up for it with his dashing good looks and fine figure." Again, we both giggled at the expense of Reverend Plumb.

"I have not seen much of you since Master Gideon fell ill," I commented.

"Aye. Lady Blanche took up all my time, she was a holy mess. But I don't blame her, she was worried she might lose her puir wee boy."

"Thank goodness he is going to be all right." And he was, the last I had seen him, Gideon had been literally jumping on his bed. I recounted this to Campbell. She grinned.

A cart trundled towards us, and I saw it was Johnny, the stable lad from the manor heading into Swanage. He touched the peak of his cap in greeting as the wheels crunched by, and we waved back.

"How long have you been at Mowbray Manor, Campbell? Look, I cannot keep calling you by your surname, I would much rather use your first name, and have you use mine." I pleaded. "At least when we are not at work. Do you agree?"

"Aye, I do. It's Moira."

"And I am Kathryn."

"Well now that's settled," she said. "So, let's see, how long have I been here—almost three years now. Though it seems a wee while longer. Working for Lady Clayton day in and day out can be a challenge. But she treats me well overall, and 'tis no' so bad as some other places I've worked."

I could not imagine being in such proximity to

Lady Clayton, it would be tantamount to torture. Moira gained my respect for being able to stand the woman, lady or not.

"What about her daughter? Did you know her well?" I waited to see if Moira reacted like everyone else at the mention of Aramintha. Much to my relief, she did not bat an eye.

"Ah, Miss Aramintha. She was a lovely lassie to be sure. Pretty as a snow queen with her pale hair and ice-blue eyes." She sighed. "I can't believe she's dead—such a tragic, senseless loss. I used to be her maid as well. She was a sweet girl, liked to dress herself mostly and just have me help with that beautiful hair."

Aramintha's face flooded my thoughts, and I almost caught my breath at the memory of how lovely she had been. Moira had grown quiet, and I wondered if she might be remembering the same thing. "Do you think she killed herself?"

Again, Moira did not flinch at my question. "Aye, though it pains me to say it. The lass hadn't been happy for a while. She spent a great deal of time alone, even withdrew from the family an' took her meals in her room."

"But do you not find it strange no one is supposed to speak of her, as though her existence has been erased from history? I find it quite unnerving."

"Aye." Moira agreed. "But who are we to dictate how a family mourns the loss of their own? We might not agree with their methods, but they're doing what they can to cope." She nudged my arm. "Anyway, what about you? How do you find working here now it's been a while? Surely you've met everyone by now. I know you've grown close to wee Gideon, but what do you think of the other boys, Gabriel and Benedict?" Her question gave me pause for thought. I did not want to confide in anyone yet, though I still preferred to be honest.

"I have met Benedict on a few occasions. He's tolerable enough, a bit stand-offish, but overall pleasant. At least he appears more sensitive to those of us who are not family."

"Aye, you're right about that, he's a bonnie man as well if you like your men tall, dark and handsome." Moira nudged my arm. "He'd look good in a kilt too. And what about Lord Clayton, a handsome wee devil if ever there was one, and the most eligible bachelor in the county of Dorset." She gave a knowing grin and tapped the side of her nose with a finger.

"Well," I began, "there's no denying his good looks. You would have to be blind not to appreciate them. Lord Gabriel seems a nice enough chap though, always happy and friendly. He obviously dotes on his mother and brother and has been kind to me as well."

"Och, he looked as though he was being very nice when I interrupted the two of you in the schoolroom." And much to my chagrin, she winked at me. The implication was obvious, and at once I felt embarrassed.

"Then you have greatly misunderstood the situation," I stuttered. "Lord Clayton had just told me of his brother's rebound from the illness, I thought him tired and was only giving him support."

"I'm just joshing with you, Kathryn, don't take on so." She laughed and grasped my hand as Mowbray came into view. "'Tis what friends do, tease one another. Now, let us become serious before we reach the end of the drive so dear old Baxter will no' become agitated."

Upon our arrival, I was delighted to hear from Cook that Master Gideon was up and about and allowed out of the sick room. As Moira and I hung up our cloaks, Cook exclaimed he was "lookin' like his old self."

This pleased me to no end. I was relieved the boy had recovered. In truth, I missed his company, his conversation and pleasant countenance. I parted with the others and made my way up to the schoolroom to ensure I was prepared for the next day's tuition, after which I planned a lazy afternoon with Miss Austen and *Pride and Prejudice.*

As I approached, there came a noise from the room. I smiled, Gideon was probably hunting for a new book to read, no boy of his age would be able to be still after a week cooped up in the house. I walked into the classroom with a greeting on my lips and stopped in astonishment to see Benedict Swan rifling through my desk.

He started in surprise as I walked in and quickly snatched his hands away from an open drawer and closed it. His dark blue eyes caught mine, and I was shocked to see no guilt there.

"May I help you find something?" I asked, my voice tight with anger. My mind formed images of him in my room, stealing my letters.

"That will not be necessary, thank-you, Kathryn. I must have misplaced the item."

I raised an eyebrow. What could Benedict possibly have in my desk? "Perhaps if you tell me what you seek, I can assist?" I stepped towards him, and immediately his demeanor changed.

“It is of no consequence, just an old pen of my father’s—I thought it here.” His voice had become authoritative, and he endeavored to put me in my place. I would not have it.

“It must be of some importance if you feel bound to go through my things in order to find it?” My voice was laden with annoyance. He acted surprised, yet unaffected.

“I apologize for the intrusion, Kathryn. I thought the desk common property of the schoolroom, not a place for one’s personal items.” Did I imagine it, or was there the play of a smile about his lips?

My anger ignited and my cheeks burned. “Sir, though I am but a servant to Lady Clayton, I still command this classroom,” I snapped. "Therefore, common property or not, all matters within this classroom are under my charge. In future, I would request you do not take the liberty of going through my desk without my permission.” My chest rose in rhythm with my speeding pulse, and I fought to keep my voice from shaking. I was livid. I wanted to shout at the man, ask him what he had done with my letters, yet I did not, I held my tongue.

Benedict walked around the desk until he stood close enough for me to see the thick swath of his black lashes. His nearness caused me discomfort as my senses battled to read his intention. My heart still hammered, and my breath came short. My lips felt dry, and I moistened them with my tongue. His eyes flickered to my mouth.

“Bravo, Kathryn,” he said softly and reached out a finger to touch my cheek. “I knew there was a little tiger in there somewhere.” He dropped his hand and walked out of the room. I stood like a rooted tree after a gale, unmoving, yet still trembling. My emotions scattered like pollen as I tried to comprehend what had just taken place. Quickly I gathered my composure. I would go to my chamber immediately. But I was to be thwarted, for as I left the room, I walked straight into the path of Gabriel.

"Kathryn, are you ill?" His face showed pointed concern as he looked fixedly at me. I must still have been flushed from my encounter with his brother.

"Should I get a glass of water, perhaps?" He gently cupped my elbow as though I might suddenly drop to the floor in a faint.

"No, Lord Clayton, I am fine, I assure you. I just felt a little warm, but it will pass."

"Then let me take you to your room at least?"

I smiled at his kind consideration. It was uncanny how Gabriel, with his light blond hair and sky-blue eyes, was the antidote which removed the cloak of darkness Benedict had shrouded around me. My spirits lifted. "I might take a breath of air first, and then retire."

"Well, allow me to escort you outside." Gabriel tucked my arm in his. "Hold on to me until you are steady." We walked down the hallway to the stairs.

I will admit to enjoying the feel of his strong arm beneath mine, an anchor to a boat unmoored. He felt solid and safe.

"I saw Benedict come from the schoolroom. I trust he did not upset you in any way?" he remarked casually as we descended.

"Not at all. He just startled me. I had not expected to find anyone in there."

"I see." Gabriel stopped our descent and turned to look at me. "Kathryn, you would tell me if my brother had done something to upset you? Benedict is an unusual fellow, half gentry, half farmer. Sometimes his ways are not those of a gentleman and can be—" he cleared his throat, "unexpected. You are a very lovely woman, and Benedict has an eye for a pretty face."

I gasped. I do not know if it was his compliment or the insinuation of his brother's motives which affected me more. Nonetheless I was taken aback by both and at once yearned to be away from all things male. I quickly pulled my arm from the nook of Gabriel's elbow.

"Gabriel, please excuse me, I have changed my mind and should like to go to my room."

"Kathryn?" He seemed genuinely surprised as I turned toward the servants' staircase. Paying him no heed I hastened away but paused briefly as the sensation of being watched pricked the skin on the back of my neck. I glanced over my shoulder to see Gabriel still stood where I had left him observing my departure, while unbeknownst to him, his mother waited at the foot of the stairs glaring up at me with naked contempt.

****

I chose not to join the servants for dinner that night. I was not hungry and felt an urgent need to burrow in my room away from everyone. I plagued myself with the events of the schoolroom, repeatedly going over my encounter with both brothers.

It now seemed likely Benedict had been the thief of my letters. This I based upon his behavior, his arrogance as he searched my desk, and his general demeanor. Benedict always kept some distance from me. He extended the hand of friendship, yet somehow remained guarded. Why? For some inexplicable reason I did not sense he meant me harm, for when Benedict touched my face it had not been with malice, but rather—what exactly? More importantly, I had not felt scared, and I knew how it felt to fear a man—I had Billy Scruggs to thank for that. But I took no solace from it all. I thought of Benedict in my bedchamber going through my belongings to steal my treasured letters. Who else could it have been? Gabriel?

No, that was ridiculous, for Gabriel was the Galahad to Benedict's Black Knight. He emanated harmony, reassurance and all manner of putting things right. He had lost his sister, what interest would he have of my things? Lady Blanche? I remembered her words of warning to stay away from her son, and her fierce expression from the bottom of the stairs still haunted me. Why would she want the letters, to what end?

It always came back to Benedict, the image of him at my desk replayed again and rendered me uncomfortable. I reached in my pocket and my fingers touched against the diary like a talisman. I gasped, perhaps it was for this he searched? Of course, it had to be! The excuse of a pen was too weak, too forced. Benedict must have been looking for the diary. A bolt of excitement ran through my body at this revelation. But then a trickle of apprehension crept up my spine. How would he know I had found it? And then I remembered that day and the sensation of being watched as I left Aramintha's room. I shivered. Why should Benedict seek the journal? There was little in there of him. Unless Benedict Swan was the mysterious 'A.'

****

My student appeared happy to be back in the schoolroom. He was busy expounding upon the virtues of going off to sea to search for buried treasure.

"So, you think the life of a pirate worthy of your aspiration?" I asked.

"No silly." He grinned that charming Clayton smile, so like Gabriel's and Aramintha's. "Of course not, for I would not wish to be hung as an enemy of the British crown. I should prefer to be an explorer, like the great Henry Stanley, the man who found David Livingstone in—"

"Africa. Yes, I know who he is. I am glad to see you have enjoyed your reading. Are you in need of a new story?"

"No, thank you." His face shone, "Benedict brought me a book to read and it's smashing! It's called *Kidnapped,* and I'm almost halfway through. It's by the same chap who wrote *Treasure Island,* you know." I did know. Robert Louis Stevenson was a popular author, most beloved by boys of Gideon's age.

"Excellent, I shall be glad to hear your thoughts when it is all read. For now, we must forget exotic seas and dead men's treasure chests. It is time to think about Latin."

Gideon heaved a massive sigh, and the lesson began.

****

We finished early as I noticed Gideon's pallor growing wan as the afternoon passed. Once I excused him and tidied up the classroom, I went down to the kitchen for a cup of tea. The young maid, Sally, was in the servants' dining room on her break, and I asked if she would mind my joining her. She gave me a friendly smile and said she'd be pleased to have the company.

"By the way, I wanted to thank you for taking good care of me since I have been at Mowbray. I do appreciate how hard you work, Sally."

Her face shone like a flower under the sun at my compliment, and I perceived she was not the recipient of much praise.

"I don't mind workin' for people like yerself, miss, those who understand just how long a day is when you're a maid. Though I'm not complainin' for 'tis a good job I have here."

"Are you a local, Sally?"

"That I am, miss, from Swanage. My da's a fisherman an' my mam, she stays home with my five brothers."

"Five boys, that is a handful." I sipped my tea.

"To be sure it is. My poor mam, she'll be thirty come Christmas, an' she says she feels more like sixty if she's a day."

I could certainly understand why. Hearing stories such as Sally's made me remember just how fortunate I really was.

"Are you likin' Mowbray, miss?" Sally took a biscuit from a saucer on the table and dipped it into her tea.

"Yes, thank you, Sally. Although it is a bit of a sad house, isn't it? But I suppose that's normal after what happened."

The maid's eyes grew dramatically round and she glanced towards the open door. "I wasn't here back then. I only come along a few weeks after the young lady died. I had to wait for my fifteenth birthday before comin' to work for the Claytons."

I felt a fleeting disappointment. I had hoped to glean more information about Aramintha.

"I were so happy to get the job, it helps my family, one less mouth to feed an all."

"So you never knew Lady Aramintha?" I said casually as I finished my cup of tea and set it down on the saucer.

"Not as such, course sometimes I saw her when she was in Swanage." Sally's expression softened with admiration. "She were lovely with that pretty yellow hair, and oh, the fine dresses she wore." She smiled. "'Twas no wonder all the gentlemen in these parts wanted to marry her."

"Really?" I kept calm, I desperately wanted her to keep talking.

"Oh yes, miss. There were Sir Malcolm Terris from Dorchester, and Mr. Buckley, he were a merchant from Poole, but the one who wanted her the most, why that were Mr. Munt, he were smitten that one, well so my ma said."

It was news to me. "Did Lady Aramintha return his sentiments?"

Sally laughed. "Not her. Accordin' to Cook, she had another who had her affection, though none seem to know who he was. 'Tis such a shame, when I go in her chamber to dust and see all her pretty things just lying there wasted, it makes me sad."

"I can imagine," I stated, remembering my own examination of Aramintha's bedroom.

"I'll tell you her room was a mess when I first went in there. Like someone had been angry and tossed everythin' on the floor and the bed. I thought it might have been the lady herself, you know, before she jumped off that cliff. But one of the other maids told me it got like that after Lady Aramintha died. It were strange though, but even Baxter didn't think anythin' of it."

"Sally, where are you?" At the cook's call the girl hastily got to her feet. She bobbed a curtsy and went back to work.

Aramintha's room had been a mess *after* she died? That could only mean someone had been inside her chamber. I felt the comforting weight of the journal in my pocket. Perhaps they had gone in there to find what I now had in my possession? Again, my mind conjured up a raven-haired man with dark blue eyes. Had Benedict been looking for her diary? It made sense, after all he might have been careless how he searched? The room had been put back to rights by the time I had visited, yet I had a clear memory of the desk drawers, they had been untidy, as though someone had rifled through them. Whoever had been in Aramintha's room had missed the hidden shelf. It had been barely visible to my eye, and only discovered because I had crawled underneath the bureau to find the dropped pen. If Benedict had simply felt around the desk, the compartment would have gone undetected in its position far at the back. His search would have been fruitless.

The importance of the journal in my pocket felt worrisome. The theft of the letters, the apparent hunt for the diary could only mean Benedict was trying to conceal Aramintha's condition, keep her pregnancy a secret to protect himself and hide their incestuous relationship. I left the dining room and made my way up the stairs to my room. Incest was illegal. It stood to reason Benedict would want no one to know, at least until he and Aramintha could run away together to the Continent.

I sank onto my bed. A nagging tiredness behind my eyes made me close them, but my mind would not quit. If Benedict Swan was the mysterious 'A' in Aramintha's diary, he was guilty of incest and would not want another soul to know of it. Her pregnancy would only validate the affair. If discovered, Benedict would be arrested, and would bring shame to the Clayton name. At the very least, both he and Aramintha would be cast out of the family, left penniless without a home nor income. This was indeed strong enough inducement for him to keep their relationship a secret. I recounted Aramintha's excitement at the prospect of her baby—my eyes flew open as a horrible possibility dawned. Dear God, had Benedict pushed my darling friend from the cliff that night so no one would learn of their affair?

Chapter Twelve

At breakfast the next morning, an air of frivolity filled the kitchen. Even Cook had a smile plastered across her face, and I would swear Baxter whistled in the pantry. I collected a cup of tea and went into the dining room to eat a piece of toast. Today we had kedgeree, bacon and eggs, leftovers from the breakfast upstairs. It was still early, unusual that the family had already eaten their meal.

Moira was not yet in the dining room. I helped myself to a plate of food and then set about eating. I had just finished the last bite when Cook joined me. She pulled out a chair at the head of the table and sat down with a happy sigh.

"You seem pleased, Mrs. Oldershaw, in fact all the staff are in fine spirits this morning."

"Yes, miss, it's going to be a good week at Mowbray. Viscountess Geraldine, the old master's sister is on her sickbed, and Lady Clayton has gone to tend her. Got a telegram last night asking her to come."

"Oh. I am sorry to hear the lady is unwell, does she live nearby?"

"Goodness no she don't. She lives in London in a big fancy house. Her husband, afore he died, was Viscount Valkenberg. A Dutchman would you believe, but a nice enough fellow even so." Fanny reached over and poured a cup of strong tea. "Lady Blanche will be gone a week, maybe more if the old biddy pops her clogs."

I chuckled, though I did not wish the lady ill. Now I understood why I had not seen Moira. They must have departed early this morning.

"That just leaves Master Gideon to cook for, because Lord Clayton's gone off to the Munts. There's a shooting party spending the week at his place, an' that means we all get a bit of a rest." As if to emphasize her point, Cook swung up her thick calves and placed stockinged feet on a nearby dining chair. She emitted a large and content moan of pleasure. I rose and gathered my empty plate.

"Well, I must be off. Master Gideon still has to work on his lessons." I grinned. "But we might skip Latin and mathematics this morning and go for a long walk instead."

****

I kept my promise to Lady Clayton and did not take Gideon along the cliff path. Instead, we took a brisk hike into Swanage. I liked the place very well. So typical of a quintessential British seaside town, yet due to its small size, Swanage lacked the hustle and bustle of other places like Brighton or Dover. The main street was full of a variety of shops, which catered to summer visitors as well as supplies for the residents. There were several hotels close to the sea front, although most were empty this time of year.

The wind rolling off the water had a vicious bite, and Gideon and I had not lasted long on the beach. We took refuge from the elements in a small café, both content as we ate steaming fish and chips. Gideon had a rapturous expression painted upon his face as though he might have ascended into Heaven. Though I had not considered eating a religious experience, apparently today for Gideon, it most certainly was.

"And you are sure this is the first time you have ever tasted fish and chips?" I could not believe the boy had lived so close to the sea and not had them before. They were considered a staple of all seaside restaurants in Britain.

Gideon rolled his big eyes. "Mother does not allow me to eat food she considers 'common.' She says we don't know what's in the recipe and it might be unhealthy."

"What nonsense." The words slipped out before I could arrest them. I looked guiltily at my charge. "Sorry, your mother does what is best for you. We will consider this a study in economics. Today you have learned one of the prominent industries in Swanage besides tourism is fishing."

Gideon giggled and almost choked on a chip. He recovered and sipped tea from a cracked mug his mother would have censored. "You're not like most tutors, Miss Westcott, you're more like a friend really. You remind me quite a bit of Minty."

"Minty?"

"Yes silly, my sister. We all called her Minty. She was a lot like you, well not to look at, she was heaps prettier, but she acted like you sometimes."

I laughed. His honesty though brutal, was accurate, Aramintha Clayton was stunningly lovely. If I were considered half as attractive, I would be proud. "She sounds like a nice sister to have had, Gideon. I am sure you miss her."

"Rather a bit actually." He paused, and then as all

young men have wont to do, immediately chased away his maudlin thought and scarfed down another fat chip. "Gosh, this malt vinegar is jolly yummy on the chips. When we get back, do you think we could ask Mrs. Oldershaw to learn how to make chips? I'm sure Mother would come around to it if she got a taste."

I could imagine Lady Blanche Clayton sitting at dinner in her fine gown, tiara, and silk gloves eating fish and chips. Perhaps it had been a mistake bringing Gideon here after all. I might be for the chop if Lady Clayton found out.

"Miss Westcott, don't look so aghast! I won't tell anyone where I tasted them, I'll just say I read a story about it. They'll think I got it from *Treasure Island.*" Sometimes Gideon Clayton was far more devious than he appeared. I finished the last of my tea and told him to eat up as the hour grew late and we should set off back to the manor.

****

Though a cold time of year, Gideon and I made the most of our days while his mother stayed in London. We explored as many places close to home as possible, even as far as Lulworth and Smugglers Cove. The effect on the young boy was positive, he radiated health and appeared happy, very different from the lad I had met just weeks ago.

Gideon rode most afternoons when our lessons were finished. His horse was one of the greys I had seen in the stables. When we were leaving the schoolroom the fourth day of his mother's absence, he asked if I rode.

"Yes, but it has been a while. Why?"

"Oh, Johnny Dainty told me you've been spending

time in the stables as you are fond of the horses. I said I'd ask you to go riding with me." He smiled at the idea. "If you have a mind to, I'd like it, miss. Otherwise, Johnny has to go with me, and though he's a splendid chap, it would be super to have someone else's company for a change."

Within the hour, and under Gideon's firm instruction, Miss Tricklebank begrudgingly procured an old riding habit which once belonged to Aramintha. It fit well enough, though it had certainly seen better days. It mattered not to me; I was happy for the chance to be on horseback. I was to ride Jezebel. Gideon mounted his own mare Allegro, a grey with a calm and sweet disposition, and I trotted after him as we left the stable yard and out down the driveway. The afternoon was certainly chilly, but the sun valiantly pushed its way through the bullying clouds. The warmth of my horse and thick tweed of my clothes kept me comfortable enough.

I followed Gideon, assured in the knowledge he knew the fields of the estate far better than I. We left the lane and began a slow canter into the lush green grass which ran parallel to the hedgerows. The sensation of the horse beneath me was invigorating, it had been far too long since I'd ridden. I could feel the bunch and stretch of the steed's powerful muscles as she easily bore me in a steady gait.

Though winter was here, the scenery was still quite lovely, a far cry from the smoky, foggy London streets I had grown used to. We both began a gallop and charged up the slope of a small hill which had a thatch of trees upon its crest. As we reached the top, Gideon pulled in his horse and waited for me to arrive.

I drew up level with him, and we both took in our surroundings. In one direction you could see the rooftop of Mowbray Manor, the stables and the barn, the dark sea behind, while in the other, the small hamlet of Mowbray Village, a jumble of shapes and sizes.

"What a spectacular view," I remarked, as Jezebel snorted steam from her nostrils after the climb.

"I love coming up here," Gideon said softly, "Minty liked it as well. She and Gabriel rode here most days, every so often they'd let me tag along."

I felt the pang of loss yet could not share it with the boy. Perhaps my hidden sorrow was why he felt a kinship with me?

"You are right to remember those you have loved and lost, Gideon. As painful as memories can be, it is important never to forget those who are gone before us."

He turned his face to me with tear-filled eyes. Whether from the cold air or sorrow, I knew not. But I reached my hand out to pat his arm. "Do not despair, Gideon. You have a good family and friends who care a great deal about you. In time you will be able to think of your sister and not feel heart-broken." Gideon wiped his eyes with the back of a gloved hand.

"Well, now, what's all this?" A booming male voice made our horses start, and we turned in unison as two men crested the hill from the other side. Royston Munt and closely behind him, came Gabriel. My heart gave a little leap as I saw the familiar handsome face. Gideon was delighted, all traces of sadness gone as he beamed at the sight of his brother. The men dismounted, and as I began to climb from my saddle, a pair of hands encompassed my waist.

"Allow me, Miss Westcott," Gabriel said as he helped me descend. The touch of his fingers burned through the fabric of my riding coat as though his skin had brushed against my flesh. Warmth rose to my cheeks as my feet touched the ground, and we stood so close I could see tiny green flecks in his blue eyes.

"Haven't we, Miss Westcott?" Gideon had asked a question and I had heard none of it. I moved away from Gabriel.

"Haven't we what, Gideon?"

"Haven't we just had a marvelous time with my mother away in London? I hope Aunt Geraldine gets a lot worse, then Mother will have to stay longer."

"Indeed," I replied with some sternness to my voice. "We have enjoyed the week, but we certainly want Lady Clayton's aunt to make a speedy recovery."

"I don't," Gideon said dully, and we all laughed.

"Royston has been entertaining me all week," Gabriel remarked. "We have been to Dorchester, and tomorrow we are off to Bath."

"You lucky dog," Gideon whined. "I wish I might go to Bath; I never get to go anywhere."

"That is not entirely true, Master Gideon, we have been to Corfe, to Lulworth, and Swanage."

"That doesn't count, Miss Westcott, I can go to those places any time. But Bath?"

His brother went over and gave him a playful cuff on the ear. "Judging by the looks of you, Gid, I'd say the only bath you should visit is the one in the washroom. You've avoided that since Mother's been gone, haven't you?" At this truth, Gideon grinned, and his angelic face suddenly transformed into that of an imp.

"Perhaps," he admitted sheepishly.

"Miss Westcott." Gabriel turned his attention back to me. "I did not know you rode." His eyes met mine, his expression soft and thoughtful.

"You did not ask." I smiled. "And it is seldom I am able to as I own no horse. But I have enjoyed borrowing one of yours. Jezebel is of fine stock; a strong Arabian mix I would suspect."

Gabriel was impressed. "Indeed, she is. An English thoroughbred, though her lineage is heavy on the Arabian side, well spotted, miss, well spotted." His face shone with approval.

"What's this?" Royston stopped conversing with Gideon. "Is our Miss Westcott a connoisseur of horseflesh as well as school lads?" His tone carried a hint of a sneer. It affronted me, I could take a jest as well as any, but my work as a teacher was not to be mocked.

"Why, Mr. Munt," I replied coolly, "it takes skill to have expertise yielding the whip *and* the chalk. Tis only some of us who can master both at once." I cocked my head like a bird and pasted an innocent smile on my face.

"Well said, Miss Westcott." Gabriel laughed and slapped his companion on the back. "Face it, man, you've been bested by the lovely lady." I looked over at Munt, and he glowered at me - no friend there. The pleasant interlude had ended, the atmosphere now charged with something uncomfortable. I wanted to leave.

"Come, Master Gideon, let us be off back home. Mrs. Oldershaw will have those tarts out of the oven by now." The mention of Cook's famous jam tarts was temptation enough. We both said our goodbyes, and as Gabriel assisted me in mounting Jezebel, he allowed his hands to linger longer than necessary upon my waist. Our eyes met and, somehow, I knew he understood why I needed to go.

****

Friday morning a telegram arrived to say Lady Blanche would return the following day on the London train, and Viscountess Geraldine would accompany her. Johnny Dainty was dispatched to the Munt place where he was to advise Gabriel of the news.

Gideon and I made the most of our last day of freedom and spent it down on the sandy beach where we hunted jellyfish and collected interesting shells. The wind was tame, a blessing considering the cold season, and by the time we trekked up the winding cliff path, we both puffed out steam into the chilly air. Gideon held a bucket with our impressive finds, I carried the net and our spades. As we reached the clifftop, a figure came towards us—Benedict, whom I had not seen all week long. Though I had read the diary every evening and thought of his role in Aramintha's life, I had given him no other thought.

"Kathryn, Gideon." He gave us a friendly smile. "It looks as though you have been on another adventure."

"Yes," Gideon agreed enthusiastically. "We've hunted shells and been looking at jellyfish. Did you know in some countries people actually eat jellyfish? I think they would taste revolting. Although not all things from the sea are horrid, I mean, those fish and chips were smashing—"

"Yes, Gideon, thank you." I stopped him before he inadvertently blurted out our secret meal. "Go along, and I'll catch up with you." The boy shrugged. We both watched him walk away and then Benedict turned to look at me.

"You've been so good for Gideon, Kathryn. He looks the happiest I've seen him since Aramintha died. Thank you for that." His words were kind and the smile which accompanied them carried sincerity.

"He is easy to be around, Benedict. Gideon is a delightful boy and will be a fine young man, a credit to the Clayton family," I said. He nodded in agreement, but I noticed a flash of something in his eyes. Sadness? His role of always being the outsider and never quite good enough?

"I have not seen you all week, Benedict, have you been busy in Lady Blanche's absence?"

"Indeed. I traveled to London and went to the Agricultural Society. I attended three lectures on farming the African Continent."

I was impressed. "It must have been fascinating."

"It most certainly was. But there is much to learn."

His expression belied his passion for the continent. As I observed him my confliction battled within. How was it so easy to converse with a man I also suspected?

"Miss Westcott!" Gideon had stopped on the path and waved at me to join him.

"I should go, Benedict. Perhaps we can speak of this another time." He nodded his dark head and we went our separate ways. As Mowbray came into view, I found myself wondering if the real reason Benedict Swan planned a future in Africa, was to escape the past and what he might have done to Aramintha?

Chapter Thirteen

Late Saturday afternoon, the Mowbray carriage was dispatched to Swanage for Lady Clayton and Viscountess Valkenberg. However, when they arrived from the station, the Clayton carriage was followed by a procession of carts filled with different suitcases and valises. I peered from my vantage point of the schoolroom window, aghast two ladies traveled with so many possessions. I could not help my curiosity though, I stared transfixed as Lady Clayton stepped out from her carriage. Once she had alighted, a footman went to the vehicle's door and was handed a ball of light brown fur, followed by a lady's gloved hand.

I could not see details, but the woman who stepped onto the driveway did not resemble an invalid to my eyes. Tall, her fur-covered back was held ramrod straight as she walked unaided into the house. I ran at once to the hallway and got close enough to the stair bannister to eavesdrop and not be seen. I heard a furor of haughty voices, the subservient tones of Baxter, and then light footsteps upon the stairs. I quickly made to move away, but then saw it was only Moira Campbell, Lady Clayton's maid.

I was pleased to see her friendly face again. I had missed her company even though we were barely known to one another. She saw me, and instead of stopping on the second floor, she ventured up another flight to where I waited.

"Welcome home." I greeted her as she reached the landing, and we gave each other an awkward hug. "You are a sight for sore eyes."

"Och, listen to you blatherin'," she said shyly. "I'm sure you've all enjoyed the peace and quiet. I wish I'd had a wee bit of that."

"How was London?"

"Exhausting." She rolled her eyes. "Between Lady Blanche and Madam down there, I needed an extra pair of legs. Now Lady Geraldine's maid has gone off home to a family funeral, so I've the pleasure of taking care of the old battleaxe here as well."

"Campbell, where are you, girl?" Lady Geraldine's authoritative voice called out from downstairs.

Moira's eyebrow arched. "See what I mean? Look, I'd better go and unpack their things."

"By the looks of all that luggage, it might take a while," I joked.

"Aye, you're right about that." Moira sighed and went back down to join her ladyship.

I carried along the hallway and down the servants' stairs to the kitchen. Mrs. Oldershaw ran on full steam, and her kitchen staff were busy preparing the evening meal. Apparently, the Ditton-Jones family were also invited for dinner, an unexpected plan which had thrown Cook's menu out the window. She was red in the face, barking orders like an angry terrier as her staff scurried around in a frantic mob. I offered my help and before long found myself assigned the task of peeling potatoes, and then I whisked egg whites for Cook's famous meringue. Surprisingly I found the work rather a nice change from the schoolroom, and I was glad to be of help, especially with no actual responsibility for the meal.

Tonight, our own dinner was delayed until after the family had dined. By the time we finally sat around the table to eat leftovers from upstairs, everyone in the kitchen was exhausted. But the filet of sole, beef Wellington, roast potatoes and parsnips were worth waiting for. Everyone was hungry. Alas, the merengue was gone, but we sufficed with delicious spotted dick and creamy custard for pudding.

"Well, I for one am glad this blasted night is over with." Mrs. Oldershaw accepted a glass of sherry from Miss Tricklebank, who also passed a glass to Baxter. Everyone else held a glass of milk or water, and we all gave a jolly toast to a meal well prepared.

"Did my Lady Geraldine have any comments on the food?" Mrs. Oldershaw asked Baxter at the other end of the long table. Judging by her expression, she expected a negative reply.

"She did indeed."

Cook frowned. "And pray, what didn't she like this time?"

"The merengue," Baxter said in a monotone voice.

Her voice was flat and toneless. "You mean the merengue that was completely devoured, and the plate all but licked clean?"

"Yes." Baxter gave a rare grin. "Apparently it took Lady G two helpings to decide she didn't like it at all."

Everyone at the table burst out laughing, I along with them.

****

Sunday morning Miss Tricklebank announced all staff were required to be present for the morning church service. The only people excluded were Mrs. Oldershaw, who would remain home to prepare luncheon, Baxter, and one of the kitchen maids. I did not relish the prospect, but nevertheless, I met Moira at the back door, and we walked with the other servants down the driveway to the lane.

"We missed you last night at dinner," I said.

"Och, sorry. I was done in from the trip."

"Understandably," I commiserated. "Has Lady Geraldine recovered from her illness?"

"Oh aye, if she *was* sick. That woman was the picture of health when we arrived in London." Moira shook her head. "It would take the bubonic plague to kill her off." She gestured back to the manor. "Our dear Lady G has the stamina of a bull and the constitution of a rhinoceros. She was nae sick at all, she was bored."

I laughed. "Oh Moira, I cannot wait to see this lady. We'll have to sit in a pew near the aisle so I can watch her when she comes in."

"Aye, and in case we want to make a quick escape during the sermon." We giggled like a couple of silly girls, and it did me good to feel lighthearted.

The Claytons were the last to arrive at the church, and every single head including mine, swiveled around as they walked down the aisle. I had thought Lady Clayton an imposing figure, but the dowager woman who walked by her side made Lady Blanche look like a kitten. Geraldine, Viscountess Valkenberg, strode between the pews, her gait slow and purposeful, with the dignity and deportment of a queen. She was exceptionally tall and big-boned, and her height was emphasized by the shockingly high hat placed upon her white hair. Her face was long and serious, her nose hooked, and her chin practically pointed upwards. The title of Viscount might have been more fitting.

I shared the collaborative tensing of muscles in the congregation as the ladies passed, followed closely by Gabriel, Gideon and Benedict. They took the family pew on the opposite side of the aisle to my vantage point and I studied them intently, though I could only see the back of their heads.

What an odd assortment they were. Lady Blanche and her secrecy, Gabriel and his radiance, Gideon and his boyish trust, and then Benedict. I struggled to determine his role with Aramintha. Though I had caught him searching my desk and suspected him as the thief of my letters, was he in truth my friend's lover and potential murderer? As though he read my thoughts, his dark head turned suddenly to look directly at me. I almost gasped out loud, and quickly averted my eyes. Moira must have felt me start, and she looked at me with a questioning glance. I smiled, and we both returned our attention to Reverend Plumb and his awful sermon.

After the service, the congregation waited politely to allow the Claytons to leave first as their rank demanded, before following them out of the church. Outside, both Moira and I slipped past Reverend Plumb and went over to his wife, whom I introduced to Moira. Avril was delighted to make a new acquaintance and insisted I bring Moira the next time I came to tea. I agreed before moving on, so others might speak with her.

We set off for Mowbray and had not gone far when we realized someone was coming up behind us. I turned with surprise to see Gabriel and automatically slowed my gait.

"Good day to you, Campbell and Miss Westcott," he said congenially as he joined step with us. "I see you survived your week in London, Campbell, hat's off to you, can't have been easy." Moira was too polite to respond, she gave a weak smile and averted her gaze, her cheeks a warm shade of pink.

"Is your aunt still unwell, Lord Clayton? She appeared quite robust this morning at church," I enquired.

Gabriel gave a hoot of laughter. "Aunt Gerry is as healthy as a horse. Though it's quite unusual for her to come to Dorset. I'll warrant she's up to something. Normally you can't pry her away from London and the theatre."

"Perhaps she wanted to be here for the Christmas season?" I added. After all, it was only a few weeks away.

"I believe that's part of it, and she has some business with Entwhistle, our family solicitor. Change of will or some such thing."

"Does Lady Geraldine have children?" I'd never thought to ask before.

"Good God no," Gabriel said with relief. "I don't think the world could cope with more than one like Gerry. She's a bit of a handful to say the least. Don't worry, you'll find out soon enough." We continued along and Gabriel made polite conversation to include Moira. It did not take long to reach the manor. As we approached the house, he gave us a formal bow.

"Thank you for the delightful company ladies," Gabriel said with a flash of his handsome smile before leaving us to go in through the front entrance of the manor while we walked around to the rear.

"What was all that about?" Moira directed a frown at me as Gabriel walked away.

I was puzzled. "What do you mean?"

"Och, don't play the innocent lassie with me, Kathryn, the man acted interested in you. And if my eyes aren't deceiving me, I think you might feel the same way?" Much to my consternation I felt my cheeks warm.

"Kathryn." Moira stopped and touched my arm. "He's engaged to be married. You know that, don't you?" Her face showed irritation.

"Of course," I snapped, and then instantly felt remorse. "I do like Lord Clayton, how could you not? But I am no silly girl, Moira. I am well aware of his position and also mine. I have no grand delusions there."

Her face showed relief. "Aye, well I'm glad to hear it. He's handsome, there's no denying it, but he's still a man, one who likes to get his own way. Be careful there, friend." She squeezed my arm and then left me alone on the driveway with my thoughts.

****

I allowed myself to enjoy a wonderful lazy afternoon. We had eaten Mrs. Oldershaw's delicious roast lamb dinner at luncheon, and I had retired sated to my room. I sat at my desk and read through Aramintha's diary once again. I ruminated over her words and reread them countless times as though the ink might suddenly change into a concise answer to all my questions. Benedict and Aramintha? If I assumed they were in a relationship, albeit an immoral one as they shared a father, why would Benedict have wanted to harm her? This nagged at me, because what would Benedict gain by murdering his lover? Surely it would be Aramintha who stood to lose more? Her reputation, her inheritance, but Benedict? His plans were to leave England and strike out a future in Kenya. This was obtainable, perhaps even easier with Aramintha at his side? There they could have posed as anyone they wanted to be, and none would be the wiser. It made no sense.

"Miss?" A rap on the door announced Sally.

"Begging your pardon, miss, but Lady Geraldine sent for you, wants to see you in her bedchamber."

"Me?"

"Yes, miss. She asked you come at once, miss." I tucked the diary inside my pocket and followed Sally out into the hall and down to the second floor. She knocked on a closed door. It opened to reveal Benedict, his face stern. My surprise must have shown on my face because he quickly remarked.

"My aunt is ready for you now, Kathryn, please excuse me." He brushed past and walked away. Sally bobbed a quick curtsy, and I went into the room.

"Ah, Miss Westcott." An imperious voice emitted from an enormous canopied bed. Lying propped up in the centre, a small wriggling ball of fur on her lap, sat Geraldine Clayton Valkenberg. "Do come in," she gestured to a chair next to the bed, "and have a seat please." I obeyed her request, but I wondered why on earth I was there, and why the lady was abed in the afternoon?.

"You must be puzzled why I have summoned you?" Her eyes were sharp as a bird of prey, sparkling brown and close together over her beak of a nose. She was not an attractive woman, yet the character in her face promised much intelligence.

"Do you have a voice, gal?" I was so lost in thought I had forgotten to answer her question.

"Oh, indeed Lady Valkenberg, pardon me. Yes, I did wonder why you would want to see me."

"Well, it's about Gideon, of course." She patted the little animal on her lap, and I realized the scruffy ball of fur was in fact a small dog. By the flatness of its face, I recognized it as a Pekinese.

"Gideon?"

"Yes, my youngest nephew. I have been worried about him since the loss of Minty, and I would like your opinion to his welfare. Benedict tells me you have been rather a good influence on the boy. How is he? Speak up, gal!" she barked.

"I believe Master Gideon is much improved my lady. He has been quite affected by his sister's death, but keeping his mind occupied with studies and challenging lessons allows it to heal."

"You don't say? It sounds perfectly sensible to me, well done young lady. I am pleased to hear it."

Lady Geraldine granted me a smile which rendered her face even less attractive if it were possible. I returned the gesture, appreciative of her praise.

"I would like a regular report while I am here at Mowbray. I want to know his mood and also how he does with his lessons. His mother has been far too lenient on the boy, in my opinion." She stopped and read my expression. "Oh, you think me rude to speak thus and to a member of staff? Tosh, what rubbish. Since the death of my dear brother, Blanche has spoiled all her children and encouraged them to favor a weakness of spirit and mind which I find abhorrent. It is time Gideon grew up. But she won't send him off to Eton so he can become a man, she hides him here at Mowbray to cosset and coddle. Ridiculous." She reached over to a side table next to her bed and rang a small bell. The dog barked. "Oh, hush Genghis, please."

I hid a smile as I looked at the scrap of a dog who bore such a massive name. Moments later a knock came on the door and it opened to admit Miss Tricklebank. Unusually flustered, she stepped into the room.

"Yes, my lady?"

Lady Geraldine held out the squirming dog. "Here, Tricklebank, please take Genghis to one of the footmen and ask that he be walked. He might need to tinkle as well."

The housekeeper grimaced at her use of language but scooped up the yapping dog and left the room. As soon as the door had closed, the old lady sat up straighter.

"Don't look so scared, girl, I won't bite." Lady Geraldine reached over to her nightstand, opened a wooden box and extracted a cigarette. She placed it in a slim holder, then struck a match to light it. She sat upright in her bed, her bearing regal, her posture straight as a woman half her age and most certainly not at the mercy of any illness. She inhaled deeply and blew the smoke up into the air.

"Miss Westcott, I take it you have become acquainted with all of the family?"

"Yes, my lady, I have."

"What about that Munt fellow, and Lucy?"

"I have met them both, though briefly."

"Hmm." She took another puff of tobacco and blew it out. Her complexion was as rugged as the cliff face. I knew Lady Geraldine was near eighty. In many ways, she owned every single day of them. Her skin, her hair, her imperious demeanor. But her sharp attention and directness belied her age. Not much would escape this woman's attention.

"Tell me, what think you of the boys?"

"I beg your pardon?"

"Miss Westcott don't be coy. I am curious to know what you think of my nephews?"

"Well—" I searched for the correct words, what could I really say? *Gabriel's charming but your other grandson might be a murderer?*

"Oh come, don't be missish. I would like your honest opinion."

My heart sank, this was a strange conversation indeed. More than anything I wanted to escape. Lady Valkenberg's dark eyes bored into my face, willing me to respond. I really had no choice.

"I think Lord Clayton a fine gentleman, courteous and considerate, he takes a keen interest in his brother's education."

"Carry on."

"Mr. Swan is a very dependable person. He seems to have the estate's prosperity at heart and is always concerned for the family's welfare."

She did not comment. What had I said wrong? Her face gave nothing away. I continued.

"Master Gideon. He is a delightful boy, almost a young man really. He seems a little lonely, but has a bright disposition, full of curiosity and kind at heart. Obviously, I know him better as I spend time with him each day."

"Indeed." She placed the cigarette in the crystal ashtray. "You have been told about Aramintha?" Her direct question caught me off-guard. I rallied quickly.

"Yes, but very little. In fact, Gideon told me, no one else would speak of it."

"Preposterous." The old lady spat. "Sometimes I think my sister-in-law has addled her brain. This ridiculous act she insists upon does more harm than good. Now I have it from Benedict you are a sensible gal, which is why I am speaking with you about the matter."

That surprised me. "Benedict?"

"Yes, my nephew. I have enlisted his help, and now yours, to encourage Blanche to accept what happened to my niece and cease this attempt at concealment. God knows it broke my heart to lose her, but facts are facts. If Aramintha decided to end her life, well that was her choice. Now I think it high time we moved on."

I was not sure I understood. "What exactly is it you want me to do?"

The old lady gave a heavy sigh. "I want you to try and find out what really happened that night. You are an employee of the house, but are intelligent and can be trusted, well according to my nephew you can. In your capacity as tutor, you interact with the staff downstairs. Therefore, I wish you to learn about the events which precipitated whatever put my normally level-headed niece into such a state that she felt suicide her only option."

"But Lady Geraldine—"

She held her hand up. "No, please do not argue. I

have given this great thought. If my brother Nigel were alive, none of this would have happened. But it has, and I want to get to the bottom of it. Miss Westcott, there is a dark cloud hanging over this house and it needs to be gone. I'll not rest until it has." She waved a bony finger. "I will expect you to keep me informed of any information you may have to achieve this end. Benedict will do the same. That is all, you may go." And with that, the conversation was at an end.

I left the room. My head spun. I had been enlisted to help solve a puzzle alongside the very man I suspected of causing the demise of Aramintha Clayton!

Chapter Fourteen

My dreams were full of disturbing images of Aramintha and Benedict. I awoke before dawn, and as I took breakfast with the other servants, I drew an obvious conclusion. I could no longer carry the weight of Aramintha's burden alone. I needed someone to help me with this quandary, especially now Lady Geraldine had made her own demands.

But who to trust at Mowbray Manor, Gabriel? No, at least not until I felt more certain. I was employed by his mother and could not risk the wrath of Lady Clayton by confiding in her son. The more obvious choice was Moira. She had befriended me so readily, and though we had spent little time together, I felt a kinship with the young Scotswoman.

When Moira sat down with her breakfast, I was almost finished with my own. She took a seat beside me and I turned to her and spoke quietly. "Can you come to the schoolroom after three o'clock this afternoon? There is a matter I want to discuss with you."

"Aye," she said between gulps of tea. "Whatever is wrong?" Her face betrayed concern.

"Nothing serious. But we should speak in private. Meet me, and I will explain."

I left her with a quizzical look stamped upon her face and departed to the classroom and my awaiting student.

Gideon and I had a full day. We read about Queen Victoria and the expansion of the British Empire during her reign. He regaled me with stories from Benedict about his exploits in South Africa. It seemed, at least according to Gideon Clayton, that his half-brother had fought battles without the aid of modern weaponry. Apparently, Benedict Swan was a dab-hand with a machete.

"Goodness." I had exclaimed, the image of the dark-haired man who at this point was at the top of my list of potential n'er-do-wells now brandishing a menacing and deadly knife. "That sounds terribly barbaric."

"It jolly well is," Gideon confirmed. "The blade is so sharp it can whack off a man's head with one swoosh." He leapt to his feet and swung an arm as though about to decapitate me. I sat back in my chair to avoid getting close.

"Whoa there, Gid. Are you trying to hit your tutor?" Gabriel entered the room and raised his eyebrows in warning at his brother.

"Don't be daft, Gabe," Gideon soothed. "I was just showing Miss Westcott how Benedict used his machete to cut off the heads of the Boers in Africa."

Gabriel ruffled his brother's curls. "Not sure if the military is in your future brother dear. I think you might stay with the navy, probably safer at sea."

"Ahoy, matey." Gideon saluted. "Fifteen men on a dead man's chest. Yo ho ho and a bottle of rum."

"I don't know about rum, Gid," Gabriel teased. "But Mrs. Oldershaw might spare you a glass of fresh milk to eat with one of her yummy scones. You can smell them all the way up the stairs."

Gideon's eyes sought mine and begged for permission to leave for the kitchen.

I glanced at the time—it was close enough to three in the afternoon and I expected Moira at any moment. "Off you go then, Master Gideon." He gave an un-gentleman-like whoop and hurried from the classroom.

"I didn't have to tell him twice." Gabriel smiled, and I returned the gesture. I rose from my seat and went to the chalkboard to wipe away the notes from the day's schoolwork and also to stay occupied, unsettled at his presence.

"Kathryn, would you care to ride out with me later today? I saw how much you enjoyed yourself on Jezebel, why don't you join me?"

I placed the rag down and tapped the chalk dust from my hands. I wanted to answer a resounding yes, but I was uncomfortable, unsure of my place. He saw my perplexed expression and read my concerns.

"I assure you it is perfectly acceptable for you to ride out with me. You are not one of the maids, Kathryn, but tutor, and your rank affords you some privilege." He moved to stand in front of me, and my senses warmed at his nearness. "You are a good horsewoman, and your skills should be utilized, not left to wither. Jezebel is a fine mare, and in need of exercise. So, let us leave it at that. As your employer, I command you to meet me at the stables in one hour." He flashed his white teeth, and his blue eyes gave a mischievous twinkle. With that he spun on his heel and left me standing bemused. I readied myself for Moira's visit.

"Lord Clayton passed me just now, and he was whistling." Moira glanced over her shoulder with a frown. "Do you ken what he's so happy about?"

I shrugged. "I wouldn't know."

She arched one brow and then just as abruptly shrugged it off. "Well now, what is it you want to talk to me about?"

Her tone was unusually curt, and I detected something guarded about her manner. But now was not the time for speculation as there were important things to tell my friend. I took her hand and guided her to the window seat overlooking the front gardens and driveway. We sat down upon the padded cushion on the thick ledge.

"I wish to share a secret with you. If you tell another living soul, I will lose my position at Mowbray, so it is imperative you keep this to yourself."

Her expression changed to one of consternation and she took a deep breath. "Aye, all right, Kathryn. Whatever it is you need to say, you've my word I'll not repeat it to another."

With my voice low, I recounted my story to Moira. I told her of my friendship with Aramintha and the reason I had come to Mowbray Manor. I paused momentarily and allowed her to absorb the first part of the tale before I continued. I explained the theft of my letters, and then finally told her about the diary. She did not utter a single sound. Moira listened intently as I explained my suspicions that Aramintha might have been pushed off the cliff.

"But why would anyone harm the lass?" Moira spoke then, the shock of my words rousing her to speech. And then I delivered the last part of my story, that Aramintha Clayton was with child. Moira's mouth fell open, her jaw hung slack as though I had slapped her with the palm of my hand and not my words. She blinked several times, swallowed and then took hold of me.

"Och, Kathryn, you must not have made this all up. I beg of you, if you are joshing with me tell me now."

I shook my head. "I only wish I were and that my friend was still here." A knot tightened in my throat, speaking of Aramintha out loud had loosened the thread which kept my emotions bound securely.

"But this is awful. If someone killed her, she with a wee bairn in her belly—" She trailed off, her face still pale as she digested the story.

"Yes, it is. Which is precisely why I must find out what really happened to her that night. If you will help me, perhaps we can discover the truth!"

"Help you? I don't know what I can do. What is it you want of me?"

I composed myself and squeezed Moira's hands tightly. "I am not certain. You could think about what happened back in June, see if you remember anything about how Aramintha behaved. After all, you must have known her a little. Did she ever speak of her beau? Had you noticed her affections being placed on anyone, or perhaps Lady Clayton mentioned something about her which might be of use? What were the servants saying about Aramintha falling to her death the night it happened?"

"Goodness, 'tis a lot to think about. I trust you don't expect me to answer just now?"

"No." I smiled. "More than anything, I wanted to tell you the truth about why I am here and have someone I could confide in. It has been a heavy burden to bear, all these thoughts and ponderings Moira. You have no idea how much it helps simply being able to speak of my worries."

She nodded her dark head, and her eyes shone warm as brandy. "Och lass, stop your blatherin'. A trouble shared is a trouble halved as they say. Let me think on what you've said for a wee while. We'll speak again soon."

With that, we rose from the sill and left the classroom. Taking Moira into my confidence was a gamble in her role as Lady Clayton's maid, and I hoped I would not regret doing so. As if she read my mind, Moira threaded her arm through my own and smiled. We headed down the hall and turned into the servant's staircase. A strange, uneasy feeling slithered across the back of my neck, and I stopped.

"What is it, lass?" Moira's brow rose in question. My eyes darted around. I was certain someone stood in the shadows of the hallway.

"'Tis nothing," I said complacently. But I lied. We were being watched.

****

As before, I slipped on Aramintha's tweed riding habit. My emotions felt as though they had been tossed into a sack and shaken violently. I knew a sense of excitement, the anticipation of spending time with Gabriel, a man who I could not deny feeling an attraction towards. Yet I also felt a tug of apprehension. Now I had shared my knowledge of Aramintha with another I felt uneasy. The truth was a fragile thing. In my heart I believed Moira to be honest and loyal, yet turmoil rushed through my breast now I had revealed my secret.

I met Gabriel in the stables. Gideon had already

gone out riding with Johnny, but Jezebel was saddled and ready. The mare was in good spirits, and as we left the courtyard, I could feel the knot of her muscles beneath my thighs ready to spring into a run. Gabriel rode his mount, Pharaoh, a beautiful black Arabian stallion, whose hooves barely touched the ground as he broke into a gallop.

As both the horses increased their gait, I forgot where I was, who I was, and became one with my horse. I welcomed the sting of cold air on my face, my body melted into the rhythm of Jezebel's movements, and I was at once a girl again, riding my grandfather's Andalusians through the arid Spanish hillside.

I matched Gabriel's speed, and when we came to a small hedgerow, I dug my heels into the mare's flanks and felt the rush of wind as we sailed over the bush. I turned to look back only to see Gabriel do the same, and I slowed Jezebel so he could catch up with me.

Pharaoh chewed on his bit and his snout blew steam into the damp air. His beautiful coat shone like wet coal, and his thick mane hung like fine braided rope.

"Good God, Kathryn, you took that jump like you were born to it." His blue eyes were bright with excitement, his breath as labored as his mount's.

I was light-headed, giddy with exhilaration from my ride. "Perhaps I was, Lord Clayton." I laughed, "there is nothing like riding in the wind."

Gabriel slid off his horse and walked closer to Jezebel. He gestured for me to dismount and grasped the slack reins. "Come, let us walk a while and let the horses cool down." I joined step with him through the thick grassy field.

"You know, Kathryn, I believe there may be more to you than meets the eye," Gabriel said. "On the exterior, you present yourself as a serious teacher, so conservative and proper."

I arched a brow. "What is this, Lord Clayton? Do you accuse me of being a fraud?" I smiled warmly, enjoying the banter.

"Tis Gabriel when we are alone, remember? I tire of formality, for it provides obstacles when one wishes to speak free and clear. I do not call you a fraud, Kathryn, indeed, quite the opposite. You are a refreshing touch of reality in a world of actors in a monotonous play."

"Goodness," I exclaimed. "Is your life at Mowbray so dull, the company of a simple teacher renders it lively?" I laughed at the prospect, but Gabriel's voice was serious, he did not jest.

"You know I appreciate the privilege of my birth - I want for nothing. Yet the price paid for such position comes at a cost, one that is not monetary."

"Do you seek my sympathy, Gabriel? For you will not find it. The trappings of your obligation as a member of the nobility seem miniscule to a person who cannot feed their family, to a mother who watches her child die from malnourishment."

He stopped and turned to me. "Do not condemn me for the accident of my birth. Of course, I recognize how fortunate I am with my lot. Yet should I be frowned upon for wishing to have the freedom to choose my future, carve my own path? 'Tis every man's desire to seek his destiny. Much harder to stay within the dictates of family and title. Would that I was Benedict."

He was quite crestfallen, and at once the mask of

the man slipped to reveal the face of a boy, full of dreams and ambition. I do not know what took hold of me, but instinctively I reached out and lay my gloved palm against his cheek. I only wished to show compassion, but Gabriel lifted his own hand and covered mine. We stood frozen in the moment, as the connection between us grew stronger.

"You are a beautiful woman, Kathryn," he said softly, so close to me that I could see the blond tips of his lashes. His free hand found the curve of my waist and his fingers pressed hard against me. I gazed into his hypnotic eyes as my pulse danced and my lips parted. But at once, the image of Lucy Ditton-Jones seeped into my thoughts and I quickly withdrew my hand as though stung.

Gabriel's chin lifted in defiance at my action, and I knew he comprehended where my mind had ventured.

Suddenly I felt the urge to get away, escape from the invisible web Gabriel had somehow cast around me. I was being ridiculous. I had allowed my romantic notions to get the better of me. For goodness sakes, I was but a tutor, what would a man like Gabriel Clayton want with someone like me?

I caught my breath and turned away. "I should like to return to the house, Lord Clayton." More than anything I needed to place a physical distance between me and this man. He frowned at my use of the formal title, dictating a return to his role as my employer. Gabriel gave me a stony look as he watched me mount my horse. I did not wait for him but dug my heels into Jezebel, and galloped back to the stables as though I was being chased by the hounds of hell.

Chapter Fifteen

Later, at dinner, I became aware of being the subject of several sly glances, followed by hushed whispers. I ignored them. Their tongues were wagging because I had ridden out with Gabriel on my own. That he was my employer and therefore bound me to do his bidding mattered not. As far as the rest of the staff were concerned, I had fraternized with the Lord of the house and therefore was no longer considered 'one of them.'

This perturbed me to no end, for I had done nothing wrong and did not wish to be labelled with any negative connotations they might construe. Perhaps I had been careless in riding without even Gideon as a chaperone, but did that make me a harlot? The double-standard appalled me. I was certain no one would think ill of Gabriel Clayton.

I tried unsuccessfully to stop brooding on my dilemma. I ate my dinner as the others finished theirs and left the table, leaving me alone until Moira sat down beside me.

"Well, Kathryn, it seems you have created quite the stir." She appeared tired and somewhat sullen as she ate a piece of steak and kidney pie.

"Yes, it appears so. Though I did not have much of a say in the matter Moira, I should like to see any of them tell Lord Clayton 'no' when he bids them to do something."

But she remained unsympathetic. "Perhaps. But you should know his mother is most displeased. She gave him a stern talking to once he returned. Lady Geraldine spotted you both and questioned why Gabriel would ask you to ride unchaperoned." Moira frowned. "Care to answer that lass?"

I groaned. "He asked me because he knows how much I love to ride and never have the opportunity. He meant it as a kind gesture, perhaps even in gratitude for my work with Gideon. I am sure Lord Clayton thought little of being alone with his brother's tutor. He is engaged to be married, and I am an employee after all. It obviously looked bad, but nothing was meant by it."

Moira's face softened. "And he didn't compromise you in any way?"

This time it was my turn to be irritated. "No!" I said vehemently. "Not in any way. Now please, can we discuss the matter at hand?" I heaved a sigh, more than ready to change the subject. "Have you thought about our conversation earlier or remembered anything?"

"Aye," she swallowed a sip of milk. "I did. When I first came to Mowbray Manor, I tended to Lady Aramintha's needs when she was home, but you ken she was away at school a great deal. Och, she was friendly enough towards me, but always kept me at a distance. I put it down to the fact I was her mother's maid. She probably didn't trust me because my loyalty would always be to Lady Clayton first." Moira took another bite of food. I waited patiently.

"After she'd left school for good and finally moved home, she had changed. I helped her dress and arranged her hair most days, but I never really got to know her, and she didn't say much to me at all. Then once she was back a few weeks, she suddenly became more outgoing and really happy." Moira thought for a moment. "Come to think of it, she took more interest in her appearance and her clothing too."

"It must be when she started the relationship with the man she calls 'A.'"

"Aye, I think it's a fair guess."

"And you have no idea who the person could be, Moira?"

"No. I've racked my brain since we spoke, but no one comes to mind at all, not even Benedict. Maybe it's someone neither of us knows?"

"Perhaps," I replied glumly. "We should expand our search and discover if there were any men in the village with whom she might have formed a liaison?"

"It would be difficult. There were few visitors to the manor, but I'll try and remember who came to stay and make a list for you."

"Thank you so much, Moira."

A bell tinkled on the wall and displayed Lady Blanche's boudoir. "I'll be off." Moira wiped her mouth with a serviette and got to her feet. "Time to get her ladyship dressed for dinner."

****

I struggled with lessons the next morning, my mind unable to settle on one thought for long. Gideon picked up on my mood and enquired if I was all right.

"Yes, Master Gideon, thank you for asking. I did not sleep as well as I might." The answer satisfied him enough to drop the subject and return to his book.

As a thick frost covered the ground, an escape from the confines of the schoolroom was not an option. I went about planning afternoon lessons when Lady

Geraldine walked briskly into the schoolroom.

"Good day to you both," she barked, going over to Gideon to read over his shoulder. "What is that you are reading?"

"It is a Jules Verne novel, Aunt, all about a fellow named Captain Nemo."

"Sounds like a lot of codswallop," Lady Geraldine complained. "Where's your Latin, your Greek studies?"

I intervened. "Gideon is studying the classics my lady, as well as history, geography, arithmetic, English, French and composition. He is allowed an hour of free time each day on a subject of choice."

"Tosh," she snapped. "In my day we had no such thing as free time. The boy should be at Eton with others of his age, not hiding away up here in the country." She pointed at her nephew. "You'll not develop as you should."

Poor Gideon examined himself as though he might be physically disfigured from being educated at home. "Aunt Gerry, I am not malformed. I look like all the boys in the village."

"Not your body boy, I refer to your mind. 'Tis critical you mix with others. How else shall you be part of society if you are a recluse at twelve years of age?"

"Thirteen," he argued.

"Is there something you required, Lady Geraldine?" I steered the conversation away from Gideon. "May I help you?"

"Yes." Her face registered the memory of her reason for the visit. "I wish you to take luncheon with me today. Twelve sharp, in my room, if you please."

"Lady Geraldine—" I stammered. My mind raced to find an excuse to decline.

"I'll not take no for an answer, my girl. Twelve o'clock if you please." The old woman gave me a haughty glare, nodded at her nephew and trounced out of the classroom.

"Crikey," said Gideon with great sympathy, "You're for the high jump now."

****

Therefore, with much trepidation, I knocked upon Lady Geraldine's door as the large clock downstairs chimed twelve o'clock.

"Come in," she responded. The austere aristocrat sat at a small table placed by her balcony window with a view of the gardens and the stables. A silver tray held a plate of sandwiches, and a delicate cake stand with a selection of *petit fours* cakes arranged for our luncheon. Lady Geraldine gestured for me to take a seat, and she poured tea.

We both selected a sandwich and began to eat.

"I saw you ride out yesterday with my nephew, Miss Westcott."

I took a breath, here it was then, the disapproval. "Indeed, Lady Valkenberg. Lord Clayton invited me, and I did not like to decline."

Her eyes narrowed. "And you found it appropriate to go out unchaperoned with a man affianced to be married?"

My patience snapped. Inside my mind a small flame ignited. I was not the submissive type, yet had kept my disposition calm and polite since arriving in Dorset. Frankly, I was tired of playing the role. My posture stiffened. "It did not cross my mind. Lord Clayton is my employer, when he required me to go riding, what was I to do, say no thank you and get into trouble? Besides, I find it interesting that you question my etiquette as a lady. Do you take me for a strumpet, my lady?"

Much to my surprise, the old woman burst out laughing. "Ah, now there's some backbone finally." She sipped her tea and took a cake from the stand. "Dear gal, I do not believe you did anything improper for it is Gabriel who is at fault. He should know better than to place you in a difficult position. My nephew is a delightful fellow, every silly gal's dream of a handsome swain." She dusted icing from her fingertips. "But alas, he is also a vain, egotistical specimen of the male gender. Confident in his ability to woo anything in a skirt."

I could feel warmth spread across my face like ink on blotting paper. I disliked being included in a gaggle of adoring females.

"Oh, come, Miss Westcott, don't be embarrassed, you would not be human if you did not fall for such a man. Goodness knows were I in your shoes, I would have already gone to bed with the fellow."

I gasped at her bluntness. It was poor taste to speak of the physical act between a man and woman, that a lady of her rank should do so—I was astounded. "Lady Valkenberg, I am offended by your—"

"Tosh," she snapped. "Don't be ridiculous. If men can discuss these things, then why cannot women?" She helped herself to another cake. "Besides, I asked you here to speak frankly, Miss Westcott. Seeing you with my nephew disturbed me. Oh, he is a fine fellow, but it will matter little to him if he collects yet another broken heart. I think you a sensible gal, and I like what you have done for dear Gideon. So here is my warning. Do not fall for Gabriel's silver tongue and pretty speech. Let him go down the path he has chosen and do not become a minor distraction while he plans a wedding to another. He and that silly Ditton-Jones gal are a good match. If you've a need for a man in your life, I would suggest you look to the brother."

I almost choked on my sandwich. "I beg your pardon?"

"Benedict. Now there's a good fellow, chip off the old block, more a Clayton than all three of Blanche's put together."

The woman was a raving lunatic. One riding adventure with her nephew and she had Gabriel labelled a philanderer and Benedict a potential future husband.

"Dear gal, I only tell you this as sound advice from one who knows the family. Blanche believes Gabriel a saint, and she will not allow anything to deter her from securing this successful marriage for the boy. Why do you think Aramintha's suicide has been hushed?"

Though I thought the woman as crazy as a bat, I had to concede her point. Perhaps there was more to this arranged betrothal between Gabriel and Lucy Ditton-Jones than met the eye. I decided to change tack, if the woman could be open with me and speak her mind, then two could play that game.

"As we are speaking frankly, Lady Valkenberg. May I ask a question?"

She nodded, her mouth full with yet *another* cake.

"What are *your* thoughts about what happened to your niece? Are you convinced she jumped to her death, or do you suspect foul play?"

The intelligent eyes became thoughtful and I could almost hear her mind ticking over. She dabbed at her mouth with a linen serviette.

"In truth, Miss Westcott, I cannot say for certain. I know my nephew and Doctor Beedles were in attendance that night, and therefore must trust their findings. Yet Benedict has spoken of things which cause concern. I plan to remain at Mowbray until I reach my conclusion. Now." She gave me a hard look. "What have you discovered that I should know?"

I hesitated, yet instinct willed me to trust the old woman. She appeared to have good intentions, though her obvious affection for Benedict niggled at me somewhat. I already had Moira on my side, perhaps another ally would not hurt?

"It appears Lady Aramintha may have had a gentleman friend, a *secret* friend."

She digested my words and their insinuation. "I see. And do we know who this person might have been?"

"We do not. She referred to him only with an initial, an 'A.'"

"Ridiculous," Lady Valkenberg muttered. "How childish of the gal. I do not recall any young men of connection hereabouts with that initial. Do you?"

"No, I do not. But I am new here, and also a member of staff. I am not privy to know who Aramintha socialized with." The lie tripped off my tongue, and Lady Valkenberg swallowed it whole.

"Hmm. I shall consider this, Miss Westcott. I will ruminate on your information and summon you if needed. That is all."

I raised my eyebrows at her curt command, the woman should have been a navy admiral. But I did as I was told, leaving her alone by the window, deep in thought.

****

When our lessons were finished that afternoon, I took the familiar walk to the chapel. My conversation with Lady Valkenberg had whipped my thoughts into knots and I needed fresh air to clear my head.

I had been disturbed by her account of Gabriel. Though loathe to admit it, I had begun to develop feelings for the handsome man which were more than platonic. I was no silly girl given to romantic whims. There had not yet been anyone who had captured my heart, no Mr. Darcy had ever crossed my path. But Gabriel? He was so enigmatic. He oozed charm and warmth like honey from a honeycomb. Yet his aunt's words rang true, and much as I hated to accept the fact, I had to. Though Gabriel Clayton might be a flirt, surely even a ladies' man could fall in love?

I reached the chapel, and though I yearned for time alone, I was still pleased to see Juniper Blessing attending the flowers on the altar. She flashed a look at me and then continued with her task. There were sprigs of cut holly on the altar, and she placed them into a large urn.

"Hello, Miss Blessing," I said, walking down the aisle.

"Hello yerself, Miss Kathryn." I was taken aback by her use of my Christian name. "How is it up at the manor with that old banshee up from London?"

I grinned. "You refer to Lady Valkenberg? Actually, I think she has livened the place up a tad."

Juniper placed more holly branches in the pewter vase. "Don't surprise me none, always was a busy body that one."

I sat down in the front pew, “You know her, I take it?”

“Tsk,” the older woman said, “know her? Why ’twas she who was responsible for Lord Nigel leaving Lavender at this very altar, fat with her babe she was, an’ he never showed up.”

“Lord Nigel Clayton planned to wed your sister, Benedict’s mother?” This was news to me.

“Why yes,” she said. “He were, until that one stuck her pointy nose into the matter. My sister would’ve been the lady up at the manor, and everythin’ would have been different. Lord Nigel was a fool, he told Geraldine what he was about, and she ran to their father and tattled the tale. Nigel Clayton was sent off to a relative in York an’ my sister was left with no husband and no future.”

“My goodness,” I exclaimed, processing all she had shared. Juniper finished her arrangement and centered the urn on the altar. With her ungainly gait, she walked over to where I sat and joined me on the front pew.

“That there family in the manor, ain’t none of ’em worth a thing, ’cept Master Gideon. Lady Blanche, she’s a ha’penny short of a shilling, and her oldest isn’t interested in anythin’ but his own reflection.” I winced at her words about Gabriel, Juniper Blessing held no love for the Claytons, that was obvious. Hardly surprising if she felt her own family had been slighted.

“I know what I saw, after all, an’ so does he.”

She spoke in riddles. “What? Did you see something Juniper? I don’t understand your meaning?”

She rose to her feet, her black eyes shone with anger. “I’ll not speak a word of it to anyone. I’ll not say."

"Say what to who?" I rose to confront her, my heart pounded with the anticipation I might finally be getting somewhere.

"I'll not lose my place here!" she said passionately. "I promised—an' I'll take it to my grave."

Chapter Sixteen

The more I learned of Araminta and her family, the more confused I became. I had no idea what Juniper hinted at. Had she seen Araminta with Benedict? I had not been able to get another word from the woman, and frustrated, left the chapel and walked into Mowbray Village.

I stopped at the vicarage. I thought perhaps a cup of tea with Avril Plumb might be a welcome distraction, but alas she was out, visiting a sick farmer's wife. Undaunted, I made my way towards the post office, there to console myself with a small bar of toffee. As I passed across the street from the Bull and Boat, the inn door swung open and Benedict walked out into the street. He was not alone, Doctor Beedles stood by his side, and there seemed to be a serious conversation taking place. Benedict's brow was drawn, and he was angry. In contrast, the physician's face appeared devoid of expression. I wondered what they discussed.

I made no purchase and left the post office to return the way I had come. As I passed the vicarage, I heard my name called and I stopped, already knowing who it was.

"Kathryn, it seems we always run into one another in the village." Benedict drew alongside me. "May I walk back with you?"

"Yes, of course."

"Have you been shopping?" He saw my basket was empty.

"Indeed," I said with a smirk, "I have purchased some air." He chuckled at that, and we continued out of the village and down the lane.

"And you?" I queried. "What business did you have in Mowbray?" I was curious how he might answer, and for some strange reason I hoped he would not lie.

"I met with Doctor Beedles," he said matter-of-factly. "Aunt Gerry sent me to riddle the man with questions about Minty and the night she died."

With difficulty, I kept my countenance as calm and uninterested as possible. "Indeed? And was the doctor able to answer any of them?"

"No." His voice carried displeasure. "He did not. It was a most unsatisfying meeting. My aunt will be displeased."

I studied him as he spoke. Benedict Swan had the kind of face which was difficult to read. I could not decipher if he was being truthful or if he actually might be in cahoots with the thin doctor. "Considering your aunt requested I help with this matter, can you share your conversation with Doctor Beedles, or was it confidential?" Lady Geraldine had to have told him of our conversation. After all, he had been the person to recommend me to the old woman in the first place.

We kept our pace constant as we went on towards the manor. Benedict glanced at me and gave his broad shoulders a shrug. "There is no secret. I asked Doctor Beedles to describe the extent of Minty's injuries. I wanted to know if they were consistent with a fall. He believed they were and was not very forthcoming. I am sure he is under direction from Lady Clayton not to discuss my sister's fate, and her command will trump mine on any topic."

"Tell me, Benedict. Do you suspect foul play?" It was a risky question.

"I am uncertain, and that is all I can say at this time."

Not an answer in either direction to be had then? What had I expected? A full confession of his unnatural love for a half-sister, a girl so distraught by his rejection she jumped to her death? Or a girl set on revealing their relationship and therefore had been killed to maintain her silence?

My thoughts swung like a clock's pendulum. So many facts pointed to Benedict's involvement in Aramintha's fate, yet still he did not have the countenance of someone so dastardly, and I had no proof. As we reached the manor and bade each other farewell, I was consumed with disappointment at my lack of progress.

Instead of going up to my bedchamber, I decided to seek out Moira. It was still early, and she would not be needed to dress Lady Blanche for another hour. I had not yet been to her room but knew roughly where it was located—in the servants' quarters upstairs.

The passageway was well lit, but narrow. The floor separated into two wings, one for the male servants, one for the women. A door divided them, and I went through into the women's wing. I could not distinguish who slept in which rooms, so I rapped lightly on each until a voice bade me to come in.

"Miss Westcott." Sally greeted me with a look of

utter surprise and then a broad smile. "What brings you up to these parts then?" She sat on her bed in stockinged feet with an open book before her.

"Hello there," I said, feeling guilty for disturbing her. The poor girl had little time to rest during the course of a day as it was. "Sorry, but I was looking for Campbell, and do not know which room is hers."

"Of course, you wouldn't, miss, they all look the same, don't they? But you're not far off. Moira's the last one on the right, just near the back stairs.

"Thank you, Sally. I'll let you get back to your reading." I smiled and left her room.

There were seven more doors until the end of the hall. Moira's was the last, with none opposite, just the staff staircase that ultimately led down to the kitchen. I approached the door and raised my hand to knock when I heard muffled laughter. I paused, knuckles in mid-air and leaned closer to the door to hear better. I should not want to disturb Moira if she was busy. I listened intently, there came another giggle followed by a voice saying 'sshh.' Frowning, I put my ear boldly against the wooden door. Moira was definitely not alone in there. Should I knock anyway? My curiosity was piqued. Moira had not seemed friendly enough with the other servants to invite one of them into her room. But no sooner had the thought crossed my mind when there came yet another sound. It was so brief I almost believed to have imagined it. I snapped my head away as though slapped because there was no mistaking what I had heard. Moira Campbell was with a man.

****

I dreaded seeing Moira at dinner that night. I was in such a dilemma, for what could I say? That I had spied on her, suspected she was entertaining a man in her room? Fraternizing with the opposite sex was strictly forbidden and an offense which could terminate her employment. I resolved to say nothing yet could not shake it from my mind.

Who was the man though? Several male servants in the house admired the pretty Scot. Thomas the footman, and Jarvis, Lord Clayton's valet, just to name two. I contemplated them, replayed scenarios where both myself and Moira had been in their company.

"Och, I've a rare hunger on me tonight." Moira set down a plate full of steaming shepherd's pie. "Have you already finished your meal, lass?"

"Yes, I came down early. I went into the village and got back a short while ago. How has your day been?"

"Busy as ever. Lady Blanche wanted me to look through some new dress patterns she received from London. She's arranged for a dressmaker to come next week with fabric samples. She's a wee tyrant today, full of vinegar."

"Have you remembered any else about Aramintha?" I asked, finding it awkward to meet her eyes as I wanted more than anything to blurt out *'who was in your room'*?

"No, sorry I haven't, Kathryn. I've not been much help." She ate a forkful of dinner. "What about you, any luck?"

"No. Though I did bump into Benedict in the village. He met with Doctor Beedles." I kept my conversation with Juniper to myself.

"Benedict was with the doctor? Why?"

I shrugged. "He had questions about the night

Aramintha died, though I don't think he learned more than he already knew."

"Oh aye?" She continued to devour her meal.

I struggled with a sense of loss I couldn't quite explain. I liked Moira very much and had been so happy to find an ally in a house full of strangers. I had confided my secrets to her, which I had never done except with Aramintha. Two women who I called friends, yet both withheld something from me, Aramintha had told me nothing of her love affair with 'A,' and now Moira hid the fact she kept company with a man.

It saddened me to think this way, but I had to face up to the truth. I was still alone in my quest to discover Aramintha's fate. And now I had another worry. Who on earth was Moira involved with and what would be her fate should she be discovered?

Chapter Seventeen

I was summoned to Lady Blanche's drawing room the next morning. It had been several days since I had seen her, which suited me perfectly. After our previous meetings, I was more than happy to keep my distance.

I followed Baxter down the familiar hall. He admitted me into the room and then left us alone. She was seated in her usual place at the bureau, pen in hand.

"Ah, there you are, Miss Westcott, do come over here where I may see you better." I approached with trepidation and wondered why she had asked for me. I steeled myself. I would not allow her to bully me again.

"I understand my sister-in-law has been in communication with you several times?"

"Yes, my lady, she has." I was not expecting this.

She rose from her seat and shot a glance at me. I felt the ice of her cold blue stare like a rush of winter air.

"Why has the Viscountess been meeting with you?"

"I beg your pardon?"

"You heard me quite well, Miss Westcott."

I had—but was desperately trying to formulate an answer. "It was regarding Master Gideon," I said quickly. "Lady Valkenberg had concerns for his well-being. She wanted to formulate her own opinion of my credentials for teaching your son."

Her chin rose slightly and then one eyebrow. I could not tell if she believed me. But I was not being untruthful, except by omission.

"And what else has she asked of you?" The ice-maiden's face began to thaw as color bled into Lady Clayton's cheeks.

"That I keep her informed of Master Gideon's progress."

"Miss Westcott, if Lady Valkenberg has invited you to partake in one of her schemes I tell you I forbid it. Whatever she might have requested you to do it would serve you to remember I am your employer, not her." The imperious voice grew louder. She was obviously upset with someone and had chosen me to vent upon.

"Lady Clayton, I—"

"Do not interrupt me. I will not have you skulking around my home—"

"Blanche? Goodness, I can hear you all the way down the hall." Lady Valkenberg stepped into the drawing room and I was never so happy to see another soul. She crossed the carpet and joined us.

"What is amiss?" she asked innocently, a watery smile painted on her thin lips.

"Tis nothing," Lady Clayton said sharply, collecting her wits. "I was reprimanding Miss Westcott, but it was a misunderstanding."

Lady Geraldine's bird-like eyes glanced from her sister-in-law and back to me.

"Dear Blanche, if you are concerned with my spending time with young Miss Westcott here, please do not worry yourself. I have only wanted to enquire about Gideon, and if I am honest, have rather enjoyed speaking with her on a number of subjects. We have a shared love of geography, and I have bored the poor gal with my tales of traveling in Holland."

As the older woman spoke, the anger drained from Blanche Clayton's face. Why was she in such a foul temper?

"Miss Westcott, it must be time for lessons. Are we finished here, Blanche?"

Lady Clayton did not do me the service of bidding me farewell, she simply nodded and turned away. Lady Geraldine inclined her head towards the door, and I did not wait a moment longer.

I was relieved to escape back to the schoolroom, here at least I was not out of my depth as downstairs in the drawing room. I set Gideon arithmetic revision, and then examined what had just taken place. Lady Blanche must suspect I was being underhanded, with Lady Geraldine as my ally. But what would make her think that? Indeed, even if I was, why would she care? Lady Geraldine was family, not foe. She would only have the best interests of the Claytons at heart. As with so many other things, it made no sense.

"I am riding this afternoon, Miss Westcott, and have permission from my brother to ask you to be my escort," Gideon said as he placed his pen down on the desk. "I hope you are willing to accompany me as we had such fun last time. Will you go?"

A ride in the fresh air would be the perfect antidote for the harsh words of the morning. I grinned. "I would love it, Master Gideon, but only if we can race!"

****

This time I was to ride Copper, a young chestnut mare.

“Now watch her.” Johnny Dainty warned. “She’s a bit flighty at times, an’ easily spooked. She’s not as placid as good old Jezebel.” Jezebel was at the blacksmith’s getting shoed.

Gideon set off on Allegro, with me following behind. Copper was certainly skittish. She had a spring in her step and would not settle. I caught up with Gideon.

“Copper is pulling at the reins. I am going to give her a fast run and see if it will pacify her jitters. I will wait for you to catch up.”

Gideon nodded, and I gave the mare her head. She took off like a kite in the wind, her hooves kicked up mud, her body taut, straining with the desire to run. I felt her energy pass through her hide and into my body, as though her release was also my own. We jumped a small hedgerow, and once she had her footing, I wheeled her around to wait for Gideon before we reached a small thatch of woods nearby. Copper still pranced, which surprised me as I thought she had run off her agitation. I strained my eyes to see Gideon. He was a good distance from reaching me.

Copper’s ears came back, and she would not still for me. What was wrong with her? I decided to dismount and check her bridle and bit. I let loose of the reins and grabbed the saddle horn while lifting one leg out of the stirrup when a loud crack reported in the air. Copper raised her forelegs and bolted. I was half out of my saddle as she went straight into a dead run. I could not get my foot back into the stirrup and try as I might, could not gain purchase with the reins. As she made for the hedge, I frantically tried to hang on to Copper’s mane as she leapt into the air to clear the branches. I clung to her neck as she sailed over, and then landed sure-footed, thank goodness. She kept at a full gallop, but I managed to right myself in the saddle, and kept leaning forward, speaking softly to her until at last she began to slow down. I found the stirrup and guided her to a stop. I could feel her lungs grasp for air. I slipped off her back and grabbed the reins, all the while speaking calmly and stroking her froth-flecked neck. I looked at the saddle, it had become crooked, and as I righted it, Copper shifted. What was amiss here? Without hesitation, I unbuckled the saddle to see blood on Copper's back. What had happened? I dropped the saddle to the ground and turned it over. Stuck inside the leather were two small pieces of glass. I felt sick.

When Gideon found me, his face was ashen with fear.

"Are you all right?" he shouted as he neared me, quickly dismounting and coming to my side. I had not put the saddle back on Copper, the poor creature had suffered enough.

"Yes, but you must ride back to the stable and fetch Johnny and another horse. Copper cannot be ridden, and she is hurt."

Gideon mounted Allegro and raced back to the manor.

****

By the time we returned to the stable, it was already getting dark. I sent Gideon up to the house and watched as Johnny took Copper into a stall to tend her wounds. I showed Bert the saddle.

"Who would do such a thing to an innocent beast, miss." He shook his head while at his sides his meaty fists clenched.

"I do not know, Bert. But someone did, and poor Copper was the victim, though I believe it was me they wanted to hurt."

"What do you mean, miss? That don't make any sense."

"Bert, I am an experienced rider. The constant chaffing of the glass, and the gunshot which startled her, would have been enough to throw anyone from the saddle. I can ride bareback, which is the only reason I managed to stay on Copper when she bolted. If not, I would have broken my neck."

"Then I must speak to Lord Clayton at once," Bert said solemnly. I thanked him and checked with Johnny to ensure the horse would be all right.

"Them's nasty cuts, miss," the young lad said. "But we got a nice thick balm on 'em, and we'll let her heal good an' proper 'fore we put another saddle on her." I thanked him sincerely and made my way to the house, though my heart still raced.

****

I took a hot, soothing bath, and then dressed in my nightgown with a warm shawl across my shoulders. I was still shaken from what had happened and its ominous meaning.

Sally delivered a tray from the kitchen as I had missed dinner. My appetite had deserted me, but I sipped the beef broth just to take the chill from my bones. Mrs. Oldershaw had sent up a small glass of sherry on the tray, a rare treat indeed. Once finished, I snuggled under the covers of my bed. I was not at all sleepy but felt the need to be secure.

Time and again I replayed the entire episode in my head. Now the reason for Copper's skittishness was all too apparent. The poor horse had been gouged by the glass at every step. I shuddered at the thought of her suffering. Someone had intentionally done this with the knowledge the irritation would cause the horse to be unmanageable. If not for my expertise, I could easily have been killed by the fall, or from Copper's hooves. And what about the gunshot? Where on earth had that come from? If anyone from Mowbray had been out hunting, Bert would have warned us to take a path in the opposite direction. Besides, it had been too late in the day to shoot. I was convinced the gun was fired intentionally to spook my horse. The fact I had survived was only because of my prowess at riding. I had my mother to begrudgingly thank for that.

Later, as my eyes became heavy, I heard a knock at my door.

"Kathryn," the voice whispered. "Tis Moira, may I come in?"

"Of course."

Moira entered my room, closing the door behind her. She came to the bed, and I patted the quilt to encourage her to sit. She did, and grasped my cold hands in hers.

"Och, lass, I heard what happened to you from Johnny Dainty. You've had such a fright, how are you?"

"I am fine," I said with a shaky voice. "But it was a close call, Moira. Someone set out to do me great harm."

Her face registered shock. "Och no, why would anyone want to hurt you?"

"I do not know."

Moira's brown eyes showed compassion. "I canna

believe someone would do that to you, it's despicable. Have you spoken to the family?"

"No. I did not feel up to it tonight. Tomorrow I shall meet with them and tell them what occurred. Perhaps they will call in the constable?"

Moira shook her head, a deep frown painted on her brow. "I don't like this one wee bit. Kathryn, if you are in danger, perhaps you should think about leaving Mowbray? If it is not safe, you shouldn't stay."

As she spoke, the Spanish blood heated in my veins. I looked fixedly at my dear friend and my chin rose in defiance. "Absolutely not," I said vehemently. "For that is exactly what someone wants me to do."

****

"The constable must be sent for." Lady Geraldine paced before the hearth, her unattractive face balled into a knot of consternation. "This smacks of intrigue, Miss Westcott. Apparently, you know something which threatens this…this despicable criminal." She looked at me. "Are you sure you are unharmed? We can send for Beedles."

"No!" My tone surprised her, and the old woman pushed her disgruntled Pekinese down from the armchair to the floor and took his place in front of the fire.

"So passionate, Miss Westcott? Might I enquire why you would not wish to see the doctor?"

"I do not trust the man," I stated flatly. "He knows more than he lets on regarding the night Aramintha died."

"Interesting. Benedict has said the very same. He spoke with Beedles the other day and found the fellow reluctant to say much. As long as you do not feel unwell, we will keep the doctor out of this." She rose again as though her nerves could not be stilled. Genghis immediately leapt back onto the vacant chair.

"I believe I am missing something, Miss Westcott. You are a tutor to Gideon, and forgive my saying so, but in the grand scheme of things, why should you be the target of this evil?"

My conscience fought with what I should reveal. In truth, I could use the support of someone in the household who yielded more power than a lady's maid.

"I have an idea why." I let out a sigh, and Lady Geraldine returned to her seat, much to the chagrin of the dog.

"Aramintha and I were friends at Brampton."

The older woman's face did not register any surprise. "Go on."

"We corresponded for many months once she returned to Mowbray until her letters suddenly ceased. Aramintha was good to me, she helped me through many dark days. It was unlike her to stop writing, and I became worried. I thought perhaps she had married or gone to the Continent. There had to be a reason she would disappear from my life. I wanted to find out what had happened."

"And you applied for the tutor's position?"

"Yes, and then Gideon told me she had died. I was devastated."

"Good God," Lady Geraldine said, "what a palaver." She rose once more and paced. "Whoever tried to harm you must know your true identity and wonder what you are about."

"Not necessarily," I replied. "Aramintha always called me by a nickname, she knew her mother would disapprove of our friendship. I brought her letters with me, but they were stolen from my room several days ago." I hesitated. "And that is not all."

"There is more?" Lady Geraldine's snaky grey eyebrows rose incredulously.

"Yes," I said boldly. "I have discovered Aramintha's diary."

Chapter Eighteen

My heart raced as I awaited Lady Geraldine's response. And after what had just happened to me, I was justified feeling vulnerable. I fervently hoped my instinct was accurate, and the woman could be trusted. My primary concern was her fondness for Benedict. Should he in fact be the secret lover Aramintha referred to, he could be the person who had harmed her and attempted to hurt me as well. I desperately wanted to convey this to Lady Geraldine but was unsure exactly how to broach my concerns.

I took a deep breath. "Lady Geraldine, there is something else I should tell you, but I do not know how to say it as it may anger you. And you must not repeat it."

She tilted her imperious chin. "Whatever you say, I give my word I shall not speak of it without your permission."

"Thank you. It is regarding the identity of 'A.'"

"Go on."

"I believe it might be Benedict."

The atmosphere changed immediately. Lady Geraldine rose swiftly to her feet and marched over to the window. She turned back towards me, fury in her eyes.

"That is a preposterous suggestion and highly offensive. How dare you speak of my nephew in such a disparaging manner."

"You think I say it lightly, my lady?" I rose and went to the fireplace. I lay my hand against the cold marble, and its solid mass gave me the stability I needed. "I have been led to this conclusion by my observations, I have no actual proof or evidence. I hoped you might—"

"Might what, agree with you? Say the one person in my family I respect is capable of an incestuous relationship with his half-sister, perhaps be responsible for her death and the attempt on your life? The same man who could not speak highly enough of you when first your name was mentioned?"

I lowered my eyes. For a moment, I felt shame, but not for long. A rush of emotion passed through me, a rising tide of all which had transpired since my arrival at Mowbray.

"Yes, the very same man. And not because I sought to lay the blame at his feet, quite the contrary." It was my turn to be annoyed. The heat rose in my face. "I like Benedict Swan. In truth, he was the only person to make me welcome here. He alone made me feel an equal, gave me respect for the work I was here to do. I take no pleasure drawing these obnoxious conclusions, but draw them I have." I took a step towards her.

"I do not ask you to agree with me, I would rather encourage you to prove me wrong, for it would please me greatly. But now there is a problem at hand. I alone have suspected wrongdoing in Aramintha's death and have been singled out as a recipient of an attempt on my life. If you think to protect the good opinion you hold of your nephew in exchange for my life, then you are not the intelligent woman I mistook you for." My breath came faster than I could take it.

Lady Geraldine stood with her profile facing me. I did not wait for a response but turned on my heel and walked out of the room.

****

By the end of the day, I was half-tempted to pack my bags and return to London. I was weary, and the events of yesterday had claimed a grip on my mind. Whoever tried to warn me off was gaining ground. The village constable had been to the manor and interviewed me, but in truth, I believed I had better odds determining the culprit than Constable Harkles. Nice as he was, the middle-aged man did not seem to be the sharpest mind in the village.

I sat alone in the schoolroom, my head in my hands while thoughts swam around my head like fish in an eddy.

"My but you look all done in." I glanced up as Gabriel came into the room and approached my desk. He leaned against its side and gave me a sympathetic smile. "I heard about what happened yesterday. I would have come sooner, but I was at Munt's. Are you all right?" His tone was warm and caring.

I looked up and much to my astonishment tears welled in my eyes. In a flash he was in front of me, kneeling on the floor. He grasped my hands in his own.

"Kathryn, please do not cry. I hate to see you in such distress. What can I do? Tell me, and it is done."

Through my tears I saw compassion shine in those lovely eyes. His face was so close. He raised one hand and delicately cupped my chin. Gabriel leaned forward and softly touched his lips to mine in the most tender gesture I had ever known. I closed my eyes and allowed the tears to run down my face. The moment was magical, all my thoughts, my fears, everything in my mind disappeared except the heady, wonderful sensation of his gentle kiss.

Too soon it ended, but he did not stand, Gabriel stared earnestly into my face, concern etched upon his worried brow. "Dearest Kathryn, I was terrified when I found out what had happened. Who would want to hurt you, do you have any idea?"

"No." I shook my head and then wiped the tears from my face. "I do not."

"Why would anyone seek to do you harm? It makes no sense." He frowned. "What are you withholding from me, sweet Kathryn? You are Gideon's teacher, are you not?" He grinned. "Unless you are masquerading and are really a spy!"

I smiled back as it was difficult not to. My mind waged a battle. Part of me wished to spill all I knew to this dear man, share the burden and enlist his help. I took a breath to do exactly that, yet I hesitated. Gabriel felt my struggle. I could see it in his expression, the slight raise of his eyebrows as he anticipated that I was going to share a secret.

"No, Gabriel, I am not a spy. Perhaps Gideon has hired someone to scare me away, so he does not have to suffer through our Latin lesson."

Gabriel's countenance changed abruptly. He rose to his feet, his disappointment apparent at my lack of trust. He wanted to be my confidante. I could not commit - not yet.

"Kathryn, are you here?" Moira came into the room and stopped short as she saw Lord Clayton. "Oh, begging your pardon, my Lord, I can come back later."

The look of annoyance upon Gabriel's face surprised me. His eyes became hard.

"Tis no bother, you interrupt nothing." And without another word Gabriel left the schoolroom.

Moira flew to my side. "Is something wrong, what has happened?"

"Nothing." I assured her. "Lord Clayton heard of my accident, he was being considerate and asked after my welfare."

Moira's dark eyes flashed a hint of annoyance, then softened. "Och, I angered him by being here. I interrupted—again."

"Nonsense." I rose from the desk and moved away lest she see my embarrassment at the memory of Gabriel's kiss. "Gabriel—Lord Clayton was trying to help me, he wanted to know why I thought someone might wish me harm."

Moira caught up with me and grasped my wrist. "Did you tell him anything?" Her voice seemed to have an edge to it, her breath quickened. I frowned at her.

"No, should I have done?"

Her hand dropped from my wrist. "Of course not. I think this better between us, the fewer that know, the less guarded they are."

"I spoke with Lady Geraldine early today."

She gasped. "What about?"

"Everything. The woman is no fool, Moira, and after what happened to me, she was most insistent I tell her the entire story."

She bit her lip and contemplated my words. "What did her ladyship say?"

"It was awkward. At first, she was interested in what I told her. But she was furious I should suspect her family members."

The maid's eyes grew large. "You told her your suspicion of Benedict? You wee fool, have you lost your marbles? She'll have you thrown out of the house for that. He is her darling." Moira was incredulous.

My temper flickered. "And so be it if she does. Frankly I am tired of everyone proclaiming their opinions upon me. All I have sought to do is the right thing. I have no desire to hurt anyone nor destroy this family. But dear God, Moira, I lost a very dear friend. Is there no other to champion Aramintha?"

Moira came to me and grasped my hands much as Gabriel had done moments earlier. She squeezed my fingers. "Och, I'm sorry lass. I didn't mean to be so harsh. I'm worried as I know you need the work, and besides," she flashed me a grin, "you're my one friend here in England an' I'll no lose you when I've just found you!"

I smiled at her. She truly was my only real ally in this house. "Thank you, Moira. That means so much to me." But as we left the schoolroom, I wondered that each time Gabriel and I were alone, she often was the one to discover us.

****

At dusk I took a quick walk about the gardens, the family would be inside dressing for dinner, and therefore no one would mind. I loved the gardens at the back of the manor. The elongated pool which I could see from my window, the thick expanse of lawn. I went along the path towards the view of the distant sea and marveled how fresh the evening air invigorated my senses. There was a stark comparison between the beauty of Dorset and the bustling city of London.

When the silhouette of two figures walked towards me, I stopped immediately and turned to move briskly away. But Lady Geraldine's command for me to wait for them halted my escape.

"A word, Miss Westcott." She drew alongside, her arm linked in Benedict's. He said a good evening to me. I responded with a nod of my head.

"I have taken a turn about the garden with my nephew, I found the house suffocating." She eyed me intently to convey her reference. "Now, I am much relieved."

"I am pleased to hear it, Lady Geraldine." I wanted more than anything to get back to the manor. It was difficult hiding my discomfort.

She turned to Benedict. "I shall go the remainder of the way with Miss Westcott here. Thank you for your company, Benedict."

"My pleasure, Aunt. I will see you at dinner." He glanced at me, his handsome face serious. "Goodnight, Kathryn." With that, he departed.

Lady Geraldine and I resumed walking back up the path to the house.

"The matter we spoke of earlier?" she began. "I have given it much thought, and though it disturbs me greatly, I have decided to go along with you and keep your secret to myself."

"Thank you Lady Ger—"

She threw me a harsh look. "Do not thank me, gal. For I still find your accusation hideous and insulting." She cleared her throat. "However, in light of the severity of the situation, I agree the fewer people who know your true identity, the better." She glanced at me. "Have you spoken of this to anyone else?"

"Yes," I replied honestly. "To Moira."

Lady Geraldine stopped. "Blanche's maid?"

"Yes."

"That is unfortunate." We had reached the French doors. Lady Geraldine climbed the steps without another word and left me on the path, trying to understand her meaning.

****

As I dressed for the day, my thoughts were of Aramintha. Now I understood more clearly how she must have been so troubled faced with her predicament of pregnancy. These musings pervaded as I joined the staff for breakfast. I was so thoroughly distracted I did not notice Moira until she nudged my arm.

"You're miles away lass."

"Oh," I started, "sorry. I was lost in thought."

"You can say that again. How do you feel this morning, any better?"

"Yes, thank you." I was improved, though I could not say why. We ate companionably, our conversation light as we interacted with Sally and Mrs. Oldershaw who breakfasted with us. I kept returning to my conversation with Lady Geraldine and her parting comment about Moira. Perhaps the old lady simply did not care for the young Scot? I would enquire at the next opportunity.

We left the dining room together, Moira to go up and see to Lady Blanche, and me to the schoolroom. As we climbed the narrow stairs my foot caught in the hem of my dress, and I stumbled and impulsively reached out to grab Moira's forearm. I steadied myself but let go quickly at her gasp of pain.

"Oh, Moira, have I hurt you?"

She recovered quickly, too quickly. "Och no lass, you just caught me by surprise." We reached the second floor and parted ways. I did not continue on but peeked around the corner as Moira walked down the hall to her Mistress's room. She had not ventured far when she stopped and bent her head to inspect the arm which she held as though injured. I withdrew before she might see me watching. I could not have hurt her, because I had gripped her arm in a normal manner. So, what was wrong with her arm, and why had Moira lied to me?

****

The remainder of the week flew by. Gideon and I spent it indoors as the weather had turned bleak. We had little snow, but the wind howled off the sea and brought cold fingers to wrap around our bones. As Christmas was three weeks away, our conversation turned to decorations and gifts. Gideon owned little money, so he had decided to make presents for the family. I encouraged this, and we spent an enjoyable time pouring over books and magazines for ideas of what he might make.

He was excited at the prospect of decorating the house. Gideon would accompany Gabriel and Benedict to select a spruce tree for the drawing room. The event was planned for the next day, a Saturday. I did not have to work, and Gideon invited me to go along with them to cut the tree. I thanked him and declined. Instead, I looked forward to a trip into Swanage to do my own Christmas shopping. I had asked to ride along with Johnny Dainty, who took the cart each Saturday into town to purchase items for Mowbray which could not be delivered during the week.

Saturday was very cold, but the brave sun cut the

frost and softened the cold snap of winter. It would be a brisk, but nice outing. I liked Johnny, and had come to know him from my frequent visits to the stables.

The Dainty family were of Scots ancestry, which accounted for his thatch of ginger hair and freckled skin. Johnny's eyes were blue as the bluebells in the woods, and his gap-toothed grin would brighten even the grumpiest of spirits. I sat next to him in the cart as he guided Domino along the well-worn lane. Johnny had a gift with horses, he could settle a fretting mare, calm an angry stallion with soft whispers and his gentle touch. I considered you could tell a great deal by the way people treated animals. I liked the boy immensely.

Copper was not yet fully recovered from her wounds. I frequented the stables each day to check on her and give her a treat, and I still could not help but feel responsible for her suffering. I usually stopped for a chat with Johnny when doing so and our mutual love of horses had shaped a friendship.

"Have you much shoppin' to buy, miss?" Johnny asked as we went along, his warm breath steamed in the cold air.

"Not really. I want to purchase a Christmas gift for Master Gideon and a few others."

"He's a good fellow, that 'n," Johnny remarked affably. "Always polite and don't treat you like a servant. Looks after his horse too, I respect him for that. More 'n I can say for some of 'em."

"Really? Like whom?" I rubbed my gloved hands together to keep them warm.

Johnny shrugged his thin shoulders. "Not my place to say miss but seems the higher up a man rises, the further behind he leaves his manners."

Such eloquence from a stable lad impressed me. "Nicely put, Johnny, and I assume you refer to Lord Clayton?"

"Yes, miss, and a few others like him. Not too fond of the Munt fellow neither, least when it comes to how he treats his horse. I know his stable boy, name of Andy Pollock, he has some stories to tell." Johnny fell silent and I took the moment to contemplate what he said. His comments about Royston Munt did not surprise me, I was not too fond of him either. But I did not want to consider Gabriel to be cut from a similar cloth.

"Lord Clayton has been most kind to me, Johnny, I am disappointed to hear you find him lacking."

Johnny tutted and glanced my way. "'Tis not that I don't like his lordship, miss. It's more he don't see things normal, like the other servants and me. We're not people to him, more like he owns us. Do you understand my meaning?"

I did, and one of the petals so recently bloomed in my heart wilted a little. "I think so, Johnny. The gentry are a different kettle of fish are they not?"

"Yes, miss." He chuckled. "Some of 'em are eels and others are sharks, 'cept Reverend Plumb, he's more like a jellyfish!" He hooted with laughter, and it was contagious. The rest of our journey was spent amicably naming the household and the villagers for different fish and animals.

At Swanage, we parted ways with a designated time and place to meet for our return journey. I began to shop. It was enjoyable scouring the different wares offered among the variety of shops along the high street. Their windows were festive, festooned with holly boughs and ribbons, I suddenly thought of

Gideon. I wondered how he fared with cutting down a Christmas tree.

I made several purchases and then found a small tea-room to have a hot cup of tea to warm up, and perhaps even treat myself to a cream cake. I took a seat near the window where I had a clear view of the road leading down to the sea. I devoured my food and relished the tea. It was fortifying after my excursion. I looked at the clock on the wall, it was too early yet to meet Johnny, so I ordered another pot of tea. As I waited, my mind checked over the contents of my basket to ensure I had covered everyone on my present list, when a familiar figure caught my eye.

Across the street a woman emerged from a bookstore, her hooded cloak drawn tight about her. Moira? I would know her in a heartbeat. I sat bolt upright with my tea forgotten, grabbed my wares and rose to leave the café. I followed Moira as she walked down towards the sea front, puzzled to see what she was about, though my conscience prickled for I kept my presence unknown. She turned at the end of the street where it met the sea, and then darted up a small alleyway. Where was she going? I did not know Swanage well and had no sense of direction here, but I kept several paces behind her and hoped she would not turn around and see me. I had not told Moira I planned to come to Swanage, because she had been absent at breakfast. Perhaps if I had, we could have traveled together?

I lost sight of her as I rounded the end of the alleyway at a road which ran perpendicular. Had she turned left, or right? A sudden movement caught my eye. I glimpsed her briefly, just as she disappeared into a building marked as a surgery. Was Moira ill? I thought of her injured arm, but she could easily have seen Doctor Beedles for that. My curiosity piqued, I drew closer to the building and read the sign in the front window and hoped she would not spot me there.

'Nurse Agnes Spooner,' it read. I was intrigued yet did not want to be discovered. Quickly I walked on and found my way back to where Johnny and I were to meet. I was still early, yet the time passed as I was completely lost in thought.

"Are you ready, miss?" Johnny's friendly voice roused me, and I realized he had drawn alongside me on the street, the cart full of purchases. He took my basket and I climbed up next to him on the cart. Johnny chatted as we rode, he spoke of his tasks in Swanage and local gossip. He had bought a fine new cap which he proudly sported on his head, and I remarked how well it suited him.

I told him where I had shopped and spoke of the tea-room and the delicious cake I had devoured.

He laughed. "Don't you be tellin' Mrs. Oldershaw 'bout that, she'll be miffed to think hers can be bettered."

I assured him I would do no such thing and then changed the subject. "Swanage is a nice town, Johnny, I imagine you know it well?"

"I should think so, miss. Been here all my life. Though it has grown much this past few years, what with the railway comin' and all. My da came here for the quarryin'as they like our Purbeck stone in London. 'Tis sent all over the country, you know."

"Indeed." I struggled to come up with a way to say what I wanted to say. "There are many businesses in town I noticed."

"Most definitely, miss."

"I wonder that Doctor Beedles does not practice in Swanage instead of Mowbray? Surely he would command more business here than in the village. I saw a Nurse's surgery while shopping, so perhaps that is why he stays at Mowbray. It was a Nurse Agnes Spooner. I have not heard anyone speak of her."

Johnny's jaw clenched at the name. "She ain't no nurse. Wouldn't send my worst enemy to that woman, she's a butcher."

I had not expected his answer to be so condemning. I was at once alarmed, thinking of my friend Moira.

"Surely not, Johnny, that is a severe opinion indeed."

The young man shuddered, and all traces of his happy countenance slid from his face. "No, it ain't, miss. She kills babies."

Chapter Nineteen

I could not get back to my room quick enough. All my joy of Christmas shopping had been annihilated by Johnny's comment. What did it mean? Was Moira with child? Had she gone to see this nurse to rid herself of an unwanted baby?

My head spun at the thought of it, first Aramintha pregnant, and now potentially Moira as well? What should I do? I ransacked my options, deliberating the best course of action to take. But how could I possibly say anything to Moira? Yet how could I not?

The dilemma stayed with me at dinner, and I found it impossible to meet my dear friend's eyes. I did however, venture to ask after her arm.

"I was worried I'd hurt you when I grabbed your arm the other day."

"Och, no, it's fine, Kathryn," Moira assured me.

"Are you certain?" She looked at me quizzically, and then pulled her sleeve up over her forearm. There was a nasty burn at least two inches long across her skin. It was red and inflamed. I gasped.

"What on earth happened?" No wonder she had flinched when I grabbed her, it must have been excruciating.

"I burned myself on Lady Clayton's hair irons a few nights ago. I was a wee bit clumsy, but no harm done."

"Oh, Moira, that looks bad. You should let Doctor Beedles give you a salve to help it heal."

She covered it back with her sleeve. "It'll be all right, lass. I've some ointment in my room I've been using. It's already healing." She continued eating her dinner, and I found myself thinking about her visit to see Nurse Spooner earlier in the day. I was desperate to ask what was going on, but if Moira wanted me to know she would tell me. Perhaps she needed encouragement.

"I went to Swanage today to do my Christmas shopping," I mentioned casually, and kept my eyes trained on her profile to see if she reacted in any way. Her small intake of breath was barely audible, but I saw no obvious change in her demeanor. Her discomfort was more evident by her efforts to maintain normalcy. Moira was hiding something.

"That must have been pleasant. I'll bet you found a few wee gems did you not?" She had recovered her composure, yet I waited to see if she would admit to being there herself. She did not. *What to do*? Should I confess I had seen her? I looked around at the sea of faces at the table, it was not the right time or place to begin such a private conversation.

Moira finished her meal. "I'm away, lass." She rose to her feet. "The mistress is dining with the Munts this evening, and I have to finish dressing her hair." We agreed to speak in the morning and Moira left the room.

I was concerned. To be with child and without a husband was ruinous. She would lose her job and perhaps forfeit good references too. And what about that awful burn? It had to be very painful and deep, almost too deep to be from the touch of a hair iron.

What was amiss with Moira? Though I had no right to intrude, as her friend, I wanted more than anything to help.

****

Sunday, after Gideon proudly showed me the Christmas tree, his family and the majority of staff left for church. I had no desire to attend. I would walk into Mowbray later in the week and pay a visit to Avril Plumb. I enjoyed the house when everyone was gone. Though Mrs. Oldershaw was probably in the kitchen, and there would a few servants remaining, the place still had an empty feel to it.

I had not seen Moira this morning at breakfast. She must have attended Lady Clayton and readied her mistress for church. I read for a while until restlessness got the better of me. I needed to get out of my room. It was far too chilly for a walk, but I could go to the stables and check on Copper.

I picked up my cloak and went into the hall, but on a whim decided to go upstairs to the servants' quarters. Something drew me to find Moira, and I had a feeling she might still be in her room. I went down the empty hallway to the last door, all was quiet. But then I heard a faint sound. Someone was crying.

Without pausing, I knocked loudly. "Moira, it is Kathryn, I am coming in." I turned the knob and opened the door. Moira sat up quickly and rubbed a handkerchief across her face to wipe away the evidence of her tears. But it was futile. Her eyes were red and puffy, her nose ran, the poor girl looked wretched.

I closed the door and went to her. I sat down on the bed and gathered Moira into my arms, holding her tightly while I whispered words of comfort into her hair. She sobbed, the sound as desolate as I had ever heard.

"Sshh," I said. "What is it, Moira, tell me, I can help."

"No, you can't," she sobbed. "No one can help me now." She continued to cry, and I stayed quiet while Moira emptied all her tears. At length she pulled away from me, dabbed her eyes and blew her nose. I waited. She would speak when ready.

"Kathryn, I am in so much trouble."

We sat side by side on the bed. I reached for her hand and gave it a squeeze. "A good friend once told me a trouble shared is a trouble halved."

Moira smiled through her tears and sniffed. "Aye, you're right, I should heed my own advice." She moved and sat cross-legged facing me. "I'm having a bairn, Kathryn," she said softly, absentmindedly placing her hand on her belly. "And I don't know what to do."

I was not surprised to hear her say those words, yet they carried no joy. My stomach clenched.

"I've nowhere to turn, and I'm so frightened. I've no money to live on, and when Lady Clayton finds out she'll turn me out without a reference! Oh, Kathryn, I have to keep my job."

"But, Moira, surely not, what of the father?"

Her face crumpled and the tears began again. "He is not in the picture."

"Have you told him?"

"Aye, of course. He wants me to get rid of it. He can't marry me and says he'll have no more to do with me if I keep it. But it's too late—I've waited too long to stop it now."

I bit my tongue so I would not curse the swine out

loud. Moira did not need my opinion or rhetoric. She was completely despondent and needed aid, sound advice and reassurance.

"You are certain he will not change his mind?"

"Aye, positive." She sniffed. "He's told me it's his final word." She touched her arm and at once I knew her burn was no accident.

"Did he burn your arm? Dear God—" Her silence confirmed my suspicion. I wanted to say so many things, but it would serve no purpose. What an absolute pig.

"And what about you. Do you want the babe?"

"Aye," she whispered, her eyes full of tears. "Of course, I do. But not enough to bring it into poverty, which is what will happen as I've nothing to live on."

I blew out a breath, what to do, what to say? "Do you have any money put by, Moira?" I knew she would not have much, but she was a thrifty girl.

"A little, enough for a train ticket back to Inverness, but my family would send me away. They'd be so ashamed."

"Would your lover help you, perhaps give you a little money?"

"No." Her voice was laden with pain. Whoever this man was, he had broken her heart.

She sniffed. "Och, Kathryn, I canna believe he's so angry with me. He said he loved me, or I'd never have—"

"Hush now," I soothed. "You do not have to justify anything to me, you are my friend. But I must ask, who is the father of your babe, Moira?"

She began to cry again. "I canna tell you."

I wanted to press her for an answer, but it would be

unkind. Moira had more than enough on her plate as things stood. The identity of the scoundrel could wait. My mind raced for a solution and found the cupboard bare. This was a lot to take in and I needed time to process all she had said. "Dear Moira," I said earnestly and touched her sad face. "Stay here and rest. I will tell Tricklebank you have the headache and you can try to sleep for a while. I am going to have a good think about your situation." I got up and helped her to lay back in the bed. I pulled the covers over her body. "Moira, you are not alone, so please do not despair, I will help you in any way I can. But for now, you must get your strength back so we can sort it all out." I leaned over and kissed her forehead. She gave me a weak smile.

"Thank you, lass."

"I will come back and see you later," I promised. I left her room. As I closed the door and crossed the landing to the stairs, I paused. There it was once again, the uneasy sensation of being observed. I spun around as quickly as I could, but no one was there. My nostrils quivered as a faint scent tickled my senses. The pleasant aroma of anise. Unfamiliar yet something nagged at the corner of my mind. I had smelled it before. But where?

****

Moira did not appear in the dining room for dinner. At first, I worried, and then realized she was probably too self-conscious as she would look as though she had been crying. I ate my meal and asked Mrs. Oldershaw if I could take Moira a tray. I carried it upstairs and took great care not to slosh the soup everywhere. I went to her room and knocked lightly on the door. No answer. I turned the handle and went inside. The room was empty. I took the tray back downstairs where Miss Tricklebank stood in the kitchen in a state of total irritation.

"Have you seen Campbell?" she barked.

"No," I replied. "I just took her a dinner tray, but she was not in her room. Perhaps she is with Lady Clayton?"

"She is not." The housekeeper was angry. "'Tis Lady Clayton who looks for her."

"Lady Geraldine then?"

"I have already checked. The stupid girl is not to be found." Miss Tricklebank marched away, issuing orders to Sally and one of the other parlor maids to attend both Lady Clayton and her sister-in-law. I went up to Moira's room once again. Still no sign of her. I wandered through the rest of the house and found no evidence of her being there. Had she gone out for a walk? Surely not, for the evening was already quite cold and almost dark. Yet as troubled as Moira had been, it would not be far-fetched for her to get some air.

I went to my room and retrieved my cloak. Then told Cook I was going out to look for Moira.

"You watch your step in the dark, girl." Mrs. Oldershaw advised. "Don't you go off the paths or you'll take a tumble-down yon cliff and break yer neck." I thanked her for her concern and left the kitchen. As I wandered around the perimeter of the manor, Benedict Swan approached. He was dressed for dinner.

"Kathryn?" He was surprised to see me out so late in the day. "Whatever is the matter?"

My face must have betrayed my concern. "It is Moira Campbell, Lady Clayton's maid. She is missing."

Dread washed over his face and I knew he thought of Aramintha. Is this what had happened the night she died? Fear gripped my belly.

"Tell me, when was she last seen?" he said.

"I saw her not three hours ago, she was terribly upset. She was to come down for dinner, but never did. She is not in her room or anywhere else in the house."

"Were any of her things gone?"

I thought for a moment. There had been clothing on a chair and a bag on her nightstand. "No, nothing obvious anyway."

"Stay here," he commanded. "Let me find Johnny and Bert so we can begin a search. She can't have gone far."

I hesitated. My instinct reminded me not to trust him. But the stables were close by, and we needed help. Within a short time, he returned with the men. They carried lit torches and set about the grounds calling out Moira's name.

I stayed with Johnny. We searched the stables, the barn and the cold house. The others walked through the gardens shouting out her name. A chill wrapped around my bones that was not from the cold.

"We'll find her, miss, now don't you worry," Johnny assured me, his voice calm as we began to walk down the drive. Suddenly, a shout rang out. It was Bert. We both took off at a run towards the sound of his voice, it came from one of the old potting sheds at the far side of the house. We could see the light of Bert's torch illuminating the inside of the wooden building, his stout figure silhouetted in the doorway. As we reached him, he turned, his face white as a ghost.

"Don't you go in there, miss," he said as I pushed

past him.

"Kathryn, wait." Benedict's voice called behind me. But too late. There, dangling like a macabre marionette, was my dear Moira.

****

I do not recall what happened next, only that I began to sob, and my knees buckled. I must have fainted, because when I opened my eyes I was in bed, my head thick and my throat dry. Lady Geraldine sat in a chair beside my bed, her face serious as it studied my own.

"What time is it?" I mumbled, disorientated and confused.

"Tis after ten o'clock, Miss Westcott, you have slept through to morning." Alarmed, I pushed my hands down and tried to raise up but felt dizzy.

"Doctor Beedles gave you a strong sedative last night, hence you will feel drowsy, but you needed it my gal." I blinked several times and tried to force away the ghastly visage which flashed before me. Moira, hung by her neck from the rafters in the shed, her feet swinging. I took a swift intake of breath. Lady Geraldine reached out and placed a gnarled hand on my own.

"Try not to think of it, my dear, not yet. It is too horrible to revisit. You need sleep and rest. Later you can dwell on what has happened." Her brown eyes radiated kindness. "Go back to sleep."

When I next awoke, she was gone. I was unsure of the time but knew it must be the afternoon. My head felt clearer, the effect of the drug finally dissipating. It took me longer than usual, but finally I dressed, washed my face and brushed my hair. I secured it into a bun and left my room to go downstairs.

The kitchen was unusually quiet. Cook stood at her table rolling a length of pastry while a scullery maid washed dishes in the large stone sink. I went to the hob where the kettle stayed warm and made myself a cup of tea. Mrs. Oldershaw heard me and glanced over her shoulder.

"Is that you, Miss Westcott?"

"It is," I replied, my voice quiet.

"Pour me a cup as well dear, and I'll take a spell with you."

We sat up to the kitchen table on opposite sides. Cook gave me a friendly smile. "Tis a terrible thing what's happened, an' no mistake. I'm sorry for us all, but specially for you as she was your friend." My eyes instantly filled with tears. I used the back of my sleeve to wipe them away.

"Poor lass," she continued. "Must have been troubled a plenty to do that, an' I for one am sorry I didn't know she was in a bad way." We sipped our tea, at a loss for words. All I could do was think of our last conversation, my promise of help to Moira. Futile, too late. Now she was dead and her innocent babe along with her. I set down my cup and looked at Mrs. Oldershaw.

"I must speak with Lady Geraldine."

****

"What?" Lady Geraldine leaned forward in her bed so suddenly, Genghis yelped as she squashed his head in her lap.

"I said I do not think Moira would have taken her life. We had just spoken about her situation, and though she was worried, even desperate, she was not suicidal."

"My dear gal, who are we to know the workings of

anyone's mind. I didn't know her well at all, but I had noticed she seemed distracted. Do you know what troubled her?"

"Yes." I stared down at my hands. "She was with child."

"Good Lord. Are you certain?"

"Indeed, I am. Moira was troubled because she was in no position to have a child, yet she could not go through with getting rid of the baby."

"You mean, have it adopted?"

"No, an abortion."

The old lady found the word distasteful judging by the look of horror on her face. Of course, she would think that. She had never faced living without an income.

"Moira needed to determine how to provide for a child. She had little money, and her family would have turned her out if she had gone home with a babe in her belly."

"What about the father, has anyone spoken with him? Did the gal tell him she carried a child?

"She did not confide his identity to me, and I had no opportune time to pursue the subject. Moira only told me of her condition a few hours before she died."

"That is unfortunate. Do you have any idea who he is?"

"No. All she said was he would not marry her and did not want the child. He told Moira he would have nothing to do with her if she kept the babe."

"The bounder," she said with disgust. "Miss Westcott, I know this is a difficult time for you. To lose a dear friend is hard enough to bear, and the manner of her death worsens the situation. But I encourage you to accept the possibility the gal was overcome with grief and worry, and in a moment of despair took the only avenue she thought available to her."

"I do not think—"

"Listen to me, dear." Lady Geraldine stared at me with what I perceived as affection. "You have already lost one friend, and you are convinced she did not take her own life. It is understandable you would feel the same about Moira Campbell. Do not torture yourself by seeking intrigue where there is none."

I looked at her, and my eyes filled with tears.

"Come, come." She handed me a dainty handkerchief. "Please do not think me unsympathetic to your views. But there is part of my mind which reminds me those who are gone can no longer be helped. 'Tis the living we should be worried about."

She was right of course, for Aramintha and Moira were lost to me. As my mind went back to the dark shed, and the shocking scene which had met my eyes, I had another thought. Who was the father of Moira's child? For surely if blame could be laid at any person's door, it was assuredly his. And I vowed at that very moment to find him.

Chapter Twenty

Gideon and I struggled through the day in the classroom. I was completely distracted, and he seemed also perturbed. He had not known Moira well, but the atmosphere in the house was dark and somber. Gideon's youth did not diminish his capacity to be affected by the morose events, especially coming so soon after the death of his sister.

In light of our reflective moods, I suggested he read from his book and then work on an art project he was sketching. It was a drawing of his horse Allegro which he planned to give to his mother for Christmas.

The cold December day mirrored my mood, cloudy and bleak. I tried to focus on my own reading. I was making notes to plan out our lessons for the following week, but it was a struggle. When the lunch gong sounded, Gideon left, yet I remained, deep in thought.

"May I come in?" It was Gabriel, and my heart gave a small leap of pleasure at his arrival, he would be the perfect balm for my low spirits. As he came into the room, my face grew warm as the memory of our last encounter passed through my thoughts, the soft touch, the tender kiss.

Gabriel came straight to me and gathered my cold hands in a warm caress. "Are you all right, Kathryn? My God, what an awful business." He searched my face with concern etched in his own. "I was at Munt's. We heard this morning, and I rode back as quickly as I could. Does anyone know why the girl would kill herself?"

"No," I replied, as the fingers of sadness squeezed my throat. I swallowed, not wanting to cry. "All we know is Moira was distressed and obviously did not think she had any option other than the one she took."

"I am so terribly sorry. I know you were friends. What can I do?" Without another word, Gabriel pulled me into his arms. I marveled at the sensation which rippled through my body. His strength and affection passed through me and I hung onto the comfort it brought. I felt safer in the warmth of his embrace.

The sound of footsteps broke the moment, and Gabriel swiftly pulled away. Benedict Swan walked into the schoolroom.

"Oh, forgive me," he said quickly, sensing the intrusion. "I did not mean to interrupt. I was looking for Gideon. I can come back later." The air was charged with my discomfort, and something passed between the men I could not identify.

"No, please come in, Benedict, I was just leaving. I called to check on Miss Westcott's well-being. I just came from Munt's once we found out what had happened here. It is a bad business, is it not?"

"Indeed." His half-brother agreed, his face set in a solemn pose. "We have sent a telegram to her family in Inverness."

"Excellent," said Gabriel, his voice lighter hearted than the situation commanded. "Let me know if I can be of any assistance. He turned back to me his light blue eyes the color of a summer sky. He smiled. "I will see you later, Miss Westcott." Much to my surprise he winked at me and took his leave.

Benedict came over to my desk. “How are you, Kathryn?” he said kindly, his face all concern.

“As well as can be,” I replied solemnly and met his gaze. I contemplated what was behind his hard exterior. Benedict’s personality puzzled me, was he a good person, or a killer? Could one tell by the look of a man? If so, then Benedict Swan fit the bill. He was dark, moody, and exuded an air of strength and danger. Certainly not a man to trifle with. But murder? Was he really capable of that?

“I know how bloody awful it was for you last night. You were in complete shock, and no wonder. I only wish you might have been spared. I should have stopped you. I am so sorry.”

“No need for you to apologize, Benedict. I made the decision to enter the shed. Yes, it was a frightful sight, one I will never forget. But Moira was my friend, no one could have prevented me from seeing her. Please do not berate yourself unnecessarily.”

His face relaxed. It surprised me to know he had been so concerned for my welfare. Yet the longer he stood by me, the more aware I became of his presence. What was it about Benedict Swan that set my steady countenance adrift? Perhaps all my suspicions of the man. Suddenly I knew the urge to get away from him and everyone else, I rose from my desk.

“If that is all, Benedict, I must go down to the kitchen for luncheon.” I went to pass him, but as I drew level, he grasped my arm gently but firmly, halting my progress.

“Kathryn, ’tis not my business, but I am compelled to speak regardless.”

I frowned and turned to face him. "What is it?"

"I worry for you," he said in an ominous tone. "Be careful with Gabriel. He plays a dangerous game." The sting of embarrassment spread across my cheeks as I realized he must have witnessed our embrace. Speechless, I pulled my arm from his hold and left him standing there alone.

****

The next day I met with both Lady Clayton and Lady Geraldine. Moira's body would be sent home, and the Claytons would bear the expense. I was grateful to hear it. I knew Moira would want to be buried in her beloved Highlands and not under English soil. I did not ask if her family had been told the details of her death. Lady Blanche was tolerably nice to me, no doubt due to Lady Geraldine's presence and being sensitive to what I had witnessed.

Late Wednesday morning, I was happy to leave Gideon in the charge of Benedict for the remainder of the day; they were going to the farm for a study of agriculture. It left me an afternoon to myself, so I sent word to Avril Plumb and asked if I might call for tea. She responded with an enthusiastic 'yes,' and I walked into Mowbray Village and felt as though I had escaped from a locked room.

I relished the intimate comfort of the rectory, the cozy drawing room with its flowered decor, the roaring fire which managed to reach into every nook and cranny of the small place. We sat eating Madeira cake with a hot cup of tea. Avril had yet to stop talking about Moira and the sordid events which surrounded her death.

"My dear, I cannot believe you were there, that you

had to bear witness to such a gruesome incident." Avril placed a chubby hand upon her ample breast. "I would have fainted, dropped like a stone if I should have seen her. 'Tis a wonder you are not still abed with shock." She took another slice of cake and her chins wobbled.

"It was awful," I replied. "I shall remember it all my days—such a senseless loss. Moira was a fine girl, kind-hearted, with a long and full life ahead of her. It is these thoughts which trouble me, Avril, for to see her light extinguished is beyond sad, it is tragic." I placed my half-eaten cake back on the plate, it had turned to sawdust in my mouth.

"And what do you think of Benedict Swan being such a friend to the girl?"

"I beg your pardon?"

Avril's button eyes gleamed with the realization she had information I was not privy to. She leaned forward with enthusiasm. "Oh yes, I had it from Plumb himself. You know how good he is, always off to visit his parishioners. Well, he walked to Juniper Blessing's cottage, and there found Benedict having tea with his aunt, *and* the young maid." She raised her eyebrows in emphasis. "Of course, my Plumb thought naught amiss there, after all, 'twas proper with Juniper in attendance. But I remember thinking to myself perhaps Benedict had taken a fancy to the girl. No harm in that."

"When was this?" My mind raced off in several directions, too many to decipher. Benedict and Moira? Surely not. I had never seen them together. She had not spoken of him nor had he of her. I was stupefied.

"Ooh, let me think now, why Saturday last I believe. I would have mentioned it, but I haven't seen you lately."

I searched my memory. That had been the very day Moira had visited Nurse Spooner's surgery in Swanage.

She leaned over conspiratorially. "There is talk she was with child. Have you heard anyone speak of it?" Avril asked in a loud whisper.

My head had started to ache, and I felt as though I had fallen into a tunnel. "No. Nor do I care to." My voice was curt, and though I did not wish to be cruel to my hostess, I had heard enough. Avril's expression registered hurt.

"Forgive me," I remonstrated. "I did not mean to bite. It has been a trying few days, and truly I would prefer to talk of other subjects. Could we speak of something happy perhaps? Indeed, that was why I came, for you are always such a tonic." My words of flattery worked, and Avril quickly moved on to discuss church events and an upcoming wedding her husband would officiate.

I left the rectory and found the frigid snap of air a welcome relief. My troubled mind cleared while I walked back to the manor. Benedict and Moira? Had it been his voice in her room? Could he be the father of her babe? I already suspected him of being Aramintha's lover, but was he the kind of man to repeat his vile behavior on an innocent such as Moira?

Upon my return to Mowbray, I went up to the classroom to retrieve a book I had left there. Much to my surprise, I discovered a small, beribboned box of chocolates laying upon my desk. A note was on top of the package, with my name. The message said, 'The best medicine for sadness is chocolate.' I picked them up and opened the lid, the delicious aroma pervading my senses, and I salivated. It had been a while since I had indulged in such a treat. Who had left them? Most likely Gabriel or Gideon. It was a thoughtful gesture. I popped one into my mouth, found my book and made my way back to my room.

By the time I went down for dinner, I had already consumed half the contents of the box, yet still found an appetite for Mrs. Oldershaw's delicious stew. Not seeing Moira at the dining table seemed so very strange. I felt her absence deeply but tried to make an effort to have conversation with some of the others who were considerate enough to respond.

I fell into bed, my head scrambled as I regurgitated notes from Aramintha's diary, my conversations with Moira, and the unsettling parallel between the two very different women. It did not take long for me to fall asleep.

I awoke with the most excruciating pain gripping my belly. Fingers made of razor blades clenched and squeezed fistfuls of my insides, and I doubled up in agony. My body was drenched in sweat while nausea rippled cramps up and down my stomach. By the time the third massive paroxysm assaulted me, I cried out in unbridled pain, uncaring who heard. I must have continued to shout loudly , because through my tears and fever, someone appeared at my bedside, and then everything went black.

Chapter Twenty-One

I had never known such a thirst. My tongue felt too large for my mouth, and I tried to moisten my lips to no avail.

"Here, drink this," came the voice, as a steady hand reached behind my neck to raise my face to a glass. Water saturated my mouth like a monsoon to a desert, and I began to cough.

"Slow down, small sips only." The voice again, such a lovely sweet sound, so familiar. Then darkness.

****

"Come along, Kathryn, try to wake up," the kind voice said, and against my own volition my eyes parted, and daylight flooded in. A broad face with concern etched into a furrowed brow studied me with great concern.

"Avril?"

"Oh, Kathryn, thanks be to God you are well." She smiled but looked strangely as though she might cry. I raised my hand and feebly touched her face.

"Do not cry, Avril. Have I been unwell?"

She gave a small sob. "Oh, my dear, we very nearly lost you to our Lord. But He saw fit to deliver you back to us I am eternally grateful. Darling girl, how do you feel?"

I frowned because my head was muddled. What was she talking about? My mind grabbed threads of memory, and slowly I began a braid of what had happened.

"I had the grippe, did I not? I remember feeling so ill and had such pains in my stomach." I moved my shoulders, they felt as though they were encased in iron. "May I sit up a little? My back aches."

The large woman leaned over and aided me so I might sit back against a stack of pillows. Once situated, Avril handed me a glass of water. "You were violently ill, Kathryn, but not from the grippe." Her face showed true fear. "You had been given arsenic."

"What?" I gasped. Panic shot through my breast.

Avril grasped my hand and squeezed it tightly to share her strength. "Doctor Beedles was called when you fell ill. You exhibited signs of having been poisoned."

I shook my head in denial. "But I ate stew, with the others—" I trailed off as I glanced at my nightstand. "Oh, my goodness, the chocolates."

Avril nodded. "Doctor Beedles took them away to be tested. After speaking with the staff, he concluded the chocolates were the only food you alone had consumed. Where did you get them, Kathryn, did you buy them in the village?"

"No, they were left for me in the schoolroom, on my desk. I assumed they were from Gabriel or Gideon. I thought them a gift, there was a note about cheering me up—" I raised my hand to my mouth. "Someone tried to kill me, Avril." Tears sprang to my eyes. "And they almost succeeded."

Avril stayed with me until dusk. I persuaded her to go to her husband then, for she had come the night I fell ill and stayed the entire time. She was exhausted, but ready to return home. I felt an indescribable amount of gratitude towards her.

That evening, both Lady Blanche and Lady Geraldine came to visit, both showing kindness and concern. Lady Geraldine's troubled eyes watched me closely, she alone recognized something was most definitely afoot in the household. My employer was as distant as always, but at least she was consistent. Gideon then came to say hello. He looked terribly worried, and I forced some joviality into my voice for fear of him becoming upset. By the time he departed his face wore less concern. The hour was late, and I had just closed my eyes when a knock sounded on my door.

"Come in," I responded, thinking it Sally with some fresh water. But it was Gabriel. My eyes grew teary at the instant relief upon seeing his lovely face. He came to me quickly and wrapped his arms about me. I took a tight hold of him, my port in the storm which had put me asunder.

A moment passed, and then he pulled back and stared into my eyes, his all concern. "Dear Kathryn, tell me you are well. Will you be all right? I couldn't bear it if anything should happen to you, my love." He gently stroked the damp hair from my brow, all the while murmuring soft words of affection.

His endearment made my heart fill with warmth and an immeasurable flush of emotion flooded my senses. "I am fine, Gabriel," I assured him. "Though truly frightened. First the riding accident and now poison. Why is someone trying to harm me?"

He shook his head. "I cannot say. How could anyone as good as you have enemies?"

"I do not know. I have only been here a few weeks

and hardly know a soul."

Gabriel pulled away, and I lay back against my pillows.

"Mother says they suspect the chocolates you ate were tampered with. Who sent them to you?"

"I assumed they were from you or Gideon. They were left on my desk with a note."

His brow creased. "Neither one of us sent them, yet obviously they were put there intentionally." Gabriel's eyes narrowed. "Kathryn, I must ask. Are you keeping something from me?" He looked at me earnestly. "Darling girl, you arrived here and have charmed both Gideon and myself. We are completely under your spell." He took one of my hands. "I know you care for me as I do you. It is time we were frank with one another, don't you agree? There is much at stake Kathryn. I am supposed to wed another in the spring. And now you are in my life and everything has become uncertain. How can I determine which path to take when I do not really know you, when you hold back? How can I protect you?"

He was right. There had been a spark between us from the start, and yet I had not been honest with him. Regardless of my caution, I should not continue to keep Gabriel in the dark about my reason for coming to Mowbray. He proclaimed to care for me, so why not take a leap of faith? I took a deep breath and held his gaze with my own.

"I have not been entirely truthful with you, and I am sorry. I will not withhold anything from you again." Perhaps it was my near brush with death, or the fact I was exhausted, alone in the world with no one to trust, no one who cared for my best interests. Or it might have been the sweet look on his face as he held my hand. No matter what brought me to my decision, I told Gabriel Clayton about my past with Aramintha, and then everything I had learned since my arrival at Mowbray.

****

For two days I stayed in bed. Doctor Beedles came each day to check on my recovery, and though I held such a negative opinion of the man, I reluctantly admitted to Gabriel he was a good doctor.

Dearest Gabriel, he had become a regular visitor to my room, so frequent was he there I know the servants gossiped. Granted he sat with me, my chamber door wide open for all to see and hear. But his marked interest in my welfare did not go unnoticed, yet I cared not a whit what others thought.

Now my confidante, Gabriel was determined to find out who had purchased the chocolates, for they had not been from him or Gideon. He had questioned the shop owners in the village to no avail and was inclined to think they might have been purchased in Swanage. He planned an excursion there the following day once I was back in my normal routine. I enjoyed his singular attention and found his conversation interesting and his wit amusing. We were never at a loss for words between us. Several times Lady Blanche passed by while her son was in attendance, and I could feel the perceptible bristle of her body as she saw Gabriel at my side. She would have been mortified to know how he secretly held my hand in his under the covers.

Lady Geraldine had left Mowbray for a short visit to a friend in neighboring Hampshire. I had only spoken with her once since falling ill. The one notable person missing from my side was Benedict. I had yet to lay eyes upon him. His absence was conspicuous.

By Monday, I was back in the schoolroom once again. My physical health was much improved, though I was still weak and stayed seated more than usual. However, the condition of my mental health was not so recovered. Mrs. Oldershaw cooked beef broth laden with vegetables, which she plied me with once I was able to eat. Initially, I was too scared to consume anything after what had happened but reassured myself the food in the house was shared by all, and therefore safe for me to eat.

Gideon fussed over me like a little bantam hen, and I was grateful he had become such a thoughtful student. In conversation with him I learned Benedict had accompanied Lady Geraldine to Hampshire, which explained his disappearance. While on that very topic, I casually asked Gideon if there had ever been a lady Benedict was sweet upon. The boy screwed up his face with disgust at the very thought, but eventually could not resist turning the tables and was the teacher to me, his student.

"Back when I was very little, after Benedict came back from Africa, he did have a lady who used to come and stay."

He had my full attention. "Indeed?"

"Hmm." Gideon squinted, squeezing the thought from his memory like juice from an orange. "I don't remember her very well, but she used to give me toffees, oh and she gave me a monkey, well a play one. She'd brought it all the way from Africa."

"Do you remember the lady's name?" I asked.

He cocked his head for a moment. "Let me think. It

was like something in the garden. Yes, an herb. That's it, her name was Rosemary."

I was rivetted, I do not know why I had not considered Benedict would have someone in his life. "Whatever happened to her?"

Gideon grimaced. "I'm not entirely sure, but I think she was run over by a train."

"What!"

He shrugged his narrow shoulders. "Yes, I remember now. She was coming here from London, and she fell under a train at one of the big stations. Honest, you can ask anyone."

We went back to our studies, but I could not concentrate properly. Mowbray Manor was a place inhabited by peculiar people. How odd to find so much misfortune all under one roof. A sudden chill crept across my neck as I thought of what had happened to me in the space of a few days, and then I thought of Aramintha and Moira. What evil ran amok at this house? I had better find out and quickly. Or I could be the next one to die.

****

After breakfast the next morning, Gideon informed me his aunt and Benedict would return from Hampshire. I received this news with mixed feelings. There was much I wished to speak with Lady Geraldine about, yet I felt apprehensive seeing Benedict, especially after what Avril Plumb had shared.

At luncheon, Gabriel sent a note and asked if I might meet him in the library. I wondered what he could want but felt inexplicable joy at the prospect of seeing him. The library was situated on the front side of the manor and a place I could spend hours. I knocked on the door, but no one responded. Slowly I opened it and went inside. No one was there.

The room was swollen to the gills with laden shelves from floor to ceiling. Other than the door and two large windows, every space of wall teemed with books from left to right. The aroma of paper, ink, leather and tobacco permeated my senses, and I was at once enchanted as though I had stepped into a fairy tale. In the centre of the room, four worn green leather chairs were grouped to face one another with adjacent small tables. A fire flickered in the grate, and I was compelled with the sudden desire to sit and read a book, curl up on a soft chair and spend some time. So engulfed in thought, I did not hear the click of the door.

Gabriel came up behind me and wrapped his arms gently around my middle. He touched his cheek against mine. "Kathryn, at last I get you all to myself." He turned me around to face him and cupped my chin in his hands. "You have the sparkle back in those lovely grey eyes." He smiled. "I am glad to see you recovered." And then without another word, he pressed his soft lips against mine.

Again, the warm rush and tangle of emotion saturated my senses, ran rampant through my veins. The kiss was so gentle, one of sweet promise and affection which made my body lean into his and relish the moment. Too quickly he pulled away, leaving me intoxicated with so many feelings, I knew not how to identify them all.

"Have a seat, dearest Kate," he said. "I have something to tell you." His face had become serious.

I sat down in one of the big chairs. "What is wrong?" My pulse fluttered nervously.

"I went to Swanage today and took the liberty of visiting all the confectioner's shops I could find. I wanted to discover where your chocolates were purchased."

"And?" I could not hide the tremor in my voice.

"I was successful. The chocolates you were given are sold in a small shop near the beach. They are a popular local brand. I spoke with the owner, and she had sold several boxes in the past week."

"I see." We were no closer to an answer.

"However, the Claytons are well known hereabouts, the family and staff are easily recognized by many of the shopkeepers. She did sell a box of chocolates to someone from the house."

"Who was it?" Dread saturated my body, and my throat became dry. I knew what he was going to say before the name left his mouth. I spoke first. "It was Benedict."

The look on Gabriel's face confirmed what I had thought.

"But why?" I looked at him, my eyes pleading. "Why would Benedict wish to harm me, I have done nothing to him?"

"Dearest." Gabriel took the chair beside me. "Of course, you haven't. But I fear he has concerns about who you are and what you know of him. There is the diary you found of my sister's."

I had told Gabriel I had it hidden. But I would not even tell *him* where.

"Yes, but—"

"Good grief, Kathryn, don't you see? Benedict must be the person Minty speaks of, the man she was in love with. It makes perfect sense!"

I rose from my seat, unable to remain still. Even with all I knew, I found it difficult to accept Benedict Swan would want to do me harm. I turned to Gabriel. "The shopkeeper, is she positive she sold them to Benedict?"

"Yes. I am sorry."

"You believe he bought them, added arsenic and then left them for me in the hope I would be killed."

"I do," Gabriel said sadly. "Though it pains me, I think that was his intention."

I felt as though I had been kicked. Tears filled my eyes. I wanted to cry, for what had been done to me and also to my dear friends.

"What shall we do?"

His brows were drawn and his face long. "I do not know yet. I need time to think, at least until morning." He rose and came to me, taking me in his arms.

He kissed my forehead. "Let us wait until tomorrow. Meet me here after breakfast. We will go from there. Will you be all right until then?" He placed a hand on each side of my face, his thumbs brushed away my tears. "Can you manage for just one more day?"

"Yes," I whispered. I felt a rush of gratitude to have him on my side. "Thank you for helping me, Gabriel. I should not know what to do otherwise." He leaned forward and brushed my lips with a kiss.

"Until tomorrow," he said.

****

I received a summons from Lady Geraldine as soon as she returned. I had expected nothing less. We sat before the fire on a cold Tuesday evening, I had finished dinner and she was preparing to go down for her own with the family.

"You are still somewhat pale, gal," she remarked, her eyes raking over me in a thorough examination. "Are you well?"

"Yes, my lady, I am much better. Doctor Beedles took good care of me."

She snorted derisively. "Well, that's something, but I still don't like the man. Now, let us get to the point. Arsenic poisoning? Nasty stuff that, and so damn easy to purchase. There's many an heir been dispatched that way, hard to trace I believe."

I nodded. Since my recovery I had searched the reference books in the schoolroom. "Arsenic is actually present in many things we eat and drink Lady Geraldine, yet in such microscopic amounts it does not harm a human being. The amount I digested would have been fatal had I eaten all of the chocolates in a short time, which I did not."

"Thank goodness for that," the old woman said. "Has the constable learned any more about who may have done this?"

I hesitated, torn between admitting the devastating truth and keeping my word to Gabriel. "No, we have no suspects yet. But it has to be someone in the house who would have easy access to the schoolroom"

"I am impressed with you gal, any other young woman with two attempts made on their life would have already run screaming down the driveway to the nearest railway station."

I raised my brows. "It certainly has crossed my mind I can tell you." My chin went up as my spine stiffened. "But that is exactly what this person wants me to do, be scared away. I refuse to be a victim. He has already taken two lives. It is time he met his match."

"Spoken like an Amazonian warrior, my dear. Yet in your capacity as a young and vulnerable woman, I suggest you hurry and determine the identity of this vulgar, cruel man. It is time to pick up the pace. Have you spoken of your findings with anyone else?"

"Yes, Gabriel. He was wonderful while I was so ill."

A shadow fell across the old woman's face.

"I am sorry, should I not have? He is the head of the family, and I thought him entitled to know what has been going on under his own roof?" I said to appease her.

"Indeed." She looked pensive. "Kathryn, I want you to be very careful, even around my family. We do not know the identity of this ill-doer. Until we do, I should suspect every single person, even those you care for, even me. Promise you will do this?"

"Of course." I stuttered, surprised at the concern for me in her voice. Benedict Swan's face filled my mind, and I wondered if his aunt would be as concerned for my welfare if she knew he had been the one who had supplied the poisoned chocolates?

Chapter Twenty-Two

I thought the next day would never arrive. By morning I could barely swallow my breakfast. My nerves were on edge, and I could hardly wait to meet with Gabriel and find out what he thought we should do. How would he deal with Benedict? I made my way down to the library and went in when I received no reply after knocking.

Much to my chagrin, Lady Blanche Clayton stood by the mantel. She waited for me like a cat under a bird bath.

"Miss Westcott. Come in and sit down." She herself took one of the armchairs. I had little choice; I did as she bade.

"I understand you were to meet my son here this morning? Well, Gabriel was called out to attend an important matter at the Munts. He will not return until later this week."

My heart sank. How could Gabriel go away now of all times? He knew it to be imperative he remain here to deal with Benedict. Yet he had left me without protection, vulnerable to the one person he knew wanted to harm me. My eyes stung with tears at his desertion.

"Miss Westcott, I do not know what you foresee in your future, but I would like to remind you it will not include being married to my son, nor will you ever bear our family name."

"I beg your pardon—" I cut in, my duress quickly replaced with irritation.

"No!" she spat. "You shall not interrupt me." She rose to her feet, her long body taut as a whip and glared at me, eyes bright with rage. "Young woman, I have watched you manipulate my son and lure him into your deceitful web. You have been very clever. First the trick with glass in your saddle and then making yourself violently ill. All pathetic attempts to gain Gabriel's attention and favor. Well, you have not succeeded!"

"What?" I rose to my feet, only two steps separated us from each other. My blood boiled. "Are you mad? How can you honestly think I would risk my life and harm an innocent animal to gain another's love? Dear God woman, I almost died!"

"How dare you speak to me thus!" Her voice escalated, becoming shriller with each word. "I want you out of here immediately. Gather your belongings and get out!" Lady Clayton brushed past me to the door, swung it open and shouted down the hall.

"Baxter! Come here at once!" The butler appeared from the foyer, his face flushed, his expression one of panic.

"Yes, my lady."

Blanche Clayton turned an imperious glare on her trusted servant. "I want this girl out of my house within the hour. Pay her the wages she is due, and one-month salary in hand. I will give her no reference. See to it." Without another look towards me, she stormed out of the door leaving her butler dumbfounded. It took every ounce of my willpower not to follow her and scream what I really thought of her, ask why she had stood by as Aramintha took her own life. I wanted to punish her for being such a horrible and vindictive woman, and I hated her for reminding me of all the reasons I could never marry her son.

I looked at the old butler, saw his obvious discomfort as he stood rigid, waiting for me to do as I had been told. I shook my head in disgust and went through the door to the servants' staircase and up to my room.

It did not take long for me to pack my scant possessions. Yet I seethed with anger as I replayed Lady Clayton's accusations. Her patronizing manner and how she had insulted me incensed me to no end. And underneath it all, was also the nagging recognition that she had not been entirely wrong. Her suspicion of my feelings for Gabriel were not misplaced, I did indeed care for him, yet to insinuate I had intentionally harmed myself for his attention was unforgiveable. I would leave Mowbray Manor and not mourn my departure. Though I deeply regretted the loss of my letters, at least I still had Aramintha's diary to take with me in their stead.

As I left my room I hesitated, then turned to take a last lingering glance at the place I had called home for the past six weeks. So short a time, yet so much had happened.

In the kitchen Mrs. Oldershaw stopped her task to come and give me a hearty hug. I asked her to keep an eye on Gideon, I felt awful leaving without the chance to tell him goodbye. My only consolation was to go into Mowbray Village and seek refuge with the Plumbs at the rectory. Perhaps I would get to see Gideon very soon. Beyond that, I had no clue of my prospects.

****

That night, my bedchamber bore little resemblance to the luxury of Mowbray Manor, yet what it lacked in finery it delivered in comfort. The spare room at the rectory was tiny, barely enough to fit a bed, wardrobe and washstand. But in the light of my lamp, I found it very cozy, and though the fireplace was barely more than a hole in the wall, it heated the space nicely and I felt safe.

Dear Avril was an absolute gem. She had taken me in without hesitation and plied me with hot tea and crumpets as I solemnly told her of Lady Clayton's displeasure. I did not allude to anything other than her dislike of Gabriel's attention towards me. I did, however, tell her of the ridiculous accusation she had made about my accidents being self-induced. Avril had gasped in horror, for she herself had nursed me through my recent ordeal and knew only too well no person in their right mind would intentionally do that to themselves.

I pleaded to stay for a few nights, enough time to plan my next move. At least I had some funds and could take a room in Swanage if I could not stay with the vicar and his wife. My main concern was the Plumbs might garner Lady Clayton's disfavor if she learned of their kindness to me. I was loathe to drag them into my situation when they depended upon her charity and kindness.

Sleep evaded me. Though warm under the goose-down quilt with the remnants of a fire which still flickered in the grate, my mind would not settle. I wondered what the rest of the Clayton family would think of my being gone. Lady Geraldine would be annoyed, Gideon would most certainly be sad, Gabriel would be confused, and Benedict? Would he try to seek me here and finish me off? Surely not, for once gone from Mowbray Manor, I posed no threat to him whatsoever.

I closed my eyes and imagined Gabriel's handsome face. I revisited his embraces and the sweet words he had whispered in my ear. My disappointment in him was uncomfortable to navigate. He had in essence abandoned me, not unlike my own mother.

And then the dark countenance of Benedict Swan loomed into view and startled me back to reality. At length, I opened my eyes and pulled myself into a sitting position. I must formulate a plan, one which could finalize my enquiries about what had happened to Aramintha and identify the father of Moira's baby. I had made little progress until now, for fear of losing my position at Mowbray. But not anymore.

****

Waking in a strange place, it took a moment to remember where I was. I had finally succumbed to sleep after much restlessness. I shrugged off the quilts, my thoughts jostled into a semblance of order. Then everything clicked into place.

Avril was still abed when I ventured down to the kitchen. Her cook, Edna, was kind enough to allow me to make tea and toast for myself while she ate her own breakfast prior to preparing her Mistress's fare. I sought time to think. My plan was to escape the cottage before Avril arose, else she sidetrack me from my course of action. I had determined to walk into Swanage and speak with the nurse Moira had sought out the day I spied her there. While in Swanage, I would also find the confectioner's shop and ask about the chocolates myself. But before I could leave the cottage there came a knock upon the door. Gabriel.

He blew into the parlor and brought the cold morning air along with him. He came straight to me and gathered me into his arms.

"My dearest Kathryn, I have just heard what happened with my mother." His pale blue eyes bored into mine. "I am so very sorry she sent you away. I cannot understand what possessed her to treat you in this manner. Are you all right? Tell me you are, I beg of you."

"Yes, Gabriel. I am recovered." I pulled away from him and bade him sit before the fire. "Although I cannot believe you left me to fend for myself. I thought you wanted to look out for me?"

I sat and he took the proffered seat and looked at my face, his beautiful eyes swimming with guilt. "Forgive me, Kathryn. Mother confronted me, and I stormed out in a rage."

"Apparently tempers run in your family because Lady Blanche is also furious with me. She believes I have designs upon you which would impact your engagement to Miss Ditton-Jones."

He groaned. "Dear God, this is such a mess." Gabriel stood again, as though he was incapable of being still. "Kathryn, my mother is not herself. Since my sister's death she has been at odds with the world. Mowbray is everything to her, she would do anything to protect the family name and home. She sees you as a threat to our prospects." Gabriel came to me and dropped to his knees. Kneeling before me he grasped both of my hands in his and raised them to his warm lips.

"Don't you see dearest? Mowbray needs money, and the Ditton-Jones have it in abundance. I do not love Lucy at all, but my mother requires me to make a successful marriage if we are to keep our family home."

"What?" I was shocked by this revelation.

"'Tis true. We have been in dire financial straits since before the death of my father. Benedict has managed to keep us going, I have no idea how. But we are not long for the axe to fall, Kathryn. We have little time before the creditors come calling. 'Tis why my mother is kind to Aunt Gerry."

"Because of her fortune."

"Yes," he said in earnest. "Mother cannot stand the old crow, but she has helped us with expenses. She thinks us wastrels, and Benedict, the only sensible one in the family." He dropped my hands and rose once again, this time pacing back and forth. "Kathryn, I have no blasted head for figures, never had. But Benedict, he was always the clever one, father's favorite." His voice was laced with contempt. "It did not matter I could outride everyone at the hunt and have a high place in society. Father cared not one whit about any of it. He wanted a son who could farm the land, wield a hoe, understand the crops and livestock. A man the villagers respected. And that was his by-blow of a son, the indomitable, Benedict Swan."

I remained silent, astonished by his words and the underlying scorn in his tone. Was there such bad feeling between the brothers? I knew they were not terribly close. They had been born on opposing sides of the blanket and would that not always cause a rift? But the bitter animosity which came from Gabriel unnerved me,

I had not seen this side of the golden, blue-eyed Lord Clayton.

"Then what would you have me do, Gabriel? With nowhere to live and no income, I cannot stay here long."

At my words he spun about and returned to kneel before me, this time his face taut, his eyes bright with pleading. "I ask you this. Could you remain in Dorset if I found you a suitable place to stay?"

"I don't understand?"

"Kathryn, I must have you near," he said dramatically and squeezed my hands in his. "I care deeply for you and cannot let you out of my life."

My mind wheeled in confusion. Was that a declaration of love? "How can I stay here? What intentions do you have towards me, you are engaged to be married."

"Yes." He sighed. "But I must have time to determine my course of action. There are others to consider who are impacted by my decisions."

I pulled my hands free, stung by his remark. "What do you mean by that?" It was a foolish question on my part for I knew exactly what he meant. "If you plan to marry Lucy, you must tell me. I will leave at once."

"No!" He grasped my arms, his eyes wild. "I cannot lose you. Please, I beg of you, 'tis too much. Give me time, surely you can afford me that?"

I was confounded by his words. What did he plan on doing? Would he break his engagement, or try to find another solution to their desperate financial situation? I moved to stand, and he released me, coming to his feet.

"Gabriel, I am all a muddle and uncertain what to

think about anything anymore. It is best you leave and allow me to clear my head."

He looked at me, disappointment etched in his face. Compassion rose in my breast and I reached out to him. We embraced and I spoke softly into his ear.

"I will remain here a few days, so do not fret. I shall do nothing without speaking to you first."

"You must promise to keep away from the manor, and my family. Especially Benedict, for I do not trust him when it comes to your welfare."

"Yes, I will stay away."

This seemed to be the reassurance he needed. Gabriel pulled back and looked hard at me. "Solemn oath?"

"I swear it," I said and tried to force a smile. He gently kissed my lips at the very moment the parlor door opened.

"Miss Westcott!" Gideon Clayton stood on the threshold. "Why are you kissing my brother?"

Chapter Twenty-Three

Gabriel quickly released me. I blushed as he went over to his brother and ruffled his blond curls.

"Gid, I was telling Miss Westcott how sorry I was to see her leave. She was sad, and I was trying to cheer her up."

"What rot," Gideon replied as he came into the room and took a seat by the fire. "I saw what you were doing. It was revolting." He looked over to me and smiled. "Golly, your face is awfully pink. Is there any breakfast? I'm starving."

A commotion sounded in the hallway, and then Avril appeared, her nightcap still perched on her head. "Goodness me." She flustered at the sight of the Clayton males. "What is afoot here?" And then she suddenly became aware of her state of undress and gave a shriek, excusing herself to return to her chamber to dress.

Gabriel took his chance to escape the rectory. He told me he was going to Dorchester but would return the next morning. He assured me I would be safe if I stayed in the cottage, and then gave a knowing nod of his head to cement our conversation. He took his leave. As the parlor door closed, Gideon spoke up.

"Mother is rotten to make you go. She told me you were a troublemaker and not to be trusted, and that is why you were sent packing."

I flinched at the brutal honesty of his mother's words and felt appalled. How could Lady Clayton see fit to slander me so cruelly? I tried to compose myself. "Have you spoken with Lady Geraldine?" Surely, she might champion my cause?

"No, but I heard her shouting in the drawing room. She was really angry with Mother. So I went into the kitchen to speak to Cook instead. She's the one who told me I'd find you here. That's why I came straight away, without even eating any breakfast," he said with pride in his young voice. "Is there anything to eat? I'm ravenous!"

When Avril returned downstairs with the vicar in tow, Edna had taken Gideon into the kitchen where she plied him with a plate of eggs and bacon. While he was occupied, I took the opportunity to go into the dining room where I could speak with the Plumbs who were eating their own breakfast.

"Reverend Plumb, a word if you please?"

I asked if I might stay a few nights, and quickly explained my friendship with Gabriel, and also my relationship with his aunt.

"My word, this is an unfortunate predicament you find yourself in," he said sternly. "Yet I do believe we can offer you shelter for a short time. After all, 'tis not only Lady Clayton's opinion which matters, Lord Clayton and Lady Valkenberg's position must be considered as well," he said generously, and then bade us farewell as he left for the vestry to attend his duties.

"My goodness." Avril was visibly flustered. "I had no idea things were such a muddle, Kathryn. To think how calm life was not long since and suddenly it has all been tipped upside down. She poured herself a cup of tea and buttered her third slice of toast. "The dust will settle, I've not a doubt. Until then, you shall stay here and keep out of sight. Let us not forget the harm which befell you."

As if I could. The memory of being poisoned was always close at bay in my thoughts. Though I would not be content to sit and dwell upon any of it, that was tantamount to torture.

"Actually, dear Avril, there is one small errand I must attend to, but I shall not be gone long and promise to take good care."

Her dark button eyes showed such concern, and my heart gave thanks for her kindness. She reached out a plump, warm hand and touched my arm gently.

"Do be mindful, Kathryn. I truly do fear for you. There is foreboding in the air."

I smiled at my friend. "I shall be very careful. In fact, I could use your help." I told her my plan.

****

My words to Avril were indeed braver than I felt. Once Gideon left to return to the manor, Avril and I waited fifteen minutes, dressed for a cold walk, and left the rectory. My intention was bold, my conviction tepid, but I was determined to go and speak with Benedict. Though my suspicions pointed directly to him, and with Gabriel's statement his half-brother had purchased the harmful chocolates, nothing would deter me from my quest to confront him. But I was no fool. Avril Plumb would accompany me. There was always safety in numbers.

We arrived at the driveway to Mowbray Manor and navigated our way through the woods undetected, to emerge at the rear of the house, by the stables and close to Benedict's residence.

As we neared, sounds emanated from the manor's kitchen window. I was confident no one would witness our passing if we kept quiet. We followed the narrow path away from the main house past the stables and arrived at the front of a small cottage.

The place looked like a gingerbread house from an old fable with its thatched roof and paned glass windows. Smoke plumed from its chimney and I guessed Benedict must be home. I gathered my confidence and gave a determined smile to Avril as she moved out of sight. I knocked upon the door.

It opened to reveal Benedict Swan, half-dressed wearing trousers, his white shirt open, displaying chest hair as wet and dark as a seal's coat.

"Kathryn?" He appeared shocked to see me perched on the step and was momentarily lost for words. He recovered himself and asked me inside.

"Good morning, Benedict," I said gravely as he hastily buttoned up his shirt. "Forgive me for calling unannounced, but I must speak with you regarding an urgent matter. Can you spare the time?"

He frowned, his dark blue eyes intense as they studied me. "But of course. Let me get you some tea, and we can sit over there if it suits you?" He gestured to a small table and two chairs placed to the side of a hearth.

I agreed and watched him go to the kitchen. I glanced about. The room was devoid of personality, it lacked a woman's touch. But the essentials were all there. Two worn armchairs and a rug. Though there was little decoration, I noticed a picture on the mantel. My curiosity got the better of me and I walked over to look.

As I stared at the painting of a woman, the breath caught in my throat. She was beautiful. With Benedict's raven black hair, thick arched brows and full mouth, it had to be Lavender Swan. No wonder Nigel Clayton had fallen for this gypsy girl, no man in their right mind wouldn't.

"Ah, you found my mother?" Benedict rejoined me, a tea-tray in his hands.

"She was lovely," I said in admiration and went to join him at the table. He poured me a cup of tea, and then one for himself. He took a sip of his, I took no chances and did not touch my own. If he had poisoned me once, he would do it again.

"Now tell me," he said softly. "What is it you wish to speak to me about?"

I took a deep breath and clutched my hands together so they would cease their trembling.

"I want to ask you about the chocolates."

"Chocolates?" He frowned.

"Yes, the ones given to me last week which almost killed me."

"You are recovered, I trust?" His eyes were soft and compassionate.

"Indeed, I am well, but I want to ask where you purchased them?"

He frowned. "Kathryn, I don't think I understand you?"

"The chocolates. please tell me where you bought them, it is important I know."

He seemed puzzled and tilted his head in question. "Forgive me, Kathryn, if I seem rude, but I honestly don't understand why you're asking me." Then his expression changed as he comprehended my meaning.

"You think I bought them?" He was incredulous. His body stiffened.

"I do."

Benedict's eyes immediately flashed with annoyance. "Wait, let me make sure I understand you correctly. You think I purchased those chocolates, laced them with arsenic and tried to poison you?" His voice was full of disbelief.

My chin came up. I would not be afraid of this man. "That is precisely what I am saying, yes, Benedict. And I would like you to tell me why you wanted to hurt me, before I speak with the authorities."

His countenance grew taut. He clenched his jaw, and his eyes were almost black. I was grateful Avril stood right outside the door listening.

Benedict was getting angry and his voice became quieter and somehow more intimidating. "You honestly believe me capable of doing something so despicable? You think me a monster who would harm another human being just like that?" He snapped his fingers and I started at the sudden sound. His chair scraped loudly on the floor as he rose abruptly. He glared at me. "Good God, Kathryn, you must think ill of me indeed. Why on earth would I wish you harm? *You*, who have brought a semblance of happiness into this miserable place. *You* who has given a sad young boy a reason to smile once again?" His voice grew louder, and I fought my impulse to flee. "Answer me, Kathryn, how could you accuse me when all I have offered you is the hand of friendship?" His eyes flashed with a moment of hurt.

My breath came fast as I tried to suppress the rising panic in my breast. I got to my feet prepared to run if needed. "Because of Aramintha!" I blurted.

The room stilled. He frowned at me once again as though trying to decode my words. His voice became quieter. "Aramintha? What has she to do with any of this?" He seemed puzzled.

"I know about you and her," I stated flatly. "I found her diary."

His expression was one of confusion. "What the devil are you talking about?"

"Her diary, Benedict. I know she was in love with you and that she carried your child. That is why you killed her!"

"What?" he said with disbelief, his tone appalled. "That is a despicable thing to say about her. How dare you insinuate something so distasteful. What is wrong with you? Dear God, you have a perverse and disgusting mind." He walked to the mantel as though he could not stand to be near me. His breath came fast as his chest rose, he struggled to compose himself.

I followed. Reckless of my safety, glad to finally have the chance to speak my honest thoughts.

"I am not perverse. I only speak of that which I read. Aramintha Clayton was my dearest friend. I knew her long before I came to Mowbray. I was shocked to hear of her death, and even more concerned when I found her diary and read its contents." I took a step closer, my fear receding as my own temper found a hold. "But you already know this, Benedict, because you stole the letters she wrote to me which were hidden in my room. You knew I was suspicious of her supposed suicide, and once I had her diary, it would only be a matter of time before I put it all together. Yes, I realized she was going to have your child, a child you could not afford to let another soul know about." My heart hammered with anger at the injustice of it all.

"A child? Aramintha was with child?"

I ignored the question. "You pushed Aramintha from the cliff that night to keep your ugly secret. You murdered my friend and then you tried to kill me so I could not tell anyone what you had done!" Tears streamed down my face unheeded as my fury unleashed against the man who had hurt my dear friend. All the rage I harbored towards him and his family burst forth as the fragile dam I had built began to crumble.

Benedict shook his dark head and held up a hand as though to keep me away. "Stop! For Christ's sake, Kathryn, how could you even think such terrible things of me?" His voice was low and quiet, and through my blurred vision I could see him sickened by my words. He stared intently at my face. "You have it all wrong, Kathryn, so wrong that if I were not so appalled, I might laugh at the complete ridicule of your thoughts."

I started to speak, but Benedict got there first.

"Please, allow me the chance to defend myself against the list of foul accusations you have thrown at me. Although I am not sure where to begin." He paused for a moment. "Aramintha Clayton was my half-sister, but a beloved sister all the same, though she and I were never as close as she was to Gabriel. We had a kinship which evolved in the schoolroom and continued as we grew up. Gabriel went off to Eton, I was sent to school in Dorchester, and eventually Aramintha to Brampton as you know already. After she returned home early last year, there was a change about her, but I thought it the blooming of a bud to a flower, chrysalis to butterfly. I suspected she had found love. I was curious but determined to mind my business. As long as she seemed happy, I would not pry. But in the spring, her demeanor underwent a sudden change. She became withdrawn and looked unwell. I asked her several times if she was ill, if Doctor Beedles should be called? But she would not have him near her. Aramintha assured me it was a cold, then a chill. There was always a ready answer whenever I showed concern." He ran his fingers through his dark hair, his face anguished.

I listened intently.

"I became side-tracked," he continued. "Spring on the farm is a busy time with livestock birthing, planting the fields and all the other activities needed. My attention was distracted, and it is something I shall have to live with the rest of my days because I do feel some responsibility for what happened to Aramintha." He shook his head. "Do not think it means I played any role in her death. I was just not paying enough mind to what went on at the manor. I had no idea she might be with child. Damn it all, if I had been watching, I might have noticed something amiss, and perhaps she would not have taken her own life."

"She did not kill herself!" I shouted at him. "She would never have harmed herself and certainly not her babe." My heart hammered in my chest. "Aramintha is the last person who would do such a thing. She would have been far more likely to run away, start a life elsewhere with her child, but she would never"—my blood boiled—"never hurt her baby. Yes, she was foolish, young and inexperienced. But one thing she was not and that was a coward."

We stared at one another. My breath coming quickly, his all spent. I believe we both took a moment for the conversation to penetrate our thoughts, link all the perceptions we both had about Aramintha Clayton. I cannot explain, but as I watched Benedict Swan and saw the pain etched across his face, I began to believe him. The more I thought about him, the less likely he appeared to be the kind of man my friend would have formed a romantic attachment with.

"Jesus, Kathryn, what possible motive would I have had to hurt her?" He must have read my mind.

I scoffed. "Other than the fact you would be shamed, and she ruined, having a family would impede you from your plans to travel to Africa."

His anger returned, and he snapped back. "Don't be ridiculous, if I was to commit incest and marry my own sister, where better to run than to the bloody African continent? Good God, woman, if I were responsible for my sister's death, I would have fled to Kenya months ago."

I had to concede the point. Suddenly it seemed there were fewer reasons for Benedict to have harmed her.

"But the chocolates, and my riding accident?"

"Those damned chocolates. Are you not listening? I did not buy the blasted things, and I don't understand why you are convinced I did." Benedict's eyes fastened on my face and I felt my skin heat.

"Then tell me, why did you not come to my sickbed?"

He rounded on me, eyes blazing. "I did. But you had another there to comfort you already."

My breath caught in my throat. It was true, Gabriel had stayed by my side.

"And then my aunt had me go to Hampshire with her. By the time I returned, you were recovered." One eyebrow rose. "Who told you the chocolates were from me?"

I could not answer. He took a step towards me, his face thunderous.

"Who was it, Kathryn, tell me!"

"Gabriel," I said softly. "He said you bought them in Swanage."

Benedict stormed to the door and pulled his jacket from a hook. He threw it on and went into the kitchen and rummaged in a drawer.

"Come on then," he said angrily. "We are going to Swanage and we'll get to the bottom of this." He grabbed something and closed the drawer.

"But I cannot go anywhere with you."

He stepped towards me, and I saw what he held in his hand. It was a large meat knife! I had been such a fool—I gasped and stepped back ready to scream for Avril to come in. Benedict comprehended my fear and shook his head. He turned the point of the blade away from me, held the vicious article on his flat palm and offered it. "Here," he spat. "Take the knife, Kathryn. If you are so convinced I am a ruthless killer, then you can use this to protect yourself. Now come along, I tire of this ridiculous farce and I shall put an end to it once and for all." He threw open the door and met the startled, gaping face of Avril Plumb.

****

Benedict convinced Avril of my safety and sent her on her way, which she did reluctantly and only after my encouragement. Johnny Dainty hitched Domino up to the trap and Benedict thanked the stable lad and helped me up. Without a care who watched from the house, he set off down the driveway at a healthy trot.

We spoke little on the way, both of us angry and chewing over our thoughts. I was at odds with myself. Just hours ago, I had labelled him a villain, the man who had wreaked such tragedy on Aramintha, Moira and myself. Yet now I rode with him alone and vulnerable, albeit armed with a kitchen knife. Strangely enough I did not feel as though I was in danger, at least Avril knew what we were about.

If Benedict had not purchased the chocolates, why would Gabriel lay the blame at his feet? Could it just be an honest mistake by the shopkeeper?

We left Domino at the livery stable in Swanage, and walked up each side of the main street, stopping at any shop selling confectionary. This was not difficult, and it did not take long to find a window which displayed confections in similarly dressed boxes to the one I received.

Benedict opened the door to the establishment and a little bell jingled. There were no other customers inside. A middle-aged man with spectacles and a wispy patch of greasy hair surfaced behind the counter.

"Good day to you, Mr. Swan," he said pleasantly. "'Tis been a while since you had a sweet tooth." He smiled and I noticed he must imbibe in his wares for several of his own were absent.

"Indeed, Mr. Bump, I should like to buy a treat for the young lady here." He gestured towards me, and I gave a polite smile to the shopkeeper.

"But first," Benedict said, "I have a question."

"Certainly, sir, ask away."

"In the past two weeks, have you sold your boxes of chocolates to anyone from Mowbray Manor?"

The older man pursed his lips and placed a

forefinger against them.

“Hmm.” He blinked several times. “Can’t say that I have, Mr. Swan. I’m sure I haven’t seen anyone from the manor since autumn.”

My heart sank. If this were true, perhaps there might be another shop in town with similar packaging?

“Are you certain?” Benedict pressed him.

“That I am—but wait.” He turned and opened a thick curtain which separated the shop from the rest of the building. “Florrie, where are you lovey? Can you come into the shop, me dear?”

Footsteps approached, and a vivacious redhead appeared, enough rouge on her cheeks to be on the stage and dressed in a low-cut dress which left little to the imagination.

“Good morning, Mrs. Bump.” Benedict smiled kindly. Much to my amazement the woman gave him a lusty grin and a wink.

“’Tis always a rare treat ’avin’ one of you gents from the manor come by.” She practically purred as her husband gazed on in complete adoration. “What is it you be needin’ then?”

“Florrie love,” Mr. Bump said quickly, “Mr. Swan enquired if anyone from the manor been here buyin’ boxes of chocolates in the past couple of weeks. I told him no one I could recall. But then I remembered that one day my gout did plague me somethin’ fierce, and I stayed abed. You kept the shop open for me, did anyone come in from the Manor?”

Florrie Bump became sheepish, her expression similar to that of a naughty child. “He said it were a surprise and that I wasn’t to say nothin’ or else I’d spoil it.” Florrie smiled seductively, but Benedict was nonplussed.

"Please Florrie," he said sweetly. "It is very important you tell me. You won't spoil anything, I promise. Who came in and what exactly did they buy?"

She gave an exaggerated sigh and her breasts almost popped out of her dress. "Oh all right then, he bought a small box of our special chocolates." She gestured to the window. "Like them there."

My pulse raced. But I kept quiet.

"Who was it bought the chocolates, Florrie?"

She grinned mischeviously. "Why, it were that handsome brother of yours, Mr. Swan. It were Lord Gabriel himself."

****

I allowed Benedict to steer me out of the shop, because I was both light-headed and nauseous. He did not speak but guided me down the street until we reached a small tea-room where he selected a table and ordered us both tea and scones. Benedict studied me as though he expected me to faint. I said nothing but watched as he poured the tea when it was placed before us.

"Here, Kathryn." He passed me a cup and then a plate with a buttered scone. "I would encourage you to eat and drink. Because if you don't, you will most likely pass out. I can see by the pallor of your skin you are in shock. Please humor me and try?" His face was serious, his tone so professional I automatically obeyed. The tea did revive me, the scone not as much, but I ate half of it and felt my stomach began to simmer instead of boil.

"Are you ready to talk about this?" His voice was calm and quiet. I nodded.

“Tell me what Gabriel said to you about the chocolates.” I recounted the conversation between us in the library and added Gabriel had been reluctant to say anything to the constable, instead preferring to wait until the next day before he took any action.

“And that was the day Lady Clayton forced you to leave?”

“Yes.”

“Did you mention anything to her about Gabriel’s accusation?”

“No. Gabriel asked me to keep quiet.”

Benedict frowned, deep in thought. “Was that the last time you saw him?”

I shook my head. “He came to the rectory this morning, he asked me—” my voice wobbled. “He asked me not to leave, to remain close until he could sort everything out. He also told me to stay away from you.” I swallowed. I did not want to get upset. There was no time for that, I needed my wits about me. “Gabriel insinuated I should not trust you, that doing so would place me in danger.”

“Yet you came straight for my cottage this morning, even though you suspected me as the culprit who poisoned you?”

“I know it sounds reckless when you say it that way, which is why Avril came along with me. We left instruction with her maid to alert the constable if we were not returned within two hours. I also left a note in my room at the cottage which said where I intended to go and for them to suspect you, should any harm come my way.”

Benedict grinned. “Ridiculous as it sounds, I am proud of you for taking precautions, even though they were in reference to me. But to come to the cottage and confront me?"

"I was very scared, and that's the honest truth. But also sick and tired of trying to solve this puzzle. I have learned so many things about Aramintha yet have not been able to put any of it together. It is a jigsaw with too many missing pieces."

"Has it occurred to you I might have those pieces, and in turn, you could have the answers I lack?" He raised a dark eyebrow and gave me a wicked smile.

Chapter Twenty-Four

Juniper Blessing's cottage lay near the chapel, set far back from the lane and camouflaged by a natural wall of thick pine trees, bushes and ferns. Benedict tethered Domino to the graveyard gate, and we traversed on foot the rest of the way.

The place was a ramshackle building, long in need of work and attention. The thatched roof damaged, the plaster walls grey with dirt and age, but the flowerbeds which surrounded the property were neat and tidy. Benedict appeared somewhat embarrassed as we walked to the door.

"Juniper grows herbs for healing, she holds little interest for anything else as you will see once we are inside."

He did not lie. When Juniper bade us enter, we stepped into a hovel. The floor was dirt, the walls devoid of paint, and there were countless bunches of tied herbs hanging from the ceiling. Though a dismal sight, the fragrance of the room was wonderful. A plume of steam rose from a large boiling pot on the hearth, the apparent source of the aromatic scent.

"I wondered when you'd bring 'er." Juniper sat in a rocking chair in front of the hearth, a lit pipe hung from her mouth. "Took yer long enough nephew."

Benedict walked over to his aunt and stooped low to kiss her cheek. He gestured for me to approach and take the only other seat available. A worn dining chair, it was uncomfortable, but better than standing. Juniper vacated her feet from an old footstool, and Benedict folded himself down so he could sit and be at eye level with us both.

"I saw him with your friend." Her black eyes landed on my face, and I flinched.

"Who? Which friend?" I asked, at once puzzled.

"The Scot, the pregnant girl. Mister Gabriel an' her, they were havin' an argument in the chapel." My eyes flew to Benedict's face. He nodded sadly.

"Juniper spoke of this after Moira was found."

"That poor girl come to me for medicine to kill her babe. I told her I couldn't help an' sent her to see the butcher nurse in Swanage. She come back again later. Ben was here too. She was askin' questions about young lady Aramintha."

I could not stop my sharp intake of breath.

"Please tell her, aunt," Benedict said.

Juniper paused and took another suck of her pipe and blew out the smoke. "'Tis like I always said to Ben." She gestured to her nephew. "He's a baddun that Gabriel. Always was. Face like an angel, heart like a demon. Can't keep his hands off the girls, that's the problem."

My heart was already saddened from what we had learned of the man I had just begun to care for. With Juniper's words, it sank further into despair.

"He would meet the maid in the chapel. Oh, I saw 'em all right, but they was so wrapped up in what they was doing they didn't notice old Juniper. You could tell she loved him though, but not him." Her black eyes narrowed. "He has no love for any but himself. They argued, and she ran off to the manor in tears."

I thought of the night Moira had died. I remembered how desperate she had been. The poor girl. And then I recalled how I had left her room and thought someone was there. The smell of anise—Gabriel's cheroots. He had watched me leaving Moira's room!

"She never hung herself, that'n." Juniper spat out the words and I physically jumped. She took the pipe from her mouth and pointed it towards me. "You mark my words, he had a hand in her fate. He done it."

I recoiled from the accusation she made. Surely Gabriel would not have harmed Moira? I resisted the thought, but then sense took hold. If he had tried to poison me, he must be capable of anything. Had he gone to her after I left her room? I shuddered.

"Tell us the rest, Juniper," Benedict, quiet until now spoke out suddenly. She hesitated, but he encouraged her with a nod. "Moira is gone, and Kathryn almost died. He's gone too far. It is time you stopped being frightened and tell us what you saw."

The black eyes glanced at her nephew and then at me. Benedict reached out to take her hand. "No more secrets, Aunt. I won't let him hurt you."

The old woman nodded solemnly and sighed. "It ain't natural what he did with the other one."

"What other one." I had a terrible feeling I already knew what she was about to reveal.

"His sister. She was a lovely thing, so she was. Pretty girl, always a smile and sometimes a coin for Juniper. But him, he put a curse on her, made her lovesick in an unnatural way. I saw 'em, but he didn't know. When she jumped from the cliff, I never told no one. Was no point. Afterwards I was too scared to tell the mother I'd seen them together, else she'd throw me out of my cottage and send my Ben away with nothing."

"Good God." My voice betrayed my disgust. At once memories cascaded through my mind, the words in Aramintha's diary, her constant comments for the brother she held in such high esteem. But my mind baulked at the very idea.

Benedict's eyes locked with mine, and I knew he felt as sickened as myself.

"It cannot be?" I stuttered. "The man in her diary was called 'A'?"

Juniper cackled and shook her head. "That was 'er special name for him, for Gabriel. She called him Angel."

I covered my mouth with my hand as it all began to fall into place.

****

I rode back with Benedict as far as the driveway to Mowbray. I did not want to see any of the Clayton family if at all possible. We were quiet, each with our own dark thoughts. We both needed time to think, and so arranged to meet at the rectory later in the day.

The trek back to the village felt like the longest walk of my life as I mulled everything over in my mind. My friendship with Aramintha, a girl I thought I knew so well, but apparently did not. Her brother, whose handsome face had bewitched me as it had so many others before. A man who took what he wanted and cast away that which he did not. And what about dear Moira? No wonder she was always troubled when Gabriel spent time with me. Her sudden appearance whenever he and I were alone was completely understandable. Pregnant with his child and in love with the man, she had been tormented by his attentiveness to me. Two women I had known, both who carried his babes and now were dead.

Had Gabriel himself killed them? Part of me still refused to accept he had. His kindness, his lovely nature, how could he be a killer? Yet I could not deny what had happened to me. The riding accident, the poison. Suddenly something snagged in my mind as I remembered the day Gideon had suddenly fallen ill. He had been sick with terrible stomach pains. Gabriel had genuinely seemed upset and frightened for his welfare. The drinking chocolate! I gasped out loud as I processed this discovery. Gideon had consumed my hot chocolate as well as his own that day. He had become violently ill from inadvertently drinking the poison intended for me! No wonder Gabriel had been distraught. He thought he had poisoned his own brother, the only person he genuinely seemed to love.

I was relieved to arrive back at the rectory. Avril exclaimed her concern as she saw my ashen face, ushered me before the fire, and asked the maid to bring tea and crumpets. I did not want to share all I had learned, instead I blamed my demeanor upon the dire straits I now found myself in. She had overheard some of the conversation between Benedict and myself but had given her word she would remain quiet about it until I told her otherwise. We had barely finished our tea when the maid announced a visitor, and before she could finish her sentence, Lady Geraldine marched into the parlor.

The older woman was extremely agitated. Her stature so tall and commanding, she immediately dwarfed everything in the room.

"Miss Westcott, we must speak at once," she said sternly, and as an afterthought greeted Avril with a cold smile. Poor Avril was flustered receiving such a grand dame in her humble home, and as she began to offer refreshment, found herself halted by the imperious wave of a glove-clad hand.

"Tosh, Mrs. Plumb. I thank you, but there is no time to dally. I shall speak privately with Miss Westcott if you please?" She directed a haughty gaze down her substantial nose, and Avril quickly took flight. As the door closed, Lady Geraldine came over to the hearth to sit.

"I've no time for chit-chat," she snapped, as though we usually indulged in mindless gossip.

"Indeed." I frowned. "What brings you here, what is wrong? Have you spoken to Benedict?"

"Benedict?" Her brow wrinkled. "Why would I talk to him? Don't interrupt, gal. I have something of great import to share." She paused and fumbled in her small reticule. After a couple of moments, she pulled out a small pile of papers and handed them across to me.

I gasped. "My letters!" There they were, a bit of a jumble, but nevertheless intact. I glanced up and she read the question in my eyes.

"Brace yourself, dear," she said. "I found them in Gabriel's room." Her face displayed an emotion which bordered between triumph and disgust.

Another betrayal from the man I thought cared for me. I felt wounded yet again, but not diminished. For each time I was hurt by Gabriel's deceit my resolve grew stronger.

"How did you find them?"

She at least had the courtesy to blush. "I waited until he had gone to Dorchester and then rifled through his things." She arched a brow. "Yes, it was very wrong of me, but I had my own suspicions. I knew from the start Benedict was not involved with any of this Aramintha nonsense, he has also been concerned with some events involving his brother." She gave a deep sigh and for a moment looked all of her years. "I have long thought something was wrong with Gabriel, noticed it when he was still a young lad. Too much charm, too much beauty in my opinion, a recipe for disaster." She eyed me. "I see Blanche ousted you for fear you were distracting her son?"

"Yes." The thought that I had been the subject of his attention, once so remarkable now made me cringe. "She believed I encouraged his affection and wanted me gone. Lady Clayton has never cared much for me."

"Silly woman doesn't like anything except her own reflection and her first-born. Now tell me." She squinted. "What are we to do next, have you made any other discoveries?"

I declined to tell her what I knew. It should come from Benedict himself. "I would suggest you meet with Benedict, Lady Geraldine. He alone knows much of what has transpired and is better suited to tell you his thoughts and opinions, of which I am in concurrence."

"Indeed?" She crowed. "This coming from his accuser, the one who named him villain."

"Tosh," I said with a cheeky smile, stealing her words.

Lady Geraldine had the good grace to laugh, and then she gathered herself and rose to leave. "I will consult with my nephew as you recommend. I have no doubt we shall speak again very soon." With that, she whirled her skirts around and departed.

No sooner had she left than Avril flew back into the parlor, her chins wobbling, her eyes bright with excitement.

"What is going on, Kathryn? 'Tis time you told me everything, I have been patient long enough."

"Sit down, Avril." And as the hour passed by, I recounted the story of my time at Brampton, my friendship with Aramintha, and the true reason for my coming to Mowbray. I stopped many times during the telling, both to answer Avril's questions, and to wipe a tear now and then. I refrained from the mention of Gabriel's role in what had happened, that must wait.

Later that afternoon Benedict finally came to call. He was most cordial to Avril, who was happy enough to leave us alone now I had given her much to ruminate over. Once she had gone from the room, Benedict removed his gloves and stood before the fire to warm himself. I could feel the chill around him and shivered.

"I spoke with my aunt," he began without preamble. "She told me of the letters, and also her visit to you earlier today."

"I did not tell her anything, Benedict. It needed to come from you."

He nodded. "I told her everything."

"Everything?"

"Yes."

"How did she receive what you said?" I was concerned it might be too much, even for the battle-axe that she was.

"Stoically, of course. Aunt Gerry is a strong

woman. Fair and honest as well. I instructed her to remain silent until we determine our next step, and she assured me she would say nothing. I believe she has told the household she has the headache and is confined to her room."

"What of the others?"

"Lady Blanche continues as usual, Gideon sulks because you are gone, and Gabriel is due back in the morning from Dorchester. He is there to be fitted for his bridal attire."

His words elicited no feeling whatsoever. Perhaps I had become numb at last? How strange was the heart to be so ready to heal and forget?

"Gabriel told me his marriage would save Mowbray from financial ruin. I was not aware the Claytons were in debt."

Benedict's brows furrowed. "Ruin? That's ridiculous. Mowbray's coffers are the fullest they have been since before my father died. No, Kathryn. Gabriel has no need to marry a fortune." His expression softened as he recognized yet another lie I had been fed and had easily swallowed. He commented no further and I was grateful. What little pride I held on to was tenuous at best.

"It seems Gabriel wanted me to remain close so he could ensure my silence and keep Aramintha's diary close at hand."

"When do you expect him back at the rectory? Did he say?"

"Yes. He is supposed to call tomorrow morning."

"Well then." He took a seat. "There is little time and much to discuss, Kathryn. We must make plans." His eyes scanned the room.

"I think we are going to require brandy."

Chapter Twenty-Five

The atmosphere in Lady Clayton's parlor the next morning was tense. Benedict paced back and forth in front of the hearth like a wildcat trapped in a cage, while Lady Blanche stared out the French windows, her eyes nervously scanning the driveway for signs of her beloved son.

"Hmm. They have opened the underground electric railway," Lady Geraldine commented as she read the paper. "Trains under the streets of London? Ridiculous notion, it will never catch on," she said with disdain.

"Here is Gabriel, at last," Lady Blanche announced nervously, turning to look at us. "I am still baffled why you all wish to speak with him. And Benedict, why it concerns this woman I do not understand." She threw me a disapproving glare.

Loud footsteps approached, and Gabriel burst through the door and strode over to where I sat. He placed a firm hand upon my shoulder. "Kathryn, are you well? I called at the rectory and Mrs. Plumb said you had come to Mowbray. What has happened??"

Before I could answer, Benedict spoke up. "I invited Miss Westcott to join us." Gabriel seemed surprised to find him there, he obviously had not seen him when he entered. His face showed a flash of confusion, and then the famous smile reappeared.

"Indeed." His glance swept across the room and

over each of us seated. Lady Geraldine put down her newspaper, his mother wrung her hands. Gabriel's eyes narrowed. "What is amiss? Why is everyone here?"

"Dearest Gabriel." Lady Blanche went to him and grasped his arm. "I do not know what is going on, but Benedict says we must speak about a family matter."

He wheeled to face his half-brother. "What is this, Benedict? What on earth are you up to?"

Benedict approached Gabriel, his gait slow yet he radiated strength and confidence. "We must speak with you about Moira, your mother's maid."

"This is preposterous!" Lady Clayton shouted.

"Oh, for goodness sake, Blanche, do shut up!" Lady Geraldine snapped at her sister-in-law, who seemed so shocked by the order that she complied.

"Gabriel," Benedict continued. "We know about your relationship with Moira Campbell. We also know she carried your babe."

Lady Blanche gasped in horror. Gabriel's expression did not change.

"Don't be ridiculous, brother, you insult me. I have no taste for servants." Nonchalantly he went to the cigar box, extracted a cheroot and lit the end. "'Twas always you who liked the common girls. Who was the little nurse you salivated for? Oh, yes, Rosemary." He strolled over to the window. "Personally, brother, my tastes have always run to a bit of good breeding." His tone was baited and offensive. I felt sickened to have ever cared for the man.

"You were seen with her, Gabriel, several times," Benedict said.

"Hah," Gabriel mocked and turned to face us. "Let me guess who told you that. Juniper, your hag of an aunt. That old witch would say anything to protect you."

"That aunt might," Lady Geraldine said, rising from her chair. "But this one would not. Stop lying, Gabriel, you were seen going into Moira's room on more than one occasion, and you were also *heard*." She emphasized the last word and there was no confusing her meaning.

Gabriel laughed and directed his gaze to Lady Blanche. "This is preposterous. Mother dear, I hope you are not as willing to condemn your son." He shrugged nonchalantly. "Oh, all right, I'll admit Campbell was a fetching little thing, and she gave me every indication she was willing." He looked to the rest of us. "Am I to be blamed for a dalliance?" Gabriel glared at Benedict. "Are you not a product of the same yourself? I don't recall my father being penalized for impregnating a gypsy girl." He smirked. "Or is it one set of rules for him and another for me?" He walked to the hearth and threw his cheroot into the flames. He did not look at me the entire time.

"You were violent with her," I spoke up and everyone seemed surprised at my interruption. "What you did to her arm? You burned her, didn't you?" I could not stop the tremor in my voice.

"Oh that?" he said flippantly. "It was an accident. She fell against a hot poker I held in my hand." He gave me a smile to emphasize his meaning, and I felt as though I might be ill. "Next, you'll accuse me of stringing the bitch up in the shed."

Lady Blanche and I both gasped in unison. Gabriel chuckled and, with horror, I realized he was enjoying himself. My God, he was insane.

"Oh, she was all for it, she just needed a little encouragement. And what's one little maid to a Clayton?" He smiled wickedly.

"And what of our sister?" The room fell silent. Birdsong, the wind, the world seemed to stop.

"No Benedict. Do not do this I beg of you," Lady Blanche beseeched.

"I said," Benedict's voice grew louder, "what of Araminta? What excuse do you make for that relationship?"

The smile fell away from Gabriel's face, and his eyes widened with intent. Everything happened at once. Gabriel charged towards Benedict with a growl of anger. They collided and began to fight. Lady Blanche screamed, Lady Geraldine stepped back, and I stood and shouted at them to stop. But they were too far gone to hear, throwing punches at one another, both hitting and missing their targets. Gabriel pushed Benedict back against the mantel with a loud thud and grabbed a fistful of his black hair. He banged his head against the marble and Benedict roared in pain, shoving his brother violently away. Gabriel grabbed at an armchair to break his fall and tipped it over as he went down. He sprang back to his feet like an agile cat and went for Benedict with his fists. But Benedict wrapped his elbow around his brother's neck, trapping him in a strong headlock. As Gabriel's angelic face contorted in the chokehold, he screamed vulgarities at Benedict. His foul words were full of hatred and venom as he spat them out at the bastard brother of the family. Suddenly the door flew open to reveal Gideon in the threshold, his eyes as round as saucers. He began to shout.

"Stop! Both of you please stop!" And he burst into

tears.

His piercing voice penetrated their rage, for both men dropped their fists to look at their younger brother, who had tears streaming down his face. Gabriel broke away from Benedict and rushed to him, all concern.

"We are stopped, Gid, 'tis all right. Don't take on so." Gabriel had a cut to the side of his left eye, and blood in the corner of his mouth. He reached his hand to take his brother's tightly.

"Listen to me, Gid. I cannot stay here, brother. Quick now, you must come with me." Gabriel pulled Gideon towards him and broke into a run, dragging his younger sibling along behind him. Gideon had no choice but to keep pace or fall over. They sprinted out of the room and into the hall. Benedict followed at their heels, and I close behind.

They ran from the house. Gabriel was fast, his body lean and athletic, Gideon easily kept pace for he was young and fit. We lagged behind but kept running. Benedict turned and shouted back at me.

"He is headed to the cliffs!"

My heart raced as I ran, but more from fear as I realized Gabriel's intent. He cleared the edge of the garden and ran down the path which led to the cliff top, the very same place Gideon had taken me when I had first arrived at Mowbray. Benedict gained on them but was still too far away to help Gideon.

Gabriel abruptly came to a stop as he reached a point where the path came closest to the cliff edge. He turned back to look at Benedict, wrapped his arms around Gideon, and lifted the boy's feet from the ground.

"Stop there, or I shall throw him over!" he

screamed at Benedict.

Gideon's face registered fear as he recognized he was in mortal danger from his own brother. He began to wriggle, desperately trying to escape his brother's vice-like grip. "Let me go, Gabriel, for goodness sakes, what are you doing to me? Please!" Gideon sobbed. "You're scaring me!" His young face contorted with fear and confusion at his brother's intent.

"Let him go, Gabriel," Benedict bellowed as I came up behind him, sickened by the sight before my eyes. Gabriel stood tall, his hair ruffled in the wind blowing from the sea, his manic eyes bright with excitement and now what I recognized as madness. Gideon cried openly, writhing to escape while he begged to be freed.

"Please, Gabriel," I shouted. "Gideon has done nothing to harm a soul. He does not deserve your hatred. Please let him go!"

But he would not release him. Instead, Gabriel stepped perilously closer to the edge of the cliff. Down below, the waves crashed angrily against jagged rocks. Gideon screamed louder and kicked, thrashing his arms and legs in unmitigated terror.

Gabriel kept smiling. "You self-righteous bastards, I will do whatever I damn well please. You can all go to—"

A loud crack split the air, and a bright red stain bloomed on Gabriel's neck. Instantly, his arms slackened, and Gideon quickly took the opportunity to scramble away. He ran like a scared rabbit straight into my open arms.

Gabriel blinked. His eyes registered shock as he gawked past me and over my shoulder. I spun around at the same time as Benedict, to see Lady Geraldine. She stood on the path, a hunting rifle in her hands which was still aimed at her nephew. As we realized what she had done, Gabriel let out a disbelieving laugh. I turned back to look at him and then watched mesmerized as he purposefully and slowly stepped off the cliff down to the raging sea below. I froze, with Gideon safe in my arms while Benedict rushed to the edge.

"Dear God, he is gone," Benedict stated flatly. His face twisted into a mask of anger, despair and grief as he stood there in utter shock.

Gideon began to sob loudly, and I wrapped my arms tighter about him though they trembled violently. I felt ill, but my mind focused upon the needs of the boy in my arms. "Come, let us go back to the house," I said gently and led him away from the ghastly scene. Benedict gathered himself and went to his aunt, who stood still as a statue, her face drained of color and tears streaming down her aged cheeks.

Johnny Dainty came running towards us, closely followed by Lady Blanche, who was screaming Gabriel's name.

Johnny stopped me panic-stricken. "Miss, miss! I heard a gunshot. Is someone hurt?"

"Not anymore, Johnny," I replied. "Not anymore."

****

I spent some time with Gideon. He trembled and cried, but eventually fell asleep as I sat and talked to him, stroking the hair from his forehead. Once assured he was settled, I went downstairs to the parlor. While I had tended to his young brother, Benedict had sent Johnny to get the constable, and Doctor Beedles. The latter was upstairs administering a sedative to Lady

Blanche, who had been sobbing uncontrollably the entire time.

Constable Harkles was leaving the parlor as I reached the door. He nodded solemnly and passed me. I was grateful not having to speak with him about what had taken place. I entered the room and took a seat next to Lady Geraldine, who nestled a large glass of brandy in her hands. She seemed surprisingly calm considering what had happened. Benedict was not there.

"How are you?" I asked. I felt bold enough to reach out and touch the old lady.

"I'll weather it." She sighed. "Only meant to wing him, I couldn't just stand there and watch him hurt Gideon." She took another sip of brandy.

"You did the right thing, Lady Geraldine. Gabriel was off his head. I cannot believe he wanted to harm his brother. It is beyond comprehension."

"Tosh," she quipped. "Gabriel loved his brother, but he always loved himself more. I pegged him for a narcissist, but I never realized how insane the boy was. Blanche has much to explain."

The door opened, and Benedict entered the room. His face was drawn, painted with exhaustion. I felt the same way and I was not even family. I could only imagine what he must be going through. And to think I had thought him the villain. An apology was in order, but now was not the time to address that. He poured himself a large brandy and tossed it back.

"How is Gideon?"

"Asleep. Hopefully for a while," I replied.

Benedict sat in an armchair facing us. "Harkles plans to report Gabriel's fall as an accident. I did not tell him about what happened with Gideon, or anything else for that matter. I would rather keep this within the family with both your consent." Lady Geraldine nodded quickly. I hesitated.

"What about Moira? Her family has a right to know of his involvement."

"I agree," Benedict said. "But to what end? We do not know all of the facts other than Gabriel was involved in an affair with her."

"The cad," Geraldine said sharply. "You do realize what I said about witnesses overhearing him in the gal's room was a bluff don't you?"

"I did, Aunt. And a very clever ruse it was."

But I was dumbfounded. I had believed every word she had said. Lady Geraldine was a very innovative woman. "What happens now?" I asked.

"There will be an inquest, and Gabriel's death will be ruled accidental. With the absence of a body, there should be no dispute. Moira's death was recorded a suicide."

"And Aramintha?" I asked.

"Doctor Beedles will join us as soon as he tends Lady Blanche. He says he wishes to discuss a matter regarding Aramintha with the family." He turned to me and his expression softened. "I would like you to be there, Kathryn, it seems you were all but a sister to her."

Tears pricked my eyes and I forced them away. I knew if I started to cry, I might not stop. "Thank you, Benedict," I said softly.

We did not have to wait long for Doctor Beedles to come downstairs. The man appeared harried as his slim figure moved like a gaunt shadow into the room. Benedict offered him a brandy which he declined.

Instead, he set down his bag and went to stand before the fire. He turned to face us as we sat staring at him, like an audience who waited expectantly for the curtain to go up and the play to begin.

His thin shoulders gave a large sigh.

"I would like to preface my comments by saying what I am about to tell you breaks the confidentiality of my patient, Lady Blanche Clayton. I do this now, only because I believe I have been misinformed in the past, and a wrong must be righted."

Benedict, Lady Geraldine and I glanced at one another, and then back to the doctor.

He sighed yet again and then cleared his throat. "It concerns Lady Aramintha Clayton, and the night she fell from the cliff."

Chapter Twenty-Six

It took us a day to reach Newcastle by train. Benedict hired a hansom cab to carry us the rest of the way to the coast. I had been in the general area before, back when my father worked for Durham University, but it had been several years earlier, and my memory was sketchy. Yet as the cerulean sea came into view, sparkling in the distance, I was reminded how lovely the place was. Visitors to the area were always pleasantly surprised an industrial city could boast such wondrous and beautiful shorelines.

We drove through a small village named Worsely. As the road wound back into the countryside, we passed a large private estate with grounds lined by a high stone wall. At a break in the brickwork, the coachman turned into a driveway. He halted at the massive wrought iron gates as the keeper asked our names and purpose for being there. I remained quiet, allowing Benedict to speak for us, I did not trust myself to remain composed.

Chalcote Mansion did not look like an asylum from the outside, it could easily pass for any ancestral home in England with its ivy-covered stone, high windows and ornate chimneys. The grounds were well-kept. Several pathways dissected the lawns, which I determined must be walkways for the patients.

The carriage deposited us at the front entrance, where huge wooden doors stood at the top of several steps. Benedict bade the driver to wait, and we rang the large bell. The door was opened by a woman wearing a nurse's uniform. She was pleasant enough and gave a welcoming smile as she ushered us inside. The foyer was stark white marble, devoid of decoration other than a few non-descript oil paintings strewn about the walls. We were led into a small room which appeared to be an office and asked to wait.

As we sat quietly, both lost in thought, Benedict's gloved hand reached for mine and held it tightly. I was grateful for the small gesture as my nerves were racked with foreboding. The feel of his touch at once bolstered and reassured me.

Before long, a woman approached. Unlike the nurse, she was dressed in normal attire.

"Please come with me. Doctor Newcomb will see you now." We rose together and followed her down the hall.

****

After the meeting, Benedict insisted I go on alone. I was afraid and unsure, but eventually agreed it was probably the best way to start. I walked down the sterile hallway past many locked doors and heard muted voices and cries behind them, which pulled at my heart. The well-built man who led the way held a large bracelet of keys, which jangled at every step. We seemed to walk forever, and then he stopped and turned towards a door.

As he unlocked the latch, my heart sped into a gallop while everything around me suddenly slowed down. My thoughts scurried into the corners of my mind, filling my head with so many images of Brampton, Mowbray, Gabriel and Moira. The heavy door swung open, and the man gestured for me to enter. Cautiously my feet stepped inside the small, bare room. There was little light from only one gas lamp high up on the wall, out of reach and danger.

She sat on her bed, her back molded into the shape of the corner where the walls met. She was dressed in a plain white gown, her hair hanging loose down her shoulders and arms. Suddenly her head lifted to see who was there. I almost cried out and wanted to run towards her. But I resisted the impulse for I did not want to frighten her.

We stared at one another and, even in the low light, I saw recognition shining in the depths of her lovely, pale blue eyes. My heart melted as her face bloomed into a smile, and her expression suddenly blossomed into life.

"Kate?" she whispered, as though she thought me a mirage.

"Yes, dearest." My voice broke as tears flowed down my cheeks. "Tis me, Aramintha. I have come to take you home."

****

Aramintha did not loosen the grip of my hand until she saw Benedict waiting in the office. She flew from me like a bird from a branch, and I found myself crying once again as I watched the two embrace. They clung tightly to one another. Benedict opened his eyes and our gazes connected. I saw the blur of tears before he closed them once again.

An hour passed before we had collected Aramintha's meagre possessions, signed all of the paperwork necessary and were seated in the hansom cab headed to Newcastle. Benedict had previously secured rooms for the night, determining Aramintha would sleep with me. Doctor Newcomb had given us both much advice, he was a kindly man. We were aware the journey would be a difficult one, for the poor girl had been locked up for several months now.

We took supper in our chamber, and Benedict joined us while we ate. The conversation was kept simple. Aramintha asked after her mother and Gideon, but made no mention of Gabriel, much to my relief. I explained I had taken a position in the house because I had been worried about her and kept the conversation busy with my anecdotes about Gideon, and the people I had come to know like the Plumbs and the other servants.

After supper, we three were all tired, and Benedict bade us good night. Aramintha and I donned nightgowns and tied up our hair, shivering as we climbed into the large bed under a mountain of quilts. We lay quiet for several minutes, and I wondered what she must be thinking? Months locked up, far away from her home and all things familiar. I reached out to take her thin hand in mine.

I listened to her breathe slowly, and then she whispered, "My baby boy died, Kate. His name was Michael." She took another deep breath. "He was dead in my belly long before I gave birth to him," she said softly into the dark room.

I rolled onto to my side to face her. "Oh, Aramintha, I am so very sorry."

"It was for the best," she whispered. "The midwife said he was not formed right, and he would not have lived long."

I struggled for the right words to say. "You must

take solace in that dearest. He died peacefully in the safety of your body, and not out here in the cold, cruel world."

She gave my hand a gentle squeeze, and I was at once reassured.

"What of Gabriel?" she said quietly.

I hesitated. What should I say to her, this poor girl who had already endured so much? But Aramintha was my friend and she did not deserve a lie.

"I am sorry to tell you, but he is dead, Aramintha. It is shocking to say, but it is the truth and you should know. We can speak of it later."

I paused, and waited for her cry of anguish, her wail of sorrow. But she remained silent. The moment grew longer, and then she said in a whisper.

"Good."

Not much later I heard the even rhythm of her breathing. Then finally, with her lying close by my side, I fell into a deep and untroubled sleep.

****

The next morning, I spoke with Benedict privately and quickly recounted the brief conversation between myself and Aramintha the night before. I believe we were both relieved the worst had been discussed.

We did not travel to Mowbray Manor that day, but directly to Mayfair and Lady Geraldine's London townhouse. She had insisted it would be far better for her niece to be told of the events leading to her rescue away from Mowbray, and all the bad memories it would harbor. We would stay several weeks, and Gideon would join us on Christmas Eve, which was only days away. It would then be up to Aramintha to determine when she wished to return home, if ever at all.

When we arrived, Lady Geraldine was beyond happy to see us, and her affectionate welcome to Aramintha endeared the old woman to me even more. I only hoped we could speak of the events that had taken place without Aramintha breaking apart. Surely the strong girl I had known still lurked beneath the quieter, frailer woman I saw before me.

We ate a hearty dinner that evening, and then Benedict explained to his half-sister the plan to remain in London with her aunt. "But Gideon will join us Christmas Eve if that suits you?" Aramintha smiled warmly at the mention of her young brother's name.

"Before he arrives in a few days," Benedict chose his words carefully, "I should like to speak with you about events which are important for you to understand. Might you be up for that Minty? I thought tonight we would all have a good night's rest and then wait until after breakfast tomorrow?"

I held my breath. This was the first indication Benedict had given to discuss all which had transpired leading up to and after Aramintha's time in the asylum. I studied my friend's face for any hint of fear. She took a sip of her claret, put down the glass and gave him a contemplative look. With a great degree of pleasure, I saw a hint of my old friend in her expression.

"Dearest Benedict, you are so like my father. Strong and capable, and you have the protective nature of a bear. I thank you for your delicate treatment. I know how difficult this must be for you, someone who had no hand in my story, and I do not wish to cause you any grief. I shall be ready to speak with you tomorrow. I am more than desirous to lock up my past and look to my future."

Benedict's face broke out in a wide smile, and his dark blue eyes shone with pleasure. I watched him, a spectator who enjoyed learning all the nuances of his personality, so many I had lost count. Lady Geraldine was correct, Benedict was a very decent man, no wonder she loved him so. He turned to look at me, and as our eyes met something stirred within me.

"Well, enough serious conversation," Lady Geraldine barked. "Have I told you about my dear departed husband's awful Dutch family? Never seen such an ugly group of people in my life, noses as big as bananas." She picked the perfect topic to lighten the mood, and the old woman had us laughing like silly children before too long.

****

"The subject is most delicate, Minty, but take courage, for you are with people who love you dearly," Benedict said kindly. "There is no judgement to be made here, simply a clarification of facts and events, which after today will be history, and no longer of importance or relevance."

We sat in the comfortable drawing room and drank our coffee. Aramintha and I on a plush red velvet settle, Lady Geraldine in a neighboring matching chair, Benedict standing as usual before the hearth.

"Let us not dwell upon your relationship with Gabriel, "Benedict began. "It serves no purpose other than to cause grief. Instead, let us start with the events which transpired after you discovered you were with child." He turned to his sister. "Am I correct in thinking when you shared your news with him, he advised you to be rid of the babe?"

"Yes." Aramintha's voice did not falter. "And I refused. Gabriel was incensed, he was terrified our mother would learn of our relationship, and he would be disinherited, our family name ruined. I suggested we leave, run away and start a new life on the Continent, go where we were unknown. But he refused."

"And you understood you were left to face your situation alone?"

"Yes. That is when I spoke to my mother." At her confession, Lady Geraldine's sudden intake of breath was audible.

"How were you received?" Benedict continued.

Aramintha paused as though she searched for the buried memory in her thoughts. Then her expression became full of distaste. "She was appalled. Mother called me a whore and told me I lied about Gabriel, that I had rutted with a common local and sought to blame my mistakes upon my brother."

I could visualize that encounter, the self-righteous Lady Blanche. Poor Aramintha to have a mother so uncaring, the woman should have protected her at all costs no matter what.

"I was distraught, inconsolable. I spent much time feeling scared and unsure what to do—little did I know Gabriel plotted against me. It was he who told our mother I had lain with another."

"He and your mother concocted their own scheme to hide your condition from society, did they not?" Benedict said. He repeated what we knew from Doctor Beedles, who explained what had happened the night Aramintha 'died.'

"Yes. Gabriel asked to meet me, indicating he had a change of heart. We met, and I was drugged and kidnapped. I awoke inside a strange carriage and then was drugged again. My fate was unclear until I awoke and found myself interned at the asylum."

"Barbaric," Lady Geraldine could not refrain from interjecting. "You poor, dear girl, I am so terribly sorry."

"I tried to convince the doctors there of my sanity, but of course they would not listen."

"You can thank Doctor Beedles for that," Lady Geraldine spat. "'Twas his signature on the papers."

"But how was my absence accounted for?" Aramintha said. "Did my mother tell everyone I had run off, or gone to live elsewhere?"

"No," Benedict answered. "She did not. I am sorry to say she announced you had died, fallen from the cliffs near the manor."

"What?" This time, the Aramintha I knew and loved came flying back. She stood up and paced angrily to the hearth. "She told people I was dead. Even Gideon?"

"All your family," Lady Geraldine said softly. "We were told you had fallen from the cliff to your death, and worst of all, she made strong insinuations you had intentionally fallen."

"Dear God! Mother put about I had committed suicide?"

None of us responded. It was the answer she expected. Aramintha returned to the sofa and sat down as though she had lost all strength in her legs. "How could she do that to me?" Her eyes filled with tears, and I placed my arm around her shoulders.

"Minty." Benedict's voice was soft and full of compassion. "May I give you my insight?"

She nodded and wiped her eyes.

"What your mother has done is unpardonable. But I beg you to consider this. Blanche has not long been widowed, and she is a woman who requires the emotional support of a man. Gabriel was that man when your father died. In him, Blanche saw the future of the Clayton dynasty, the continuance of the only life she has known or wants to know." He shook his head.

"No one recognized the deviant mind of our brother, not even his own mother. She, and then you, both became pawns in his web of control and self-gratification. Against him she was powerless, her maternal love blinded her, and Gabriel guided her down the wrong path, one that appeased him and violated you."

"But she falsified my death to save herself and the family name, though she harbored the very person who was responsible for the demise of the Claytons," Aramintha said, her voice full of disgust.

"Yes, she did. And that was wrong of her. And you became the victim, the person who forfeited their rights to satiate that need."

"And what of Gabriel?" Aramintha asked. Benedict shifted his eyes in my direction. I sensed he desired me to pick up the tale and move it forward.

"When I arrived at Mowbray, I told no one of our friendship. I brought the letters you wrote to me, my purpose being to discover where you were as you had stopped writing so suddenly. It seemed odd when I learned of your death that I could find no grave, there had been no funeral service, indeed even Reverend Plumb had not attended your body. Then I found your diary." I turned to see embarrassment spread across her face and quickly took her hand. "Do not worry, I read the pages only seeking clues, reasons you might take your own life, because the Aramintha Clayton I knew would not have done so, especially when she carried a child. You were never that selfish and I knew you would protect your baby at all costs."

Her expression calmed and I was glad to see it. I continued. "Gabriel must have suspected I knew you from our time at Brampton. He stole the letters from my room and then realized our connection. He had been in search of the diary for fear it would out him. So, he embarked on a quest to woo me, befriending me so I might become another one of his puppets."

Benedict interrupted. "At the very same time, I contacted Aunt Gerry. I suspected something foul was underfoot, and she came to stay at Mowbray, where she enlisted both Kathryn's and my help. Alas, by then, Gabriel had long been conducting an affair with Moira Campbell, your mother's maid. Moira and Kathryn were friends, and he used Moira to learn everything Kathryn shared about searching for you."

My thoughts gathered all the times Moira had seen Gabriel and me together. He had tormented her with his attentions towards me. The bastard.

Not to be left out Lady Geraldine spoke up. "Gabriel tried to kill Kathryn on three separate occasions, twice by poison, and once he tampered with her horse's saddle. He accidentally almost killed your brother who drank poisoned chocolate left for Kathryn."

"Good God." Aramintha covered her mouth with her hands.

"Moira became pregnant." Benedict picked up the

thread. "And like you, he refused to help her, this we know from my Aunt Juniper."

"I remember Moira, she was nice, but I did not befriend her because of Mother. Where is she now?" Aramintha asked. The room fell silent. I spoke up.

"We believe Gabriel hanged her." My voice wobbled. "There was nothing we could do."

"Dear God, the poor woman," she said generously. "How many lives has he ruined?" Aramintha said with a catch in her voice. We all took a moment to recover ourselves.

"When Gabriel attempted to poison Kathryn the second time, he almost succeeded." Benedict's voice was grave. "He also had convinced her I was the villain at work, and I the person in your diary. Fortunately, Kathryn survived, and together we determined the real culprit with the help of our aunt."

"I discovered your letters in Gabriel's room," interjected Lady Geraldine.

"Which helped me to realize I blamed the wrong man," I added.

"The three of us verbally ambushed Gabriel with many accusations, and once he realized we were united in our belief, he had nowhere to hide." Benedict said. "He went berserk, Minty. He took Gideon hostage and ran to the cliffs."

Aramintha's eyes grew round, her face pale.

"He was a lunatic," Lady Geraldine said, her voice laced with venom. "He threatened to throw his brother from the cliff if we tried to apprehend him. He was mad my dear, completely and utterly stark raving mad."

"But he loved Gideon!" Aramintha cried. "Surely he would never have harmed him?"

Benedict shook his head appalled at the memory. “No Minty, he would. He loved you too and look what he did to you.” She nodded at his statement, knowing he was correct.

I wanted to support Benedict’s words and spoke up.

“There is no doubt in my mind he would have tossed Gideon into the sea without another thought. He did love him, but Gabriel held his own life in much higher value than any others’. Gideon was doomed.”

“And that is why I shot him,” said Lady Geraldine.

“What?” Aramintha’s head spun to search her aunt’s face.

Her noble chin was up, her eyes bright with fierce justification. “I shot Gabriel to save Gideon.”

“Oh, my goodness.” Aramintha was visibly shocked.

“The shot didn’t kill him. I was only trying to wing him so he would let go of the boy.”

“Aunt Gerry is right, Minty,” Benedict explained. “Gabriel was but wounded, yet he chose to jump from the cliff to escape his fate. It is ironic how he chose the very death he had fabricated for you.” The room fell quiet.

“Brandy,” Lady Geraldine announced. She rose and went to a table laden with a crystal decanter and glasses.

While we waited, I pulled the diary from my pocket and turned to Aramintha. “Here,” I said. “’Tis yours and should be returned to its rightful owner.” I handed her the diary. She took it, stared at the book for a moment and set it in her lap. Our eyes met, silently conveying feelings not easily put into words.

Lady Geraldine passed us all a crystal goblet and returned to her seat.

"Well," Benedict said. "There it is Minty, the whole sorry mess in its entirety. Gabriel the villain, with several others brought into the fray through their inability to recognize his wrongdoing. Doctor Beedles is devastated to have played a role in your being sequestered at the asylum. But in his defense, he was encouraged by our family, and he believed you incapacitated."

"Fortunately, he has left Mowbray Village, and currently seeks a new appointment in another county." Lady Geraldine could not hide the smug tone in her voice.

"It is an unbelievable story." Aramintha took a sip of her brandy. "And an unexpected turn of events." She looked at each one of us. "I would like to say something about what happened between Gabriel and myself."

"You do not have to," Benedict said quickly.

"Yes, I do, Benedict. Gabriel and I were always close. When he took our fraternal relationship in another direction, he made it seem pure, loving, even natural. Though a part of me always recognized what we did was immoral, it gave me a taste of being the object of someone's devotion, something I had not felt since Father had been alive. Everything changed when Father died, so when Gabriel began paying attention to me, I was easy prey. Though short-lived, I did not really understand what we had between us." Aramintha got to her feet and walked over to the fireplace. She stared at the diary in her hand and then tossed it into the flames. Her shoulders sagged, and she turned back to study our faces.

"I have a role in this sordid story, one which carries much blame. I hope you will all forgive me, and know though I have made mistakes, I am no longer that young innocent, but a woman who shall not err in her judgement again."

"I will drink to that," beamed Lady Geraldine, and we all raised our glasses.

Epilogue

It had been a wonderful Christmas Day. Gideon's presence had transformed Lady Geraldine's palatial dwelling into a happy, loving home. His emotional reunion with Aramintha on Christmas Eve had rendered not a dry eye in the house. Since his arrival the boy had barely left her side. Gideon was such a tonic for Aramintha. Around her brother she brightened, became more like my dear friend of old. For the first time in months I finally felt at peace.

Yet I could not sleep. Though I knew it was a late hour, easily past eleven, I left my bed in search of a new book to read. Fortunately, the downstairs lamps were not yet doused, and I was in the library, determining whether to read poetry or Dickens. It seemed appropriate to choose Dickens at Christmas time.

I had just selected a book from the shelf when the door opened, and Benedict entered the room. He started, as he realized it was already occupied.

"Kathryn!" He came to where I stood.

I laughed. "Am I so frightening in my ghostly white attire?"

His eyes raked over me, and I was at once conscious of how flimsy my borrowed silk robe appeared as it touched every contour of my body. My hair hung loose down my back and my feet were bare.

Then he grinned, his generous mouth exposed a dimple in his left cheek. "Fear is the last emotion I feel at this precise moment, Kathryn. I had no idea your hair was quite so beautiful." He stared into my eyes for a long moment, and then pulled his gaze away and glanced at the book in my hand. "Ah, another in search of something to read. Are you having difficulty falling asleep too?"

"Yes," I admitted with a groan. "It has been such an eventful week and my mind cannot stop racing. Every time I close my eyes, it becomes even more frenzied."

"Mine too," he agreed, and stepped past me to run his eyes across the shelves in search of a story. He picked out a book of poetry.

"Keats?" I asked.

"Tennyson," he replied with another smile. His attention settled on my face, his expression thoughtful. "Kathryn, I've not had much time to speak to you since we arrived in London, but I want to tell you how very glad I am you came to Mowbray. Without your help, we may never have discovered my sister's fate, and who knows what could have happened. Thank you."

"Tosh," I said with a grin. "You were on the right path and would have got there eventually, regardless of me." My eyes found his. They were dark, brooding, lovely.

"Perhaps," he admitted. "But I would have been denied the friend I have found in you. From the moment we first met I have enjoyed our conversations, our many walks together."

"Even when I named you a despicable villain?"

He chuckled. "Yes, even then. You did it with such

conviction. You cannot apply yourself to anything half-measure, Kathryn, you are full on in all you do. I admire you for that." His tone was respectful.

"A compliment, Benedict." I smiled. "I too have enjoyed your companionship these past weeks. I will admit, for each blame I cast at your feet, another voice in my head questioned if I was right. It was not by choice I suspected you, far from it."

"Well thank goodness for that."

"Indeed?"

Benedict took a step forward and grasped my free hand in his large palm. He stared earnestly into my eyes. "Then I have a chance?"

I caught my breath as our eyes locked together. Something flickered in the depths of my heart, not the sudden rise of passion, nor a furious pounding, but a beat, strong and steady. A reliable, comfortable sensation I had not felt since my father had been alive. "How can you possibly care for me? After all I have said about you, after—"

He placed a finger on my lips to still my voice, and then slowly, he bent his head and gently touched his warm mouth to mine. I gave a great sigh and dropped my book. Of their own volition, my arms rose up and fastened about his neck as I leaned into his body to receive the full measure of his deep kiss. Though tender at its start, his mouth claimed mine, inquisitive, demanding. The kiss carried promise and desire. As his lips spoke to mine, they brought such emotion, and another urge so new I had no name for it.

Benedict ended the kiss and slowly pulled back from me. With our breath coming fast we stared intently at one another. He studied my mouth, swollen from the caress of his lips while I absorbed every detail of his face. The thick black hair, ripe for my fingers to rake through, his rugged good looks. Yet I dismissed them all. For what I found the most appealing about Benedict Swan lay not on the outside of his body, it was all that lay beneath his skin. His good character, his loyalty, his kind heart and giving nature. All these traits belonged to him, and I knew I could care most deeply for this man given the chance.

"Will you come back to Mowbray Manor with me when I return?" Benedict's voice broke the spell, his tone betrayed his apparent doubt.

I did not answer directly but paused. And in that very moment I thought how much my father would have liked this man, how he would have respected him for the way he treated me, his aunt, and his siblings. And then I had my answer.

My lips parted in a broad smile, and I watched as comprehension reached his eyes and they shone with fire. Boldly, I reached my hand to press against his rough cheek, and then I raised up on my toes, and kissed Benedict Swan like I meant it.

A word about the author...

Though British, my family traveled all over the world throughout my childhood. I credit my passion for writing to all the amazing places and cultures which made such a huge impression upon me. I now live in the Midwest, a far cry from London, but my mind travels home to England every day when I write.

I am a voracious reader and enjoy all genres if they are well written. My favorite authors are Robert Galbraith, Stuart MacBride, C.S. Harris, Victoria Holt, Agatha Christie, and of course the astute Jane Austen.

Find Jude Bayton at:

judebayton.com
Facebook: Jude Bayton
Twitter: @judebayton
Email: author@judebayton.com

Thank you for purchasing
this publication of The Wild Rose Press, Inc.

For questions or more information
contact us at
info@thewildrosepress.com.

The Wild Rose Press, Inc.
www.thewildrosepress.com